Trust

By Avery Woods

www.RoanePublishing.com

Editor: Lynne Street
Cover Artist: Rebecca Hart

To my mom, who opened my eyes to the world of reading.

Prologue

"Positive."

Positive. Usually positive is a good thing, right?

I mean, the word positive has a positive connotation. It's not *supposed* to be a bad thing. Being in the positive's good. Usually it means you have something. When your bank account is in the positive, it means you have money. That's a positive thing. Or, let's look at another prime example: when a couple takes a pregnancy test, a positive result is a good thing; it means pregnancy was achieved.

Now let's look at life in a general aspect. Common phrases people always use include: 'look at the positives in life', which correlates to the *good* things in life. Or when people talk about how having a positive attitude or mindset is the key to success in life. Both good things.

Positive.

Positive.

Positive.

Every time I say it in my head, the meaning of the word positive stays the same. Positive has to be a good thing.

How can 'positive' be a bad thing?

Well, in this moment, in this case, being positive, having this...*thing*...is not good.

"Positive," she repeats.

This doesn't mean what I think it does, does it? As she repeats the statement, it's this moment, I'm putting together what she just informed me...

This *can't* be right.

My heart begins to race so fast, I can feel it hammering against my chest. The pounding of blood pulsating in my ears is deafening. I fear I might actually pass out...

As I inhale deeply, I wipe an excessive amount of sweat from my palms onto my pants. I wonder if she's noticed how nervous I am.

I follow her gaze to my hands. Yup, she's noticed.

Is she concerned? Disappointed in me? I can't read her expression. She must have mastered that poker face in medical school. I wonder how many times she's had to have this exact conversation with someone? One hundred? One thousand?

As her fingers tap on her desk, I realize she is waiting for me to respond. What is the correct way to respond to something so life altering?

A frivolous thought comes to mind. Maybe, if I just close my eyes and wake up, this will all be a dream. Like it never happened. Like how it is in the movies. My subconscious could be playing a sick joke on me. It wouldn't be the first time. I do feel as though I am having an out of body experience. Almost like the night it happened. That careless night where I made the most naïve mistake. The night I would give anything to take back. Guess this is me dealing with the consequences.

I wonder if...

"Hayden, did you hear me?"

"Yes, sorry, I did," I quietly answer. "Are you sure there wasn't an error in the tests? I mean mistakes happen all the time. There could have been an error in the lab. I just read online this story about a guy—"

"Hayden. I am so sorry, but it's true. You are, in fact, HIV positive. Now I know it's hard to adjust to this new diagnosis, but we can come up with a treatment plan that we can adapt to suit your life, so you can live as much of a normal life as possible. I am not saying everything will be easy, but HIV isn't what it used to be. Although in this point of time, HIV is not a curable illness, we have options. There are medications—"

I can't do this right now. I can't even stand to listen to this.

I can't accept this.

I stand up and bolt through the door of the exam room, hearing the echoes of my doctor call after me. I know my doctor has good intentions, but I can't deal. Not right now.

How did this happen?

How did my life go from one extreme to the next? My life suddenly just got upended. Someone pulled the carpet right out from under me. It's one thing for my doctor to give me the results, but a totally separate thing to receive and deal with them. *She* doesn't have to deal with this diagnosis. *She* didn't make one stupid decision that messed up her whole life.

Trust

I make it to my car in the parking lot. I get in and burst into tears.

"Wow, Hayden. Twenty-two years old, and you've already screwed up your life."

Chapter One - Hayden

Two Years Later

> *Beep, beep, beep.*

As I turn off the medication alarm on my phone, I down my anti-retroviral medications. Yes, you heard that correctly. Medications, as in plural, not singular. I take three. Yup, that's HIV life for you. And the most important concept about taking anti-retroviral medication? Take that shit on time. Like the birth control pill, taking the medication at the same time every day is crucial.

As I make my way to the kitchen, my roommate and best friend, Cori, asks "Hey, are you going to be home tonight for dinner?"

Cori and I share an apartment, which is a ten-minute drive from the university we both attend. The apartment's nothing fancy. It's a two bedroom that consists of a living room, kitchen and a bathroom we have to share. However, sharing a bathroom is not a big deal, as Cori is one of those low maintenance girls who sticks a bit of lipstick and mascara on her face and looks naturally gorgeous. She has really intense light blue eyes, with naturally soft dark brown curls. I, on the other hand look completely different. I have long straight blonde hair, green eyes, and am on the shorter side of five-feet-three, whereas Cori is almost five-eight.

"No, I have class tonight, remember?" I don't have class tonight, but not that she needs to know. I'm actually going to my HIV support group. I know what you're thinking. 'You lie to your supposed best friend, you're a horrible friend.' It's complicated. I just can't tell her where I go or why.

Yet.

I've been meaning to, it's just hard. Like, harder than parallel parking hard. It's like jumping into a cold pool. I have to decide to commit and jump in, or bail and not do it. There's no halfway.

"You're still coming out for drinks with us Saturday night though, right?" she asks.

Like a child I respond with "Do I have to?"

"Well no, you don't *have* to, but it would be so much more fun if you do come. You used to go out all the time, and now you never come. Plus, we can find you a guy! It's been forever since you dated!"

"One, it hasn't been that long. It's been a year. And secondly, maybe I don't want or need a boyfriend."

Because the last one ended *so* well.

Why is it that every friend who's in a relationship thinks they're destined to be matchmakers, and go around trying to set everyone up? All because they want to go on stupid double dates. Being in a relationship doesn't automatically solve all problems. I get the appeal, but it's not mandatory.

I promise I wasn't always this negative about relationships or dating, but it gets annoying when everyone around you tries to set you up because they think a relationship will fulfill you, or somehow make you happier. Spoiler alert: it doesn't.

Our conversation is interrupted, as our other friend, Brennley, and her five-year old niece, Penelope, knock and walk through our front door. Good friends always knock on your door and wait until you answer it because it's the polite thing to do. Best friends just knock and walk straight through your unlocked door.

"Auntie Hayden and Auntie Cori!" Penelope yells and attacks both Cori and I with hugs and kisses.

"Hi, Penny. You're getting so big! One day you'll be taller than me." Penny just laughs at my comment.

"You can definitely count on being taller than your Auntie Hayden," Cori teases.

I send a glare in Cori's direction, but she just laughs.

"Hey, sorry to bother you, Hayden, but can you please look after Penelope while I go to class? I promise I won't be more than two hours. Our babysitter jammed out again last minute, and I can't miss another class."

"Yeah, no problem, Brennley."

Mikayla, Brennley's older sister and the biological mother of Penelope, had unfortunately gotten involved with drugs in high school. She became pregnant at seventeen, but ultimately died from an overdose only eight months after Penelope was born. Brennley's parents have custody of Penelope, but Brennley helps look after Penelope as both Brennley's parents work full time.

Also, as adorable as Penelope is now, she's a handful and super energetic, so Brennley's parents get tired more easily from looking after her, as they are both getting older.

"Thanks, I owe you one. Want a ride to the school, Cori?"

"Yeah sure, just let me grab my bag." Cori is studying to become a Chemist, whereas Brennley is in school to become a pharmacist, so they have a few classes in the same building.

Just as Cori and Brennley leave the apartment, I look into Penny's big brown eyes and ask her, "How are you enjoying kindergarten?"

"It's so much fun! We get to read a lot of books and even paint. I can print my name on the whiteboard faster than everyone, even the boys."

"Do you like any of the boys in your class?" I tease, knowing how she'll likely respond.

And I'm not disappointed...

"No! No way! Boys are gross, and they never listen!" Penny shakes her head and scrunches up her face, looking disgusted.

"Good answer, "I laugh. "Boys are too much trouble anyway. Hey, do you want a cookie? I know exactly where Cori keeps her stash. Ha! That will be punishment for that uncalled for short comment. Like what is *with* people these days? Can't come up with a better joke than to knock us for our less than average height?"

Penny jumps up and down. "Yes, please. And Auntie Hayden, it's okay if you're short. I still love you."

Oh, the adoring unconditional love kids have for you. Just for that comment, I figure I should repay her, so after giving her one cookie, I ask:

"Want another cookie?"

I know what you're thinking. Do I really needed to ask a five-year-old that?

* * * *

As I didn't take my diagnosis of HIV well, one suggestion made by my internal medicine doctor, Dr. Shields, was to join a support group for people who are HIV positive. I attend once a week, every Thursday night. I'm the youngest one who attends group, and probably talk the least, but I've always been more of a listener than a talker anyway. Although I was skeptical at first, the group has helped. More than I thought it would. It's turned out to be my safe place. My lifeboat. The place I don't have to hide. The place where people know the real me and my real struggles. The place where saying 'HIV' doesn't automatically turn into disapproving looks, or make people run in the opposite direction because they think you are a walking disease, and if they come to close, they might catch it themselves.

Billy and Mason are a married couple, both in their mid-thirties, who lead the group. They bring up topics the group want to discuss. At the end of every session, each group member writes down on a piece of paper a topic they want to discuss, and at the beginning of the next group we randomly pull one out. One common topic we discuss are tips on disclosing our HIV status to our families and our significant others. This one I struggle with the most, which is why I haven't told my family or friends. I understand that I shouldn't be embarrassed about my HIV status, and my friends and family will love me no matter what, but some part of me feels like I've let them down. It's not so much the HIV I am embarrassed about, it's more of how it was transmitted. I know my friends and family will bombard me with questions to why this happened, or they will be disappointed in how my irresponsible decision lead to this status. Every time I begin to tell them, I always back out. And, yes, I understand I have been backing out for *two years*.

"And remember, trust and safety are key when it comes to disclosing your status. It's important to trust your partner, but also to feel safe enough to do so. Hayden, do you feel comfortable enough to share a disclosure story, or any concerns or feelings you are having with disclosing your status?" Mason asks me.

Great, now everyone is staring at me. What should I say? I guess the key is to have a *positive* mindset going into it. I chuckle to myself. Nope not funny. And I don't think anyone else will find it funny.

I take a deep breath. "Nope, sorry I don't have a specific story to share. I think disclosing is a very difficult subject, which is why I am glad we discuss it."

Difficult is an understatement. The last time I attempted to disclose my status...well let's just say, saying it went poorly is an understatement. I mentally try to block the memory, but it to always seems come back. Why is it, I can't remember what I ate for breakfast yesterday, but I can recall every embarrassing or humiliating moment in my life in perfect detail like it happened only minutes ago? Life is weird. And unfair.

* * * *

Travis

"We have an announcement we would like to make." My older brother, Tristan clinks his glass with his fork.

I'm currently at my parent's house for a family dinner. We're all sitting around our dining room table, half-way through our dinner. My dad is at the head of the table, with my mom sitting laterally beside him. I'm next to my mom. Across from us is my oldest brother Trevor, and his wife Savannah who is currently seven months pregnant. At the other end of the table is my second eldest brother Tristan, and his girlfriend Addison. After everyone stops eating and looks up at Tristan he continues on. "Well, actually, Addison and I have an announcement to make."

He blushes. My brother actually blushes. He's changed so much since he's met Addison. Nowadays, it's hard to believe he's the brother who got suspended from school for kicking some guy's ass. And now he's blushing.

Great.

Tristan grabs Addison's left hand and shows us a ring that sits on her ring finger as he announces, "I proposed last night, and she said yes! We are officially engaged."

My mom shrieks with excitement, at a pitch that risks me never being able to hear again. Everyone mumbles a 'congratulations'. My mom and Savannah get up to hug Addison and check out her engagement ring. You know just to rate my brother on how well he did on picking out the ring. He sure as shit didn't ask me what I thought. He actually didn't even tell me he was going to propose, so I am just as shocked as you are. Even though I'm surprised he didn't tell me he was going to propose, I'm still happy for him. My two brothers and I are fairly close, and we were inseparable when we were kids. It might have been because we are so close in age. Trevor is twenty-nine, Tristan is twenty-eight, and I'm twenty-six. However, in the last couple of years we have drifted a bit. Ever since Trevor has gotten married, and Tristan became serious with Addison, we don't hang out as much. Trevor now is in almost full-on daddy mode, and Addison is controlling and never lets Tristan come out when the guys and I go out. She says she doesn't want him to be 'enticed' by other girls when we go out. She says it's not that she doesn't trust Tristan, she just doesn't trust the other girls. To me that's complete bullshit. It totally means she doesn't trust *him*. I mean, if it was back when we were in our early twenties, I'd see her point in not trusting us. But now that we're in our late twenties, my brothers and I have settled down and matured quite a bit. I mean Trevor is going to be a dad after all.

Even though I am not the biggest Addison fan, if my brother is happy then that's all that matters. I stand up and give my brother a smack on the back as I say "Congrats, man."

My mom breaks out a bottle of champagne which she happens to have on hand for some reason, and we toast my brother and my soon-to-be sister-in-law. I don't think my mom has stopped smiling since the announcement. It's like she has been waiting for this day for months. The rest of the dinner is followed by everyone asking questions about the wedding.

Later that night, Trevor, Savannah, and I are in the hallway entrance getting ready to leave my parent's place. Trevor turns to me and says "Me, you, and Tristan need to get together before this one comes along." He jerks his head towards Savannah's pregnant belly. "After the baby comes, I'll have responsibilities and such, and never be allowed to leave."

Savannah gasps, and playfully hits Trevor. "You already have responsibilities! One of them taking care of your loving wife."

Trevor laughs. "Yeah, that too."

Savannah gives him a smug look and puts her hands on her hips. "Keep that up, and the couch is where you'll be sleeping tonight." She grabs the keys from Trevor. "I'll meet you in the car. My feet still ache."

As soon as she is gone, Trevor warns me, "Think very carefully before you get your wife pregnant. The hormones are wild. I think almost every day this week she has threatened to send me to the couch. Yesterday it was because I picked up regular milk, instead of soy milk."

I'm confused. "Does she normally drink soy milk?"

He looks at me with a serious look. "No, she doesn't. We drink just regular milk."

I cough out a laugh. "That's rough."

"That's my point. Anyway, I'll talk to Tristan and talk some sense into Addison, so he can come out for one night. But for now, I'd better go. I don't want to see how serious Savannah is about me sleeping on the couch."

"Alright, later."

Trevor mumbles a 'later' and heads out the door. Just as I'm getting my coat on, I hear mom head down the stairs. Damn. I thought we'd all said goodbye upstairs, so I could discreetly head out the door without another lecture.

"Travis, I packed some leftovers, so you could take some for work this week." She holds out a container with leftovers. I know this is just an excuse to talk to me about something else.

"And, what did you think about the engagement news? It's wonderful, hey?"

"Umm yeah, sure."

She taps her foot and gives me that look that only mothers can.

"Doesn't it make you want to settle down? Don't you want to find a girl, get married and start a family? Look at how happy Trevor and Tristan are."

And here is it folks. The lecture I was *trying* to avoid.

"Mom, I'm not talking to you about this." I turn to leave.

My mom lets out an exaggerated breath, and I turn back to face her. "C'mon, Travis. You haven't brought a girl home since Courtney, and that was when you were in high school. I'm worried about you. I just don't want you to be lonely."

I'm appalled. "I'm not lonely."

She tilts her head and looks at me with sympathetic eyes. "You know what I mean. You're twenty-six. It's time you start getting serious about girls and think about settling down. Is it because of Courtney?"

I hold my hands up to stop her. "Okay, enough. It's not about her. I don't want to talk about this. Especially with you. I'm leaving." This time I turn to leave for certain.

"Travis please—" Her voice comes out somewhat unsteady. Almost as if she regrets saying anything. I don't care at this point though. I am definitely not talking about my relationship status with my mom.

"Bye, mom." I open the door, close it, and head out.

* * * *

Hayden

On Saturday morning, I get ready for my early morning run. I know what you're thinking. I'm one of *those* people. But I promise you it's just to de-stress and clear my head. I love running for that exact reason, which is why I run multiple times a week, down at the local track field. Today is the perfect weather for it. It's just brightened up outside, so it's not dark anymore. A clear cloudy day, which is unusual as it tends to rain here a lot in Vancouver. I tie my hair up, stick my cell phone and driver's license into my running jacket pocket, grab my iPod, and I'm out the door.

There are only a handful of people at the track, which works for me as I really don't like to run into people I know while I'm working out. As I am finishing up my last lap around the field, I suddenly feel an arm grab me from behind. I immediately scream and jump five feet in the air. I quickly leap to the side, pull my ear buds out, and turn around while swinging my arm in my attacker's face getting ready to hit him.

"Whoa. Whoa. Calm down, I promise I was just trying to get your attention." My attacker states as he starts backing away with his hands up in the 'I surrender' way. "I was running behind you and saw your driver's license fall out of your pocket. I wanted to give it back to you. I tried to call after you, but you had your ear buds on—"

"Why in the hell would you ever think it's a good idea to get a girl's attention by approaching her from behind, when she clearly can't hear, and then trying to grab her! Are you out of your damn mind!" I shout.

"In my defense, I was tapping your shoulder, *not* grabbing you."

I roll my eyes. "That's beside the point. You never do that! Do you know how many news articles there are that start with, 'attacker grabs running girl from behind'?"

"Well then, why do you run with both ear buds in, when it clearly isn't safe? You should be more aware of your surroundings, and only run with one ear bud in," he states, looking serious.

I immediately get defensive. This guy doesn't even know me. "Wow. Classic. The attacker blaming the victim, even though the attacker was the one in the wrong."

He thinks it over and looks remorseful. "Look. I'm sorry, okay? I shouldn't have approached you the way I did. I wasn't thinking. Here's your driver's license."

He passes me my driver's license, and that's when I really get a good look at him. Putting my anger aside, he is quite attractive. He's got to be at least over six-feet tall. Compared to me he's a giant, but that's not saying much. He is also extremely built. He's not overly built, but definitely toned and fit. He has shorter brown hair, and light brown eyes. I've always loved guys with blue eyes, but there's something about his brown ones... if you really stare at them, they are almost a beautiful hazel color. He looks a bit older than me. Maybe twenty-eight?

Wait no, stop!

I have to remind myself. I'm on a break from guys. Guys are trouble. Remember your ex who turned out *so* great? There's also the fact he almost attacked me. Accident or not. Great, now stop checking him out. Or, on second thought... you can always appreciate an attractive person whether or not you make a move. He keeps staring at me, and I realize he is waiting for me to respond to his apology.

"Look, it's totally okay. Thanks for my license. No one was hurt, and I appreciate the apology. I am sorry for yelling at you. You just scared me that's all," I explain.

"It's totally understandable, Hayden. Like I said, I wasn't thinking." He looks genuine.

Wait, did he just say my name? "What? How do you know my name?" I glare at him.

He chuckles. "It's on your driver's license."

"Great. Now your next joke, which won't be funny will be: 'and now I know where you live'," I half tease, but also feel a bit on edge, because I don't know this person. He totally could be a creep. Appearances can be deceiving.

His face relaxes, and he laughs again. It's then I notice he has perfectly straight teeth. And I might like the sound of his laugh. Just a little bit.

"My memory isn't that good," he points out.

"Well I don't know. Maybe you took a picture of my license on your cell phone before running over here?" Now I am completely teasing.

"Do you want to check my phone?" He reaches in his shorts pocket, and now it's my turn to hold my hands up in 'I surrender'.

"No, No, I'm just joking. I do however think it's only fair that I get your name, as you know mine."

"Fair enough. It's Travis."

Just as I'm about to tell Travis it was nice to meet him, I feel something wet land on my head and drip down my face. Oh my god. Is it starting to rain? I look up in the sky. Nope, not raining. I use my sleeve and reach to wipe the wetness off my face. The wetness is white. When I look back up at the sky, I see birds flying away.

No way!

Oh my god.

Did a bird just shit on my face? Is my hand right now covered in bird droppings? This cannot be happening. Not only did a bird shit on my face, but in front of this *attractive* guy whom I *just* met. Also add in that I am not looking my best in the first place as I am sweaty and gross from my nearly done run. That comment I made earlier about life being unfair? Well I am applying it to this situation.

"Oh my god, did that really happen? Are you okay?" Travis asks with a smile on his face.

Great. Not only do I have bird shit on my face, but this guy is trying his hardest not to laugh.

At *me*.

"I have extra towels in my car, I can go run and get one for you, so you can...ahh...clean that off?" he asks awkwardly.

This is not good.

"No thanks. I'm good." I can't even look at him right now. He has a look on his face that is half concern, half trying his hardest not to laugh. I am completely humiliated. I quickly decide to do what I am best at: running away from less than ideal situations. I immediately mumble out "I got to go" and turn and start running away from the track.

"Hayden!" I can hear him shout after me.

Nope. No way am I turning back around. If there is anything positive that can come from this situation, it's that I don't know who he is, and hopefully I'll never have to see him again. That part about life being unfair? I don't think I'm close to seeing the end of it anytime soon.

Chapter Two: Hayden

"That is the best story I've ever heard!" Brennley laughs.

Cori on the other hand is at a loss for words. She isn't just laughing; she is full out guffawing. I've just told both of the them about what I'm referring to as 'the bird incident'. It's Saturday night and the three of us are in my room getting ready to go out for drinks at the local bar. We are meeting Cori and Brennley's current boyfriends, Erik and Cooper, and some other friends from school.

"That sort of thing would only happen to you, Hayden," Brennley says as she curls another piece of her dark brown hair with her flat iron.

I agree. "I know right? Embarrassing moments, especially with guys, always happens to me."

"Hey, you're not the only one! Remember how I met my ex, Greg?" Cori finishes putting on a coat of mascara and turns towards me.

"C'mon, Cori, that doesn't really count. I think that was more embarrassing for him, not you," I point out.

Brennley frowns. "How come I've never heard this story?"

Cori finishes putting on her mascara and turns to tell Brennley the story. "I don't know. It happened first semester of school when I was at college before transferring to university. You know in college because class sizes are so small, they make you play that game where you break off with a partner, ask them questions to learn facts about them, and then the professor makes you introduce your partner to the whole class?"

Brennley and I both nod and groan. I hate when professors want you to introduce yourself or your partner to the whole class. It's like 'How about let's not?', and 'How old are we?' I internally cringe every time a professor mentions that game. Next thing you know, you'll be in college and having to do show and tell.

Cori continues the story. "Well the guy next to me at the time was Greg. He introduced himself so quickly to me, and to be honest I wasn't really paying attention to anything he said. When it came to be our turn, I accidently introduced him to the class as

'Cole'. He then corrected me in front of the whole class and said 'actually my name's Greg'."

Brennley snorts, but laughs as well. "Cole? That's not even remotely close!"

Cori shrugs. "I know, I know. I have no explanation. It just happened. But anyway, it worked out, because a couple of days later he asked me out and we dated for some time."

Brennley shudders. "Don't worry. Before having my first kiss when I was thirteen, just as I was leaning in to kiss him, the sudden urge to sneeze kicked in. I had to step back and move away just to sneeze. Not only did I sneeze, I had a sneezing fit and sneezed about five times. Talk about a mood killer. Kisses are awkward at that age, and then to have that happen. Embarrassing."

"Wow guys. Those are nowhere near as embarrassing as my story," I argue.

"All I'm saying is everyone has embarrassing stories. All you can do it laugh them off...and hope they never happen again. Also, now if you ever see this guy again, you have the perfect ice breaker." Cori adds.

I roll my eyes. "I only got his first name so, no, I don't think I'll ever see him again. And it's a good thing, because I don't think I could ever look him in the eye again."

"You're exaggerating." Cori quickly fixes her hair and walks over to my closet.

Next thing I know a green top is being thrown at my face. "Now, put this top on. The green will definitely match your eyes."

* * * *

The bar we're in is casual and low key. The lighting is dimmed, and there are a bunch of hockey themed photos and jerseys on the walls. Since it's a Saturday night, there's quite a lot of people here, but not too many where you have to bulldoze your way between people. There are lots of tables and chairs, a few pool tables, and TVs airing the hockey game. It's too loud to hear the game, the TVs are just more for visual purposes. There's also a decent sized dance floor, with a live band playing. It's still early in the night so not many people are dancing yet.

There are nine of us here, some sitting at a table, and some over in the corner of the bar playing pool. I'm sitting at the table next to Brennley who is sitting beside Cooper, with our friends Kelsey and Keegan who are also a couple. Cori and Erik are playing pool with our other friends Dominick and Cassie, who you guessed it are also a couple.

And to answer your question, yes sometimes it sucks to be the ninth wheel. Did I feel like I fit in more when I was still with my ex-Kyle? Yes. But to be honest, I'd rather be single, than be with a douche bag boyfriend like Kyle was.

Cooper and Keegan start talking sports, and I'm already out. I don't watch sports, and I can't even pretend to act like I can follow along. Brennley shares the same sentiment. She turns to me and says "Can you believe Penelope is going to be going into grade one in the fall? She's growing up so fast!"

I grin. "I know! It feels like yesterday I was trying to teach her to say, 'Hayden is my favourite Aunt'."

Yes, I'm that aunt. And I'd be lying if I said I don't spoil her rotten.

"Oh, that reminds me. Penny has a dance rehearsal at the end of next month. She wanted me to invite you. Will you come?"

Watching a five-year old at a dance recital? It's going to be both funny and cute. "Yes, of course I will. I can't wait."

Brennley rolls her big brown eyes. "Don't get too excited. She's only five, so I have no idea what to expect. For all I know it will be a bunch of five-year-olds prancing around the stage."

And they probably won't be in time with the music. "Doesn't matter, I still want to co—"

"Oh, look who it is! My baby sister," I hear a drunken voice say behind me. Before I can turn around, this person, who I am ninety-nine percent sure is my big sister Lauren, squeezes me into a hug from behind.

"Lauren, get off me!" I try to loosen her arms around me.

"What, I can't say hi to my baby sister? I thought we had this agreement now that we are older, mature adults we could acknowledge each other in public?" Lauren says, slurring her words.

Lauren is my annoying older sister. We obviously love each other, but there is no one else who knows how to push my buttons the way Lauren does. Lauren has similar long blonde hair with green eyes like me, except she is much taller and has dimples. Lauren is super flirtatious, and the classic party girl, whereas I am more shy and reserved. Lauren and I fought all the time growing up, as our personalities always clashed. I always had to work super hard for everything, whereas things just 'worked out' for Lauren. I think that's why I hold a small grudge against her. She also doesn't do the whole boyfriend thing as she likes to 'keep her options open' (her words not mine). However, it doesn't stop her from flirting with every guy she meets. Because she is quite good looking, she attracts guys like no other. This is probably why she doesn't have many female friends and decides to borrow mine every chance she gets. Cori and Brennley love Lauren because they think she's 'super fun', and they think her crazy stories are 'entertaining as hell'. It's almost like 'What will Lauren do next?'

"Hi, Lauren," Brennley says before I can answer Lauren.

"Hey, Brennley. How's it going?" Lauren looks at me and notices the glass of water in front of me. "Why aren't you drinking, Hayden? C'mon let's go get a drink and dance!"

"Absolutely not. Plus, I am the DD tonight. What are you even doing here?"

"It's Saturday night, and I came out to have some fun! It's a silly coincidence I'd run into you here." Lauren replies.

I frown at her. "No, it's not! You know if I go out, this is the bar I come too."

"It's actually a miracle I'm seeing you here. You never come out anymore." Lauren points out.

"Sorry some of us are focusing on school." I look smugly at her.

Lauren never went to post-secondary. She works full time at a high end cosmetic store.

"Wow, low blow. And not that is any of your business, but I just landed a role in a commercial the other day. Want to know how much I get paid for it?" She raises her eyebrows at me.

"Didn't you just randomly decide to become an actress the other day?" I ask.

"Yes, and look how it's worked out. It's meant to be." She glows.

Remember how I mention that things just 'work out' for Lauren? This is why. You can also add that onto the life's unfair list.

"Let me know if you need any help, or someone to practice running lines with." Brennley tells her.

Brennley was a childhood actress, and from what I hear she was quite good. She doesn't act anymore, but from the projects I've seen, I'm surprised she stopped. She said something along the lines of wanting to go to high school like a normal teenager.

"Thanks, Brennley. I might take you up on that offer. Anyway, I'm going to go hit up Cori. She's actually fun and will dance with me." Lauren says and storms away.

"Weren't you just a little harsh on Lauren?" Brennley asks.

"Nope. You don't understand. Lauren is fun when you only have to deal with her in small doses. She gets exhausting. Plus, she's not sixteen anymore. She's twenty-seven, she needs to grow up and start taking life more seriously. Anyway, excuse me while I go to the washroom."

As I try to make it to the washroom and maneuver around people as the bar has become busier, some random stranger bumps into me. It ultimately throws me off balance and I end up bumping into the back of some other guy near me. Just as I am about to say 'sorry', the guy turns around and, of course, it turns out to be Travis. *Just* my luck.

"Hayden?"

"Hey, Travis. Fancy seeing you here. I guess this time it was *me* attacking you. Sorry about that." I turn to continue on the path to the washroom, when I hear him.

"Hayden, wait."

I stop and turn around to face him. Why did it have to be him? But of course, he looks just as attractive as when I last saw him this morning. Now that I'm standing inches from him, I notice he smells really good, although I can't decipher what exactly he smells like. He is dressed casually in jeans and a black t-shirt.

Don't get distracted by him, Hayden.

Focus.

You were on your way to the bathroom.

"Why did you run away so suddenly this morning?" He looks sincere, like he actually wants to know the reason, not like he's just making small talk.

"Umm, you know, I guess you could say I was having a shitty morning." That was an awful pun. Why does this guy want to talk to *me*?

"I can't tell if that was a joke, because you said that with a completely straight face."

I can't even look at this guy. I look over his shoulder and see a guy with blond hair and bluish-green eyes who appears to be walking over to us, although at the last second it looks like he decides against it and heads back up to the bar. He must be a friend of Travis's.

"Oh, it was definitely a joke. A bad one. But definitely a joke." Wow. Apparently talking is hard. Get yourself together Hayden.

"Would you like a drink? It can be an apology drink for this morning?" Travis asks.

Focus. Now. "Umm no thanks, I'm actually designated driver tonight. I'm just here with some friends." I think that sounded normal?

"Just some friends?"

I roll my eyes. "Yes, *just* some friends. And if that was your subtle way of asking if I had a boyfriend, I'm going to tell you, that attempt was as bad as the attempt I made trying to tell a joke." I grin.

He looks a bit taken aback, as if he didn't expect me to say that. His face relaxes, and he smiles back at me. I really like his smile.

"Are you always that blunt?" he asks.

"Yup. I see no reason to hide what I'm thinking. Who are you here with?"

"Is that your way of trying to sneak in asking if I have a girlfriend?" he teases.

I'm pretty sure my face goes bright red. "Who gave you that idea?"

"Had some insight from a pretty blonde. But to answer your question, I'm here too with *just* some friends"

Yup, I'm definitely bright red now.

I'm so focused on Travis, I completely miss Brennley and Cooper making their way over to me, until Cooper crosses my line of vision and approaches Travis.

"Hey man, how's it going?"

"Not bad. How's it going with you?"

Wait, what? How do they know each other? "Hey how do you guys know each other?"

Cooper fills me in. "We've played baseball together since we were six."

"You know Cooper?" Travis asks me.

"Yes. Brennley here is one of my good friends and Cooper is her boyfriend." I point to Brennley. "Brennley, Travis. Travis, Brennley."

"How do you know Travis?" Cooper inquires.

"Funny story." I begin. "I actually met him this morning."

Brennley turns to me and gives me the knowing look. The look that tells me she has put two and two together.

"Excuse me while I use the washroom." I leave Travis and Cooper while they continue catching up.

Brennley follows me, and I know she's going to give me a hard time. Just as we're far enough from the guys so they can't hear us she asks, "That's bird guy?"

I laugh. "Do not call him that. But to answer your question, yes."

She looks surprised. "Wow. He's way better looking than you let on. I can't believe you just ran off and left. *Without* getting his number." She gives me an unimpressed look.

"Did you forget what happened during our encounter?" I tuck my hair behind my ears.

"No. But just wow." Her eyes widen. "Oh my god. Cooper and I just cock-blocked you, didn't we? Don't worry I can fix this. I'll go collect Cooper and you can continue— "

"Hey guys, what's up?" Cori does some sort of half-walk half-dance towards us. She's obviously a few drinks deep.

"Guess who we found?" Brennley taunts, as she gives me a mischievous grin.

Cori looks around the bar. "Who?"

Brennley answers for me. "Bird guy."

"Stop calling him that!" I shriek.

"Bird guy?" Cori looks confused and, a second later, figures it out. "Oh my god, the guy from this morning? Where is he? I want to see him!"

"No. Absolutely not!"

Brennley doesn't share the same sentiment. She points to the corner of the bar. "He's over there, talking to Cooper."

Cori's eyes wander over, and when it appears she sees him, she looks back to me and says "He's cute, Hayden. Does he know you're here?"

"Yes. I was talking to him."

Cori gives me a clueless look. "And you stopped because...?"

"Well it's actually my fault. Cooper and I interrupted them. Apparently, Cooper used to play baseball with him."

"And he didn't introduce us to him before when we were all single and looking for guys because...?"

Brennley shrugs her shoulders. "I don't know. That's a good question. You should ask him."

Before I get to answer, a drunken Lauren walks over and puts her arms on my shoulders, trying to use me for support to stay standing.

"Hayden, I don't feel good. Can you take me home?"

I try to give Brennley my best 'this is what I mean when I say she needs to grow up' look. How does Lauren not know her limit by now?

I groan. As much as Lauren pissed me off tonight, I can't say no. Due to sister obligation, and the fact she's picked me up numerous times after nights where I've consumed my fair share of alcohol. Plus, I honestly don't think I am even ready to think about dating again. I need to work on myself. Well that's the excuse I keep feeding myself with. I just don't want to get my hopes up and be disappointed. *Again.* I think I could start liking Travis. However, if I bail now, the potential of getting hurt is gone.

I look at Lauren. "C'mon let's go get your coat, and you can crash at my place." I look at both Cori and Brennley. "You guys want a ride?"

Brennley looks hopeful. "Aww Hayden, are you sure? Why don't you just go talk to him again? A guy like that won't be single for long? What if he turns out to be a great guy? You'll never know if you don't try."

"Nah. I'm just really tired, and Lauren needs to get home." And if we don't start getting to know each other, then we won't have to have that awkward conversation if we chose to move our relationship to the next level.

"Okay, I'll come with you. Just let me grab Cooper." Brennley walks off to go collect her boyfriend.

"Cori?"

"Nah. I'm going to stay a bit longer. I think I'm going to head to Erik's place tonight anyway. I'll check in tomorrow." She gives me a hug, and I drag a drunken Lauren through the bar, avoiding Travis on the way out.

* * * *

Travis

I can't believe I ran into her again. Hayden. What a coincidence. I wouldn't say it to her face, but her getting shat on by a bird—funniest fucking thing ever. Although I did feel bad for her too. I'm not a complete asshole. I like Hayden. For starters, you can tell she's a natural blonde. And her green eyes are different. I've never seen green eyes as intense looking as hers. She also has a killer body with just the right amount of curves. She's a bit on the shorter side, especially when comparing my six-foot-three height to her. However, there's something off about her. She seems preoccupied and jumpy. I can't tell if that's just her personality or it has something to do with me. Just a couple of minutes ago, she was adamant to get the fuck away from me. I do like that she's blunt and speaks her mind. Her sarcasm is great, even though sometimes I have a difficult time deciphering if she is being sarcastic. The comment she made about having a shitty morning was funny. At least she can laugh at the situation. After finishing up talking to Cooper, I head back to the bar to get another drink, where I meet up with my best friend Jesse.

"Hey, who were you talking to?" he asks.

I don't know if he's referring to Hayden or Cooper.

"Cooper? I used to play baseball with him. By the way, I may have signed us up to play with him on his team in a charity baseball tournament on the weekend. And before you give me that look, it is a charity for cancer, so you can't say no. Plus, apparently they are down some players, so they need us."

Jesse lets out an exaggerated groan and runs a hand through his blond hair. He used to play baseball too, so I know he doesn't mind going. "Fine, I guess I can go. But that wasn't who I was referring to. Who was the blonde chick?"

"Hayden? Oh, I randomly met her this morning at the track. She's a runner too. It's just a weird coincidence I would see her here."

Jesse takes a sip of his beer. "She's hot. You going to go after her?"

As much as I'd love to take her home tonight, based on her on-edge vibe I doubt she would be one of those girls I could get to come home with me, no matter how charming I was. She seems like the type you would have to take things slow with, and work for. Which I do appreciate and respect. I mean, she's a girl I'm sure my mother would be delighted I bring home.

"Nah, not tonight. She seems too skittish. She's playing this weekend in the baseball tournament, so I'll get to see what she's like. For all I know, she could be crazy."

Jesse nods. "Yeah, unfortunately these days most girls are. But, I'm still going to try my luck with that redhead over there." He starts walking towards her.

"Later." I mumble.

I try to look for Hayden again, but can't manage to find her. Cooper leaves and tells me she's already in the car waiting to drive him home. Something about getting her sister home. Later that night, a cute brunette makes a pass at me, but I'm not interested. For some reason, I can't shake the thought of Hayden. There's something about her that intrigues me. I can't quite figure out what it is, but it has piqued my interest. I guess I'll learn more about her next weekend.

* * * *

Hayden

On the car ride home, Brennley and Cooper are sitting in the backseat. It's kind of funny because Cooper is almost six feet seven, so he barely fits back there, but he's such a good guy, he doesn't complain. Lauren is currently passed out in the passenger seat. I'm driving, and everyone's super tired, so it's been a quiet drive.

Suddenly, Cooper breaks the silence.

"So just a reminder that next weekend is my work's co-ed baseball tournament. I've submitted everyone's names and remember it's for a good cause. It's a charity event to help raise money for cancer, so nobody can back out. "

I groan. "Aww man. Are you serious about me playing? I honestly suck. I don't know why I have to play every year. Can't I just make a donation, and cheer you guys on from the bleachers? I'll just make us lose. Some of you guys take it way too seriously and I don't appreciate being yelled at for missing the ball. I don't know how many times I have to tell you guys, I'm not coordinated."

As I mentioned earlier, I can't hold or follow a sports conversation. Let alone play an actual sport? Apart from running, I don't play sports. Trust me, throughout the years I've tried many sports. They are just not for me.

Brennley and I make eye contact through the rear-view mirror. "C'mon, Hayden. If I have to play, then you definitely have to play."

Brennley is probably just as bad as I am. Maybe even worse? Cori on the other hand is one of our best players. She grew up playing softball, and man she has a killer arm. Even the guys are impressed with how good she is.

I fold. "Fine. but I'm not going to be happy about it."

Cooper chuckles. "Also, I was a bit worried because before tonight I thought we were going to be down a few players. My cousins are out of town that weekend, so they aren't going to be able to make it."

"Wait. So, *they're* allowed to bail but *I* can't?" I let out an exasperated sigh.

Cooper rolls his eyes. "Like I said, they're going to be away that weekend. It's not like they want to miss it."

"I just remembered. *I'm* going to be away that weekend."

Brennley has a huge grin plastered on her face. "Oh yeah, where are you going that weekend?"

"I'm going away that weekend to take care of my sick grandmother." I jokingly lie.

Brennley decides to call me out on my lie. "Haven't both of your grandmothers passed away?"

"Semantics." I argue.

"Shut up, Hayden. You're going. End of story. Friends suffer together," Brennley declares.

I stick my tongue out at her through the rear-view mirror.

"There's good news though. Luckily, I ran into Travis tonight. He and his friend Jesse agreed to join our team. I've played baseball with both of them, so I know they're good players. We might actually have a shot of winning this year." he beams.

"What!?" Brennley and I shout at the exact same time.

Cooper looks confused. "What do you mean 'what'? I thought that would be okay. I thought you were friends with him, Hayden?"

"I told you I just met him this morning. Man, now I'm definitely not going." I groan.

Cooper looks at Brennley with worried eyes. "What did I do wrong?"

"Nothing. You did great, babe!" Brennley beams at him cheerfully. "You actually did something right for once."

Cooper shakes his head. "Okay, now I'm really confused. And slightly worried."

Brennley tries to reassure him. "I'll explain later."

"No, you most definitely will not." I give her a look that hopefully reads as 'hoes before bros, so you better keep your mouth shut'.

Lauren stirs and then decides to join the conversation. "Who is Travis?"

I look over; I'd almost forgotten that Lauren was in the car. "Nobody, Lauren. Just go back to sleep. It's not like you're going to remember this conversation tomorrow anyway."

Lauren must be tired because she doesn't even give me the satisfaction of replying to my comment. She just lays her head back down against the side of the door and falls asleep within seconds.

Trust

After I pull in the driveway, Cooper helps me bring Lauren inside. I decide to put her in Cori's bed since Cori is staying at Erik's. I just pray she won't vomit in bed, because Cori would freak. After Lauren is settled, I drive back to drop Cooper and Brennley at his place. By the time I get back home, I peek in to check on Lauren, and finally climb into my warm bed. I drift off to sleep fairly quickly, glad that this awful day is finally over.

Chapter Three: Hayden

"Well your viral load and CD4 count are within the target range as I would like. This is good. It means that your anti-retroviral medication therapy is working well." Dr. Shields, my internal medicine doctor who specializes in HIV informs me.

I am currently at a routine checkup. I have to visit Dr. Shields a few times a year to check in. Dr. Shields is in her late forties. She's dressed professionally in a knee-length black skirt, with a grey blouse, and a white lab coat overtop. Her black stethoscope hangs around her shoulders. She's sitting at the table with her laptop open, my blood test results on it. I get blood work taken prior to meeting her, so we can review the results and adjust treatment as needed. Because HIV is an immunodeficiency condition, hence the name human immunodeficiency virus (HIV), it is important for me to get my blood tested regularly to check on things such as my white blood cell count, and to check the levels of the virus in my bloodstream. Because HIV affects my immune system, if I were to get an infection, or not take my anti-retroviral medication according to directions, there could be severe consequences. As Dr. Shields informed me when I was first diagnosed, HIV is not curable, but the anti-retroviral medications can help control it. There is lots of ongoing testing and research for HIV. A part of me hopes that one day there will be a cure.

I am currently sitting on top of the exam table. I look down at the floor and shrug my shoulders. "Well, that's good, I guess."

Dr. Shields narrows her eyes at me. She doesn't look impressed with my answer. "Well it is good. Hayden, you can't change the fact that you have HIV, so the next best thing is, that we do have a treatment plan that's working the best it can for you right now. Is something else bothering you? You know you can ask me any questions, even if the questions are about sex. I know we've talked about it before, but I don't expect you to memorize everything after one conversation. It's a lot to take in."

I feel bad. Dr. Shields is the most understanding doctor I've ever met. She's super open, so I feel comfortable confiding in her, which is important because a lot of the questions I had were about how HIV is transmitted, and how it would affect my sex life. She explains things well and avoids medical jargon, so I can understand the concepts clearly. It's just that some days, it's still hard to take in that I am in fact HIV positive. It's almost like coming to see Dr. Shields is a constant reminder of the mistake I made that led to this diagnosis. I would do just about anything to change what happened that night.

I decide to cop out and lie to her. "No. Honestly, I'm good. I'm just feeling stressed from school. It has nothing to do with my HIV."

Dr. Shields glances down at her laptop, and then back at me. I think she can tell I'm lying, but if she does, she doesn't call me out on it. She gives me a sympathetic smile. She continues to ask me some more general questions about how I'm feeling and if I am having any new symptoms, which I'm assuming are related to my HIV.

"Well if that's it, then I can let you go. Just before you go, make sure you check in with reception and book a follow up appointment."

I get up off the exam table faster than I mean to. "Sounds good. Thanks, Dr. Shields."

She gives me a genuine smile. "You're welcome. Take care of yourself Hayden. You have my card if anything comes up, or if your health changes. You can call me whenever."

I give her an appreciative grin and walk out to reception. I book my follow up appointment and leave to head home. Once I'm home, I begin to start on my homework. Since this weekend is the baseball tournament I won't have much time to get it done, so I try to get a majority of it done tonight.

* * * *

It's early Saturday morning, and Cori and I are driving to meet our friends for the baseball charity weekend. Because we had to get up so early, I decided to skip my morning run. Also, it might have to do with the fact that I wanted to avoid Travis. Just in case. I know it makes no sense because luckily for me I'll get to see him all day today and tomorrow. I've decided I'm just going to limit the interaction between us. Be polite if he talks to me, but ultimately make sure I am never alone with him.

It's the middle of June, and it looks like it's going to be a super-hot day. The sun is out, and there are no clouds in sight, only blue sky. When you live in Vancouver, because it rains so often, you have to make the most out of every sunny day and spend it outside.

Cooper works for a major telecommunications company, with hundreds of employees. Add in the fact that the employees bring their family and friends, you can just imagine how many people are here today. There are booths and tents selling a variety of items, all profits going to cancer research. There are also booths selling food and drinks. There are people walking around selling tickets for a fifty-fifty draw. It's nice, because at lunch time Cooper's bosses put on a barbeque lunch, consisting of hot dogs, hamburgers, pop, and chips. You know, classic barbeque food.

Cori and I walk over to our baseball 'team'. Our team consists of Cori, Brennley, and their boyfriends, plus our other couple friends we went to the bar with: Kelsey and Keegan, and Dominick, and Cassie. Oh, and I almost forgot my favourite person Travis, and his friend who I've never met Jesse. Although now looking at Jesse, I realize he's the blond guy with the bluish-green eyes that nearly interrupted Travis and me at the bar. And of course, he's also super good looking. I'll keep that thought to myself. As I'm looking around at our team, I realize there are quite a few of us. Cooper thought we would be short of players? How many people play on the field at once in baseball? Seven? I'm pretty sure we exceed that number. Sorry, I'm just being bitter.

Cooper hands Cori and me a jersey with our last names on the back. I check to make sure my last name Myers is spelt correctly. You know, just in case Cooper wanted to be revengeful because I gave him a hard time about coming. I wouldn't be surprised if my jersey said Loser across it. I glance at the jersey Travis is wearing. Turns out his last name is Barrows. Cooper also passes me a baseball cap. Yes, I know it's embarrassing that we all have to wear matching jerseys and baseball caps. I don't put up a fuss though, because one: all the teams do it, and second, this tournament means a lot to Cooper. His Uncle passed away a few years ago from pancreatic cancer.

Our jersey's actually look nice. They are royal blue with white writing on them, and of course Cooper's company logo. Our baseball caps are also royal blue. I put the jersey on, over my tank top. I put the baseball cap on, as I stick my ponytail through the hole in the back of the cap. Everyone is in black shorts, so it looks like we'll all match perfectly.

Travis then walks over and approaches me. "Hey Hayden. How's it going?"

"I'm alright. A little tired, but good."

Travis looks good. I mean not everyone can pull off the baseball cap, but he certainly does. I raise my eyebrows at him. "You ready for today?"

"Yes. It should be fun. But you should know something about me. I'm pretty competitive. I definitely want to try to win." He grins.

"Well it's a good thing I'm here then. I've been MVP on our team the last few years. My stats are impressive, and my arm is just killer." I wonder if he'll pick up on my sarcasm.

"Oh yeah?" His eyes brighten. "How long have you played baseball for?"

"Actually, not that long. I just got into baseball recently. I'm a real natural. I'm actually a real natural at a lot of things."

Travis's lips turn up into a huge grin. His grin is so big, his dimples are showing.

Oh, my goodness. That came out wrong. I wasn't trying to flirt, but that's exactly what he's going to think. That I *was* trying to flirt. Damn sarcasm. I knew it would get me into trouble one day. Before he can flirt back, I cut in. "I'm just kidding. I am the worst baseball ever. I strike out almost every time. I try really hard, just my execution is lacking."

"Well we have some time before we start. I can give you some tips and show you how to swing the bat?"

I sigh. "Even with your help, I'll still fail."

"No, you won't. Come on, let's go somewhere private, and I can give you a quick lesson. We have an hour before we start. We'll be back in plenty of time."

31

Before I can say no, he picks up a spare bat, and lets the group know we'll be back soon. He reaches out to grab my hand and for some reason I let him. As we walk off, I look down at our hands and I notice how big his are. Mine are so little compared to his, you can barely see mine while were intertwined.

And no I am not clueless. I did pick up on the 'let's go somewhere private' part. I do recall the last time a guy said that to me I lost my virginity.

* * * *

"You're not positioning your feet like I showed you." Travis sighs.

Did Travis show me proper technique? Yes. Did I pay attention? Sort of. I may have been looking at him, it just wasn't to learn proper baseball stance... I was checking him out. I mean how could you not? Look at him! Every time he moves, his muscles flex, and it's quite lovely. Also, as he's wearing shorts and hasn't put on his shin guards, you can even tell how developed his calf muscles are.

"Here, maybe if I stand behind you and guide you, it will work better."

My eyes bulge. The remarks I could make to that comment are endless. Although he doesn't even seem to notice what he's said. He's serious and determined. You can really tell his passion for baseball, because he really wants me to learn.

He stands behind and grips the bat with me. He's so close to me I can feel his breath on my neck. I shudder, and immediately get goose bumps. If I couldn't concentrate before, I really can't concentrate now. He uses his own feet to spread and guide my feet out the way he'd showed me. He covers my hands with his, and lines them up on the bat the way they are supposed to be.

"Good. Now look at where our hands are placed on the bat. That's exactly how I want you to have them when you're up to bat," he explains.

Let me show you where I want *your* hands to be.

I can't help these comments. Especially when he is standing so close to me. I try to be a good student though. "Okay. Got it. Now what?"

"This is how you swing the bat." He guides me as we go ahead and swing the bat together.

"Good. Now you think you can do that on your own?" he asks.

"Anything for you," I murmur.

He smirks. "Okay, show me."

I demonstrate a few swings, until he's pleased with my technique.

"Okay, good. I think you've got it." he states.

"It's probably because I have a great teacher."

He smiles, and the dimples pop out again. "Or maybe you're just a good learner."

I smile at him. "So, do you still play baseball?"

"No, not anymore. I stopped in college because I wanted to finish my schooling."

"Oh. I see. What do you study?" I can't even begin to guess what he studies. But then again, I actually don't know a lot about him. I don't even know how old he is.

"I actually finished my master's degree. I work as a physiotherapist."

"That's a cool job. So, you still work with a lot of athletes then?"

He shrugs. "Yes. Some. At the clinic I work at we get a variety of clients. What about you? What do you study?"

"I'm working on getting my master's degree in marine biology. When I was little my parents took me to the aquarium, and I loved it so much, I knew then I wanted to get into marine biology. I volunteer at the aquarium and love it. Every summer we run kids' camps, and they are always so eager to learn that it makes working there rewarding. I might continue to get my PhD after I finish my master's, but I'm not sure yet."

He looks impressed. "Wow, that's amazing. It's refreshing to meet people who know what they want to do in life."

I don't take compliments well, so I decide to steer the conversation. "Can I ask you a question? I feel like we skipped over the part in getting to know basic information about each other, and I don't know how to ask it in a non-awkward way, without just coming out and asking it."

"Well I don't know. I guess it depends what it is", he teases.

I just spit it out. "How old are you?"

He lets out a breath. "Man, I was not expecting that. I thought you were going to ask something completely different."

Like what? "Like what?"

"I don't know. Just not that."

I cross my arms against my chest. "Well, Mr. Avoider, your age?"

"Right. I'm twenty-six. You?"

I was off by two years. Although twenty-six is closer in age to me. Wow. Twenty-six and he has his master's, which he uses to work as a physiotherapist. I'm impressed. I think it's so attractive when guys are motivated and driven. You know, guys who actually do what they plan to do, not just *talk* about doing it. And on the plus side, if I so happen to roll my ankle or screw up my knee on the baseball field, he's my guy.

"Don't you already know my age, from the picture of my driver's license you kept on your phone?" I tease.

He laughs. "Oh yeah, I forgot I had that. Give me second, and you won't have to tell me. " He pretends to get his cell phone out of his pocket, and I playfully hit his arm.

"I'm twenty-four. And don't worry, I'm fully aware I need to work on my joke telling ability."

He laughs, and glances at his phone. "Actually, we should head back now. It's almost time for the first game."

"Okay. Also, I kind of feel bad we left your friend there without him knowing anyone besides Cooper."

"Jesse? Jesse will be fine. He's an outgoing guy."

As we begin to walk side by side back to our friends, before I know what I'm doing, I automatically grab his hand. He doesn't say anything, he just welcomes my hand in his, and we walk back holding hands. Something about it just feels right.

* * * *

"So, what were you and Travis doing alone?" Cori whispers to me, giving me 'the look'. Brennley looks over and picks up on the fact that there may be potential for juicy gossip, so she comes over to us to join the conversation. I look around to make sure Jesse isn't in ear's length.

We're playing our first baseball game of the day, and Travis is currently up at bat.

"Nothing. He was just teaching me proper batting technique." I reply.

Cori doesn't look convinced. "M-hmm."

"No, I'm being serious. We talked too. We're still getting to know each other. We just met the other week. I actually don't know too much about him. I just learned that he's twenty-six."

"You like him though, right? I mean his friend's hot too. We need to keep Travis around if he keeps bringing friends over like that," Cori looks over in Jesse's direction.

"Well so far Travis seems nice. I don't know. I don't think I'm ready to start dating. After Kyle...I don't know... Let's just say my confidence isn't as high as it was." And if Kyle couldn't deal with learning about my HIV status, what's to say Travis can?

Anger builds up in Cori's eyes. "No, that's exactly the problem. Don't let your stupid ex get to you. You deserve a great guy, no matter what Kyle said. Forget about him. Look I know your break-up with Kyle didn't end well, and I know you won't tell me why you guys ended it, but you deserve a chance with Travis. You won't know unless you try. And if it doesn't work out, so what?"

I don't say anything. I just give Cori a hug.

"We just want you to be happy. That includes being happy with yourself," Brennley adds.

I extend my arms and Brennley joins in on our hug.

Just then a loud smack breaks us up from our moment. I turn to look at where the sound came from and see Travis has hit the ball and is running to first base. It's a great hit, and he ultimately makes it to third base.

I cheer and look over to Travis and give him a thumbs up. He winks back at me. Cori is next up at bat. She manages to hit the ball and get a double run. See? Look at me learning how to use sports jargon.

After a couple of our other friends get up to go to bat, it's my turn. Travis comes over and whispers in my ear "Just do what I showed you."

I'm really nervous. I don't want to disappoint him by striking out. Especially because he took the job of teaching me so seriously. I get up to bat, and into the stance Travis taught me. I'm right handed so I position myself accordingly. The pitcher on the other team looks about Travis's age. He has a smug smirk on his face, as he probably doesn't take me seriously because I'm a girl. Although he really should, considering how well Cori did. He throws the ball, and I scream, jumping forward as the ball curves to the right almost hitting me on the left side of my ribs. If I didn't move forward just in time, he would have smoked me with the ball. Asshole. And Cooper wonders why I don't want to play? The umpire calls 'ball'.

"Hey! Watch it asshole!" I hear someone shout at the pitcher.

I turn around and realize it was Travis who yelled that. It kind of makes my heart melt that he thinks he needs to stick up for me. I turn back around and get back into position. The pitcher throws the ball, and I swing the bat, getting a piece of the ball. The ball launches passed third base, and I run to first base. By the time the other team has recovered I make it to first base. Score! Not something to brag to the grandkids about, but definitely acceptable.

After the game, Travis comes up and crushes me into a hug "I told you the technique would work."

"You did." I smile and lean back so I can look directly in his eyes. They look hazel today. "And you didn't need to stick up for me to that pitcher."

"No, I did. That guy was just being an asshole. The game is only for charity and he shouldn't be doing that, especially to a girl."

"Okay. Well to be honest..." I lean in and whisper in his ear "I kind of liked it."

* * * *

Hayden

After winning our first two baseball games (go us!), we head to the barbeque for lunch. Travis properly introduces me to Jesse, as I missed out on meeting him when Travis was helping me learn proper batting technique.

I decide to go against the logical side of my brain telling me to stay away from Travis, by sitting next to him at lunch. As I'm eating my hotdog, he rips open his pack of munchies, grabs a Doritos chip, and eats it. Nope, he isn't doing it right. I can't help but tease him about it.

"Your first bite of the mix, and you chose to eat a Dorito chip? C'mon, everyone knows the pretzels are the best part of the munchies mix."

He looks at me, confused. "Umm... No way. Doritos are the best part of the mix."

"No, they're not, they're the worst. It goes in order from best to worst: pretzels, cheezies, sun chips, and then Doritos," I argue.

"No, it's Doritos, sun chips, cheezies, and then pretzels," he argues back.

"If the Doritos are supposedly the best, how come you got the munchies, instead of just a bag of Doritos, " I challenge.

"Maybe because I like variety. How come you didn't get a bag of just pretzels?"

"Because they didn't have just pretzels as an option, or I would have."

"Oh my god, are you guys seriously fighting over fucking chips?" Erik interrupts.

I chuckle. "Yes, in fact we are. C'mon Travis, let's go get you a bag of just Doritos." It's my way of getting Travis alone. I want to spend more time with him without our friends interfering. Travis doesn't argue. He just gets up and we head off away from our friends.

* * * *

As Travis and I are walking I realize I'm more nervous than I thought I would be, which is unusual for me. I've had plenty of boyfriends, and guy friends, so it's weird for me to feel somewhat uncomfortable around Travis. I decide to start the conversation safe, with something we have in common, knowing Cooper. "So, you've known Cooper a long time then?"

"Yeah, I guess. I mean we didn't hangout much outside baseball, but he's cool. He was also one of our best players," Travis replies.

"That comes as no surprise. He's good at almost every sport. It also helps that he's basically a giant. Although when he played basketball, everyone was so tall he fit in well." I laugh. "He's a really good guy, and treats Brennley well, so I like him. He's also super sweet to Cori and me. He's taken care of the three of us on different occasions after we'd had a few drinks, and he's the best person to scare away creepy guys at the bar, since his height intimidates the guys."

Travis raises his eyebrows. "Oh. So, is that why he interrupted us last Saturday at the bar?"

I chuckle. "Definitely. I just gave him our secret code hand gesture and that's why he came right over." I tease.

His eyes glisten. "Yeah, and what hand gesture is that?"

I give him a shy smile. "Well I can't tell you. I might need to use it this weekend."

He pretends to look hurt. "Ouch."

I playfully bump into his shoulder. "I'm just giving you a hard time."

He nods. "I know."

As much fun as teasing him is, I decide I want to get to know a little more about him.

"So, have you lived in Vancouver your whole life?". We head over by a tree, so we can sit down in the shade. He sits beside me, closer than I expect him to.

"Yes, I have. You?"

"Yes. I love it here. Recently, photography has become my new favourite hobby. The scenery and landscapes in Vancouver are just so beautiful, so I find it's the perfect place to take pictures," I explain.

He smiles. "Have you traveled much?"

"Yeah, actually I have. My dad's a pilot, so my family has been really fortunate on the traveling front. That's also why I developed a love for photography. When I travel, I'm always taking pictures. Although I want to travel more of South America, and more of Asia. I really want to visit Japan. You?"

He's staring intently at me. I think this is my new favourite thing about him. I keep saying I don't know him that well, but when I talk to him, I know he's actually listening to me, and he cares what I have to say.

"Well that's convenient that your dad is a pilot. No, I haven't done that much traveling. I keep putting it off. First, it was graduate high school; then, finish my bachelor's degree; then, finish my master's. Now it's work a few years. Just a bunch of excuses, I know. Someday though."

"Where would you want to go?" I ask.

"I'd want to travel around Europe. I agree with you though. Japan would be cool."

I grin, recalling all the times I got to explore Europe. "Europe is amazing. You need to go. There's always going to be a reason to not go traveling. You just need to focus on all the reasons why you should go. You earned it too, by getting your master's. It can be a late graduation present to yourself."

He leans in closer. "You keep telling me to go, and I just might."

His face is inches away from me. If I moved in just a little closer our lips would touch. I could be bold and lean in closer to see how he would react. I can't read him though, so I decide against it. Plus, if I read him wrong, it could get awkward, and I just met him not that long ago.

And you said you were off boys, Hayden.

Damn my subconscious voice.

"Good, you should." I lean back slightly and decide to change the topic.

"Do you have any siblings?" Cori would appreciate me asking him this. You know, just in case he has an older brother who happens to be just as good looking as Travis is, and if things didn't work out with Erik.

"Yes, I have two older brothers. You?"

Score. Remind me to inform Cori later. "Aww, so you're the baby of the family."

He groans. "I hate that term. Just because I was the youngest doesn't mean I got away with everything."

"So, you were a trouble maker?" I laugh.

"Well, my brothers and I just never ratted each other out, so it seemed we got in trouble more frequently. One time as kids, when my parents were out, my brothers and I were playing hockey in our backyard, as it was mostly concrete. My oldest brother Trevor shot the hockey puck, and it hit and shattered part of our kitchen window. When my parents came home, we tried to convince them that someone tried to break into the house. Obviously, they didn't believe us. Tristan and I stayed silent and wouldn't rat Trevor out, even though my mom tried to talk to all of us on numerous occasions to get one of us to spill."

"So, what happened? You all just got grounded?"

"Not only that, but the three of us had to pay to get the window fixed. My mom made each of us pay for a third of it. My chore money went to that stupid window for weeks." He shakes his head and laughs.

"You seem close to your bothers."

He smiles.

There are those dimples again.

"I am."

"Yeah, I have one older sister Lauren who you may or may not have seen in an inebriated state last Saturday night. Which is why I left so suddenly. Had to take her home. Although, Lauren and I are different than you and your brothers. It felt like I was always taking the fault when we got into trouble."

"That sucks for you."

"Yeah, but after a while I think they knew Lauren was manipulating me into taking the blame." I stretch my legs out. "Anyway, what time is it?"

Travis looks at his cell phone. "Definitely time to go back if we want to make our third game."

"Then we'd better go."

Travis stands up and holds out his hand to help me stand. I take it, and we walk back to prepare for game three.

* * * *

Travis

Trust

This weekend has been more fun that I thought it would be. So far, we've won all our games. Jesse and I have meshed well with the others. It seems like we've all been playing baseball together for years, as opposed to hours. One of the girls, Cori, who seems close to Hayden is surprising good. I was hesitant when Cooper was going to let her pitch, but she has a decent arm. Hayden is hilarious. I can tell she's trying, but you can tell sports are just not her thing. At least I have a good angle when she's up at bat. She also has the widest grin on her face when she messes up, and I can't help but laugh at her when she screws up because she is just so uncoordinated. You just can't fake that level of un-coordination.

Hayden is easy to talk to. Usually I don't like to open up and talk about myself, but for some reason I feel I can trust her. She actually asks *me* questions. You'd be surprised at how long girls can talk about themselves without stopping. Most girls do. It gets boring and I find myself nodding my head at appropriate times and zoning out. Hayden appears way more ambitious than the girls I'm used to. Because I've finished school, and have a full-time job, most girls would be happy staying home while I go to work and basically take care of them. All they focus on is getting married and having babies. I'm not hating on stay at home moms because I know they work hard. It's more of a fact that I don't want a girl who is one hundred percent dependable on me. I want a girl who has her shit together. I don't want to pick up her slack. I don't want to work hard so I can earn money, just for her to spend on herself to do her hair and buy expensive shit we really don't need. I don't want a girl who is with me to just mooch off of me.

On the other hand, I wouldn't mind spoiling the girl I'm with, and taking care of her in the sense that she's secure. I want her to be able to achieve her goals and dreams, and not settle. The fact Hayden is passionate about what she studies is a turn on. To be honest, physical attraction was important to me when I was younger. But I'm realizing that as I get older, other attributes such as ambition and being able to look after one's finances are becoming more attractive.

* * * *

Hayden

It's Sunday afternoon, and it turns out that our team has done well this weekend. We've officially made it to the semi-finals, no thanks to me. It's mainly because Cooper, Travis, Jesse, and Cori are amazing baseball players. Travis and I have spent a lot of time together. Between games we go sneak off to chill, and talk. Kind of like teenagers. Since our group's so big, not many people seem to notice when we discreetly leave. I have no doubt though, that Cori and Brennley have noticed and will bombard me with questions when we get home. I've also learned a lot more about Travis. He seems really genuine, but that's the problem. There's got to be something wrong with him. How can a young attractive guy who has his master's and a full-time job be single? I mean, maybe he just wants to be friends? He hasn't made a move on me or asked me out. Aside from our hand holding, and our near proximity when we talk, there's been no indication that he likes me. I don't know why I'm even debating this. I keep telling myself I can't get involved with another guy. Not yet.

"Are you excited about playing in the semi-finals?" Travis asks me.

"Can't you guys just bench me already? Why do we take turns and rotate our extra players out in the field? I'm a great benchwarmer." I pout.

He looks amused. "Because baseball is a team sport."

"Well next time we do a group activity. I think I should get to pick."

"Photography is not a group activity," he jokes.

"Maybe that's why I like it so much," I murmur.

"Okay, how about this. If you play well in this next game, the next time you want to go do your photography, I'll come with you."

I grin. "You would hate coming with me when I take pictures."

"Why is that?"

"Because I can spend easily an hour taking a picture of the same flower. Cori and Brennley purposely avoid coming on hikes with me, unless I agree to not bring my camera, because they get tired of waiting for me trying to get the perfect shot."

He shrugs. "It can't be that bad. What's your schedule like?"

I pause to think. "I have school almost every day, but Friday's I don't start until the afternoon."

"Well, I don't start work until early afternoon on Friday's, so why don't we go on a hike Friday morning and you can take your photos?"

I look up at him and smirk. "You know, you're going to regret asking me to come."

He beams. "We'll see."

Chapter Four: Hayden

So, we didn't end up making it to the finals on Sunday for the baseball tournament. We ended up coming in third place. The guys and Cori were disappointed, but to be honest I didn't really care how we did. It's currently Monday night, and I've just finished making some pasta for dinner. I gave Travis my number yesterday, and he texted me after I finished school asking how my day was. It's a simple gesture, but it's nice to know he's thinking about me. As I'm pouring myself a plate I hear the front door open and Cori walking in.

"You're home late. I just made some pasta. Help yourself."

She looks at me, relieved. "Aww, thanks, I will. I'm super hungry. I totally lost track of time in the lab today."

Cori grabs a bowl of pasta and joins me on the couch. Cori has been working late a lot lately. Besides this weekend, I've caught her zoning out a few times, so I decide to confront her on it because that's what good friends do. "Are you okay? You seem like you've been distracted this last week?"

Cori grabs a curl that has fallen out of her ponytail and tucks it behind her ear. "Do you like Erik?"

Wait, what? I wasn't expecting that. What do I say to that? To be honest, I'm not a fan of Erik's. He has this cockiness to him that I find unattractive. I mean he is good looking, with his dark brown hair and piercing green eyes. He's also superficial. He comes from money, so he buys Cori nice things, and takes her on trips. But it's hard to know if it's just for show, so I have always questioned his sincerity. In addition, he bails on Cori quite a bit. One time he left her alone at the bar, and I had to go pick her up. I still haven't got over that. Cori played it off like it wasn't a big deal and he's 'not normally like that', and he just 'had too much to drink.' It's not like he has done something really bad, it's just simple things like this that have happened way too frequently for my liking. I haven't mentioned it to Cori, because I know she'll get defensive; and really, as her friend, I'm just here to support whatever decision she makes, even if I don't agree.

"Well it doesn't really matter if I like him. He's *your* boyfriend. As long as you like him, he respects you, and makes you happy, then I'm happy. Where is this coming from?"

Cori shrugs, and shifts around on the couch to change her position. She's picked at her pasta, but for someone who said she's hungry she hasn't shown it. She's definitely distracted. She reaches out and puts her bowl on the table and nervously picks at her fingernails.

"I don't know. It's almost been a year since we've been together, and I just thought we'd be closer you know? For some reason there's something lacking with our intimacy. I can't figure out what it is though. I just don't always feel one hundred percent comfortable with him. I feel like I always have to be serious, and I'm not allowed to show my silly side, worried he'll just laugh at me, but not in a good way. He is sometimes rude to other people, which I don't like." Cori shakes her head. "I don't know, maybe I'm just overreacting. Maybe I'm trying to find something wrong with our relationship. I don't usually do long term relationships. This is my longest relationship I've had, so that's probably why I'm anxious. I just have to give it some more time"

I take a deep breath. Giving relationship advice to friends is difficult to say the least. It's also easier to give advice than to take it. I want to be honest with her and tell her I don't really like Erik, but I am sincere when I say it's really up to her to decide if she wants to be with him, and that I'd support her either way. I don't want to intentionally hurt her feelings, so I decide to be careful in how I word my next sentence.

"Well, you can't compare your relationship to other people's relationships. I think everyone's relationships move at different speeds, depending on a lot of different factors. It's good to be thinking about it though. You don't want to make a rash decision."

Yeah, Hayden. Take your own advice. You can't compare relationships. Just because it didn't work out with Kyle, doesn't mean it won't work out with Travis. I push that thought out of my head. It's not about me right now.

Cori sighs. "Yeah you're right. I guess sometimes it's hard to see other couples, like Brennley and Cooper. They make it look so natural and easy. And then having people our age getting married and having babies. It just makes you think."

I have to agree with her. It is hard not to be jealous when you see other couples who seem so compatible and appear to be in love. Although over the years I have discovered that people act differently in the privacy of their own homes. Kyle, my ex always acted like a gentleman when we were out with friends, but he sometimes acted differently when it was just the two of us. It was almost like he didn't try as hard when it was just the two of us. On the other hand, I know Cori knows Brennley and Cooper's relationship is not perfect. She's heard Brennley vent about her relationship frustrations plenty of times. I almost think these kinds of thoughts come forward when we aren't in the best place in our relationship.

"Well you know firsthand that Brennley and Cooper's relationship is not easy, and they have their own issues they deal with. And that's exactly my point. Don't compare your life to other people's." I raise my eyebrows at her. "Plus...do you really want to have a baby right now?"

Cori relaxes, and it's almost like I can visibly see the stress wash away from her face. "No, definitely not. Definitely need to finish school first." She beams her blue eyes at me. "I just want you to have a baby, so I can get my baby fix, and them give the baby back to you when I'm done."

I give her the bitch brow.

"Wow, how thoughtful. And don't count on it. You know we live together so the baby would live here and cry all night, so you wouldn't get any sleep. Right now, the only way I'm having a kid is though immaculate conception."

Also, I would have to do some research and talk to my doctor before ever getting pregnant, because I'm sure there would have to be important discussions on how my HIV status would affect me, and my baby. For a second, that thought makes me sad. I guess I've never really thought about how my HIV would affect my ability to have a baby. I guess that's something I can bring up with my doctor at my next appointment. Not that I'm in any rush to have a baby.

She looks mischievously at me. "Well, maybe not. Not if things work out between you and Travis."

"Wow. I see how you just slipped that into the conversation."

"Well you did spend a lot of time together this weekend." She looks hopeful. "Did you get his number?"

I look away as I tell her. "Yes, I did. And we may or may not be hanging out this Friday."

Cori perks up. "On a date?"

Are we going on a date? We haven't actually discussed where we want our relationship to go. Right now, I'd say we are just friends. Like I mentioned before, I'm not really sure if he actually likes me like that.

"We didn't put a label on it. It's just casual. We're going on a hike, that's all. I told you I'm not ready to start dating. "

Dating involves trust and vulnerability. And I can't trust guys right now.

Cori leans forward and picks up her bowl of pasta. "Okay, I'll stop pressuring you. Just please be open-minded."

I guess I could try to be open-minded. I also want to be realistic. Not have my hopes too high. I nod. "I'll try my best."

* * * *

Travis

Jesse and I decided to stop for a drink at a local pub. It's not too busy, so we grab a booth. Both my brothers are meeting me here in a bit.

As promised, Trevor was able to convince Addison to let Tristan out, since it's a Wednesday night. Apparently, it would be the end of the world if she let him out on a Friday or Saturday night without her.

I casually take a sip of my beer. "I forgot to tell you. Tristan got engaged a couple weekends ago."

Jesse looks surprised. "Did you know he was proposing?"

I shake my head. "No, he didn't tell me. I found out at our family dinner. I'm not even mad he didn't tell me. It's just that he hasn't been dating Addison for that long. It's been less than a year. She's so controlling. He does everything she says, and she makes all the decisions. He needs to grow a pair."

Jesse nods his head in agreement. "When are they getting married? Soon?"

I take another sip of my beer. "Who knows? Hopefully not soon. He'd better know what he's in for."

"What do your parents think about them getting married?"

I finish off my beer. "My dad didn't say much, and you know my mom. She's over the moon. She loves weddings. She was on my ass that night, wondering when I'm going to be getting married next."

Jesse smirks. "When are you getting married?"

I flip him the finger. "Fuck off."

The waitress comes by, and I order another beer. Jesse's face turns serious as he asks me, "So are you serious about this Hayden girl? I mean in all the years I've known you, you haven't had a girlfriend. When is the last time you've even had a girlfriend? Grade five?"

I flip him the finger again. "You fuck around too."

He chuckles. "Yeah, but I do the girlfriend thing every once in a while, too. Actually, between us, I'm been thinking about the idea of settling down. Now that we're older it seems everyone is getting married and having kids. I almost feel left out. The idea of having someone to come home to every night after work seems nice. Especially if they have dinner made."

I choke on my beer. "Wow, I think this is the deepest conversation we've ever had. What's happened to us?"

"Well in a few years' time, we'll be thirty."

I shudder. "Don't remind me." Although he has a point. Lots of my friends and brother's friends are settling down and getting married. It's not that I'm against it. I just haven't found the person I want to spend every day with.

He slants his head. "You avoided the question."

I pause for a couple beats. "Hayden's cool. She not like most girls. Although her baseball skills definitely need improvement. I like her. We haven't talked about it. I think I'm just going to see how things go."

He nods in acknowledgement. "Her friend Cori is pretty hot. She's got a killer arm as well."

"Dude, she's got a boyfriend." I point out. "But between us I was impressed as well." I mutter.

"Her boyfriend seems like an asshole. He probably won't last long. She can do better."

I guess we'll both be playing the wait-and-see game. The conversation floods into sports talk, and before I know it, Trevor and Tristan arrive. Jesse gets up and leaves, even though I invite him to stay. He says he has errands to run, but I know he's just using that as an excuse to give us some privacy.

Trevor, Tristan, and I briefly talk about our day, and things that have been going on recently. I then decide to break open the wedding topic.

"So, have you guys set a date for the wedding?"

"Yeah. We decided we're getting married at the end of August."

I almost spit out my beer. "It's almost July. That's only two months away!" What is he thinking? Is he really going to have everything ready by then? I can't imagine Addison will be ready by then. She'll have numerous demands that need to be met before she'll agree to that. They haven't even dated a year. I wonder whose idea it was to get married so soon. No, I definitely know it's her.

Tristan glances at me. "Well our wedding's going to be on the smaller side. We want it intimate. We don't want anything too fancy. You wouldn't understand, Travis. Once you find a girl that's right for you, you won't want to wait to marry her either."

Wow. Thanks for that low blow, Tristan. Notice how Trevor doesn't say anything? I wonder what he's thinking. I think he's been so preoccupied with becoming a dad, he isn't fully comprehending the situation with Tristan. I know it really shouldn't matter to me. Tristan is an adult and he can make his own decisions. I just don't want Addison to fuck him over. I've seen how some relationships end, and how ugly some divorces can turn into. To diffuse my anger, so I don't regret saying anything nasty to him, I try to lighten the situation. "Well just be careful with late August. Wouldn't want one of your best men to not be able to make it because he's too busy helping his wife deliver his child."

It takes a second for Tristan to comprehend what I'm saying. Realization hits his face. He looks at Trevor. "Sorry, man, I guess I didn't think that one through. I was thinking the baby is going to be born in September, but I guess if the baby is early it could be problematic."

Is that the only thing Tristan didn't think through?

I keep that comment to myself.

* * * *

Hayden

It's Thursday night, and as usual I sit down at group. Billy and Mason announce we have another member joining our group. The guy is in his late thirties, slightly underweight, with a military-style shaved head and brown eyes. He introduces himself as Connor. Connor tells us his full life story, beginning when he was a kid. He talks about his parents who were addicted to drugs and alcohol when he was growing up. His dad passed away from liver failure ten years ago, and his mom is in recovery, and has been for about fifteen years. Connor discusses how he became addicted to drugs at just fifteen years old and lived on the streets shortly after that. He has been sober for eighteen months now and wants to turn his life around and possibly get into social work. He explains how he contracted HIV through sharing needles he used to inject drugs while living on the streets.

His story is upsetting to hear, but it makes me hopeful when he talks about his future plans. His story reminds me how easy it is to judge people, but you can never know what they've been through. His story also reminds me a bit of Brennley's sister, Mikayla. Although she had a super supportive family with no history of substance abuse, Mikayla still managed to get involved with drugs and alcohol. The most upsetting part of her story is, that Penelope has to grow up without a mother. It's sad, because Penelope is such a good kid and she deserves nothing but the best. Thinking about Penelope makes me want to see her. I make a mental note to ask Brennley to bring Penelope over, next time we hangout.

Another guy in our group, Clayton, acknowledges Connor's story, and discusses the similarities. Clayton also contracted HIV through sharing needles and is an ex-addict. That's another thing about HIV. Although there a few different ways to contract HIV, all of our stories and circumstances are different and unique to us. I might have contracted HIV through sexual activity, but I can still empathize with both Clayton and Connor's story.

I'm walking out of group with a different perspective, and I am inspired by how some people can be so open-minded and willing to share their stories.

Just like *Travis* could be open-minded.

I brush that thought off. The building which we have group in is three floors. There are dental and doctor's office in there as well, so I don't leave group in a hurry to not be seen. It's not like people will know where I'm coming from. Not that I should be embarrassed, because I shouldn't be. As I exit the building, a few feet away I see Travis.

Of course. Why is that guy everywhere?

"Hey Hayden, I didn't expect to see you here." He comes over and gives me a quick hug. "I'm glad to see you though." Travis is a good hugger which is definitely a plus. Some guys just don't know how to give good hugs. They awkwardly lean back during the hug, or they unintentionally tense up. Or maybe I'm just dating the wrong people. It could be me.

"Oh, I just had a doctor's appointment. Everything's okay though, so not to worry. What are you doing here?"

Why did I just lie to him now? I talk about how I shouldn't be embarrassed about going to group, and then flat out lie to him.

This isn't the place to tell him, my subconscious reassures me.

He looks at me with his soft brown eyes. They look more brown today, as opposed to the hazel they were this past weekend. "I have a dentist appointment."

"Oh-h, fun," I say sarcastically. Going to the dentist is the worst. I've yet to meet someone who actually likes going to the dentist. One time I ate almonds before going to the dentist. I wouldn't recommend that. When they start flossing your teeth you realize just how much of the almonds get stuck it your teeth. Sorry, I know that was TMI. Although, Travis going to the dentist explains why his teeth are always so white and perfect. He must be one who actually goes to the dentist every six months, as opposed to being one who goes every eleven months or so. Sorry,

I'll stop ragging on my poor dental health. I promise I brush my teeth at least twice a day.

He groans. "Yeah I know. Hey look, I don't mean to be rude, but I am kind of running behind, so I do need to go." His eyes soften. "We're still on for Friday though, right?'

"Yes, of course. See you Friday." I give him a quick goodbye hug.

As Travis walks into the building, I let out a breath I didn't know I was holding. The first thing I think of is 'damn, that was close'. What if he did catch me in group though? Or if he caught me outside talking to someone from group, and something about HIV slipped. Maybe he could be understanding. It's a possibility, right? I guess I won't know if I don't try. Where is the lion from the *Wizard of Oz* when you need him? I'm looking for some bravery and courage myself.

* * * *

"What are hemp hearts?" I ask Brennley.

Our schedules have been so busy the only time we could fit in hanging out is a Thursday night at the grocery store, right after my group. Adulting sucks sometimes. Actually, a lot of times.

"I'm not sure, all I know is they are supposed to be super healthy and good for you."

Oh, Vancouver. It seems like everyone in Vancouver is always on a health food kick. That, or people just enjoy talking about doing healthy things. The jury's still out on the actual doing and eating healthy foods though.

I glance down at the grocery list she brought. "You also have here on the list 'Chia seeds' and 'Lentil Pasta.' Oh, wait here on the bottom of the list is chocolates. Now you're talking."

Brennley gasps. "Those are not for me. Penelope hates studying for spelling tests, so I bribe her with chocolates. She gets a chocolate for every word she spells correctly."

Wait, what? I don't ever remember getting chocolate for every word I spelled correctly when I was a kid. My parents just told me I got the satisfaction of knowing I spelled every word correctly.

"Talk about Penelope, I miss that rug-rat. When do I get to see her next?"

Brennley looks at me shyly. "Actually, I was going to ask if you could look after her this Saturday until Sunday afternoon? My dad is at a golf tournament, my mom's away for work, and Cooper and I wanted to go away for the weekend to my parent's cabin since the weather is supposed to be nice. We'll pay you, I promise. I mean, worst case scenario we can bring her with us; she's just a little bit of a mood killer if you catch my drift."

Sometimes I feel for Brennley. I know she loves Penelope. I would never come out and say it, but I think looking after Penelope is too much for her sometimes. I think she misses out on a lot of things because she gets stuck taking care of Penelope. Even though Brennley's parents help look after Penelope, Brennley didn't really have a say in choosing to look after Penelope. I mean her sister died, and that was hard enough. I shake my head "Nah, it's all good. And we're friends, you don't have to pay me. I'd love to have her overnight."

Brennley gives me a hug. "Thanks. You're the best."

"But on one condition. You need to buy enough of those chocolates for me too. "

She grins. "Deal. Now let's go find those hemp harts."

I groan. "Are we serious about those?"

Brennley starts to take off, and I unwillingly follow. I guess we are serious.

* * * *

On Friday afternoon, Travis picks me up and we head out to go on our hike. The best part of Vancouver is there are numerous hikes and trails to follow, so it makes it easy to switch it up. Vancouver also has amazing trails in the mountains, and when you reach the peak, the views are extraordinary.

Travis has been sweet this past week. Every day, he texts me asking how my day was, and this morning I even got a good morning text from him. It just makes me wonder what he wants from me. Friendship or more?

The day is beautiful, with a clear blue sky and nice sunshine. The air has a slight breeze to it, which helps with the heat. I'm in shorts and a tank top with my hair in a high ponytail. Travis is also in shorts and a tank top, which is nice because it's quite the view. When he isn't looking, my eyes drift to those arm muscles, so clearly taut and defined.

Within a couple minutes, I find this extraordinary looking tree, and I must stop to take a few photos of it with my very expensive camera. The tree has an old appearance to it, and the length of it goes on and on. The bark on it has ripples that make it appear as if the bark has numerous different shades of brown to it. My favourite part of it is, it's not perfectly straight. It has a unique bend to it, sort of like a Charlie Brown Christmas Tree, although it appears strong and sturdy, not as if it will fall over. The branches are wavy and have a slight inward curve to them. I stop, move my position so the angle and light hit the tree the way I want, and start snapping photos.

I'm so focused and in the zone that for a second, I forget Travis is here. After a couple of minutes when I think I have a few good shots, I stop and turn around to see him staring at me. Not in a creepy way, more of an admiring way. Okay, or maybe it has to do with the fact I'm in shorts and was bending over a little bit on those last couple shots. Because he's a guy, I'm going to go with the last one.

"Whatcha looking at? " I smile shyly at him.

He shrugs. "Nothing. Just watching you take photos. You're so focused."

"You have to be, if you want to get a good shot." I blush.

"I can tell. It's cool seeing you. Just by looking at you I can tell you love it."

I walk back closer to him. "I do. You aren't bored yet?"

He smirks. "Nope, I'm actually enjoying the view."

I giggle. "I'm sure you are. We have to move on though. We have to make it to the top of the mountain. That's going to be the money shot. "

Travis sticks his arm out. "Lead the way."

The view at the top of the mountain is amazing. We sit down on a big rock and stare out. There are so many trees, the surrounding mountains, and of course the best part is looking out at the water.

"Although I almost collapsed a few times from exhaustion walking up the mountain, it was totally worth this view." I explain.

"Yeah, definitely worth the view." he replies.

I stand up, take numerous shots of the view from different angles. Because Travis is not paying attention, and he looks so beautiful, I quickly take a snap of him. When the flash goes off, he turns towards me.

"Did you just take a picture of me?" He looks shocked.

"What if I did?" I challenge him.

"You can't do that." He looks exasperated.

"Well I just did." Just to annoy him, I start moving around and taking pictures of him. He laughs and sticks his hands in front of his face, and my camera lens, trying to ruin the photos. He then groans "Stop, stop. I'm going to take that camera from you."

I gasp. "No, not my camera." I stop taking pictures of him. I call a truce and walk over and sit beside him on the rock. This time I sit closer, so our legs are touching.

"You don't like your picture being taken?"

"No, I hate it." he exclaims.

I'm not surprised, it was always a fight to get my ex-boyfriends to take pictures with me. I don't understand. If they smile nicely for the first picture, then I'll stop. When they put up a fight, it just becomes that much more painful, and takes that much longer.

"Can we take a picture together?"

"Nice try, but no."

I pout. "You're no fun."

He grins. "I know."

Since I know he's not going to change his mind, I decide to change the conversation.

"So, you have any summer plans?" I ask.

He nods. "I usually head down to the States every summer to visit family in Oregon. I have a lot of cousins my age there, so my brothers and I like to head down there. But otherwise, not much. Just working. You?"

He was telling the truth when he said he was close to his brothers. It makes me happy he's close to his family.

"Well I start volunteering at the Aquarium at end of the month, when the kids are out of school to run the summer camps.

Brennley's family also has a cabin up north, so she usually invites a bunch of us to go camping."

"That sounds fun."

"Yeah, it is mostly. Although when there's drinking, things can turn a bit crazy."

One time, Lauren came with us, and used our camping tarps to make a giant slip-and-slide down the hill by the cabin. We had been drinking, so obviously we thought at the time that this was a brilliant idea. Lauren put on way too much soap, and some people almost got really hurt.

Don't try this at home kids.

Another time, a mother black bear and her two cubs came by when we were all sitting around the fire. We all freaked and ran into the cabin, without putting out the fire, or taking in our food. We were stuck for hours in that cabin, as the bears feasted on our food. It was awful.

He tilts his head. "Is that why you don't drink, or was it just your turn to be designated driver the night we were at the bar?"

My anti-retroviral medications don't prevent me from having a drink or two. It's just...

You made the worst decision of your life when drinking too much, my subconscious likes to remind me.

I take a deep breath and let it out. "I don't drink often. If I do, I have a drink or two."

"Well that's fair enough. So, you have plans this weekend?" he asks.

Oh look, he changed the subject. Did he not like my answer? He didn't look disappointed. His brown eyes are soft and have a gentleness to him. Maybe he's picking up on the fact I don't want to talk about drinking.

"I have to look after Brennley's niece Penelope tomorrow and Sunday. She's five, and she's so smart and adorable. I think I might take her to the aquarium tomorrow. Since I'm volunteering there I get free admission, and she loves animals. If you don't have plans you could come with us?" I try to read the expression on his face.

When he doesn't immediately answer I blurt out "You don't have to. I get it. Some people don't like kids. Or maybe it's me? I know we haven't known each other very long, and I'm not sure of the status of our relationship or what but—"

"Hayden." Travis cuts me off from my awful rambling, but I continue.

"I can't believe I just said that." I hide my face in my hands. "Why do I always embarrass myself around you? The bird shit, sucking at baseball and now this senseless rambling. I promise I'm normal."

He chuckles. "Hayden, it's okay. Honestly, not to hurt your feelings, but the bird shit thing was fucking hilarious."

I wince. "I knew you were trying not to laugh at me!"

"You're trying to tell me that if the roles were reversed you wouldn't have laughed at me?"

I chuckle. "Oh, I definitely would have laughed at you!"

He smirks. "So, then you can't get mad at me."

I guess he makes a fair point.

"Can we please try to forget it happened? It was super-embarrassing for me."

"I'm never going to forget it happened. Next time I have a bad day, I'm just going to replay that moment in my head."

I scowl at him. "You better not!"

"I won't." He winks at me.

I groan. "You're the worst. Friendship over."

He looks amused. "Anyway, back to your question—or should I say questions. Last weekend was actually a ton of fun, and that's mostly because of you, so yes I'd love to come hangout with you and your niece tomorrow."

I open my mouth to reply, but he cuts me off before I can speak

"And to answer your other question, I don't know where our relationship stands, but I thought it was obvious that I liked you. Or should I say like you."

So, he does like me. But it still doesn't answer my question if he wants to be friends with benefits or exclusive, and I definitely don't want to play games to try to figure it out. I look away from him.

"So...what does that mean?"

He reaches out his hand, and gently grabs my chin to guide my head back to face him so I am directly looking at him. Because we're sitting down we are at almost eye level.

"Well I guess it means if you're down, we can see where things go."

"Okay. I'd like that." Screw my subconscious. I said I was off guys, but I feel connected to Travis, and I barely know him. There's no harm in trying right?

He quietly murmurs a "me too", and then tilts his head slightly and leans forward. I lean forward too, and next thing I know our lips are touching. He kisses me gently and somewhat hesitantly at first, but when he doesn't feel me pull away, he tilts his head on more of an angle and brushes his tongue out against my lips, wanting to gain entrance into my mouth. I lift my hands and wrap one of my arms around his neck bringing him closer, while I place my other hand on his other shoulder. I casually shift my position to angle myself better and open up to him.

Once I open my mouth, our tongues touch, and I let out an embarrassing low moan. I can feel him smile against my mouth. He continues his exploration of my mouth. He tastes good. He must have been chewing gum earlier because he tastes minty. He then wraps one of his hands around my waist and pulls me up onto his lap so I'm straddling him. He keeps one of his arms around me so I don't fall back, while he places the other one on my hip.

As our kiss deepens, I can feel his hand move up from my hip to just under my breast, and then back down my side. After he does this a few times, he hesitantly, and ever so slowly, sticks his hand underneath my shirt by my right hip. He pauses with his hand under my shirt, as if to get permission to continue his exploration. I move my hand from his right shoulder down and cover his. I guide his hand up my body, giving him permission to continue.

Just as he's about to reach my bra area, in the distance we hear a not-so-subtle coughing noise and a whistle. I immediately break apart the kiss, pull my tank top down slightly where it has risen, and step back off Travis's lap.

A few feet away are an older couple, probably in their forties. The man has a smile on his face. The woman, however, does not. The woman looks unimpressed. If I had to guess, it was the man who whistled and the woman who coughed. I'm probably as red as a tomato right now. I grab Travis's hand pulling him a bit harder than I normally would. I just want to get out of here.

"We were just leaving," I give an awkward smile as Travis and I walk past them and head back down the mountain. When were far enough away and out of ear shot I look at Travis. "That was so embarrassing."

Travis has a shit-eating grin on his face. "Well that's another moment you can add to the 'embarrassing moments with Travis list', as you seem to be keeping track."

I groan and cover my eyes with my free arm. "Well at least that was embarrassing for both of us and not just me."

Travis casually shrugs. "That wasn't embarrassing."

I sigh. "Yes, it was. Did you see the look on the woman's face? She didn't look impressed."

"So, what? It's not like we'll ever see them again so there's no point in being embarrassed. Plus, I would never be embarrassed getting caught with you."

I don't say anything. I just blush. All of a sudden, Travis pulls on my arm, and moves us over to the left shouting "Look out!"

Oh my god! What am I supposed to be looking out for? Panicked, I yell "For what?"

He brings us to a halt and relaxes. "Don't worry, all clear."

All clear? I'm so confused. What is wrong with him? I look at him, uncertain, and frown. "All clear?"

He has the widest grin on his face, and he looks like he is going to laugh. "Yeah, sorry. A bird flew over us. I was worried you were going to be the victim of another vile attack."

He cracks up. I'm half unimpressed, and half trying not to laugh myself. I playfully hit his shoulder again. "You are the worst!"

Chapter Five: Hayden

The next morning, I wake up early and head for my morning run. I feel a slight disappointment when I don't see Travis at the track.

You're seeing him today, I remind myself.

When I get back, I shower, and make a smoothie. I change into a nice floral skirt, which I deem appropriate in length, and a matching pink tank top. My side bangs are not cooperating, so I braid them to the side and secure them with a bobby pin. Since I have time before Penelope comes over, I sit at the kitchen table and begin to do some homework, as I doubt I'll have much time this weekend to get it done. I'm able to get two hours of homework done before I hear a knock on my front door, and a second later Brennley and Penelope burst through the door.

"Hay-Hay Hayden!" Penelope yells, and launches herself at me when she sees me. I taught her how to say my name like that. I pick her up and give her a hug. Isn't she just adorable? I lean her back in my arms, and she uses her hand to push back her long brown hair out of her face. She has the biggest, roundest brown eyes I've ever seen. She's dressed in jeans and a t-shirt with dolphins on it.

"Who's your favourite Aunt?" I ask her.

"Auntie Hayden!" She exclaims. "You always ask me that, Aunt Hayden." She giggles.

Brennley rolls her eyes and I stick my tongue out at her. Brennley gives me the finger behind Penelope's back. Penelope knows that Brennley is her real aunt, and her mom is in heaven.

I look back at Penelope. "I just want to make sure you never forget."

She looks at me seriously. "I never forget. I'm a smart girl."

I laugh. I love how she's so confident in herself. I hope that never changes.

"I have to pee!" Penelope wiggles in my arms. I put her down and she runs off to the bathroom. I turn towards Brennley. "Hey, I meant to ask you something about today. On a side note, I like it when you curl your hair." I say as I step forward and grab a dark brown curl. "Trying to impress someone tonight?" I wink.

Brennley gently pushes me on my shoulders, and I fall back a touch but regain my balance. She has her hands on her hips. "Well, what's your question? And yeah, I am trying to impress someone tonight. Got a problem with that?"

"Nope, I don't. But be safe, unless you want to look after another little monster." I nod my head in the direction Penelope took off in. Trust me, be safe. I may not have a little monster, but I did get stuck with something else that never goes away. "Anyway, I was wondering if it was okay with you if I bring T-r-a-v-i-s..." I spell out his name just in case Penelope can hear me, "...with me and Penelope to the aquarium. I get it if you're not okay with me introducing Penelope to a strange guy. I know you barely know him yourself."

Brennley cuts me off. "Yes, it's totally okay. In fact, I support it one hundred percent. How guys treat children says a lot about them." She smiles. "I'm glad you're taking a chance and seeing him. Have you seen him since Sunday?"

I nod. "Yes, twice actually."

Brennley gives me the look, the look that says, 'give me details'. "And...?"

I look around the room to make sure Penelope is still gone. "Well so far he's been super nice. And we k-i-s-s-e-d." I spell again to make sure if Penelope hears, she won't understand.

Brennley gets giddy. "How was it? Is he a good kisser?"

I can't help but smile as I tell her. "Yes, he is. And now, enough about me. You need to leave and go have an amazing weekend." I point towards the front door.

"Okay." Brennley gives me a super big, tight hug. "Thanks again, Hayden. I owe you one. Again."

We both make our way to the front door. "No problem. You can make it up to me, if things work out with Travis, because I'll want to bring him when we all go up to your cabin."

Brennley turns around and glances at me. "Wow, already thinking about the future? That's a good sign."

I don't say anything. Brennley just smiles and gives me another quick hug after she finishes putting on her sandals. She yells a goodbye to Penelope and then walks out the door.

I can't believe that slipped out. I am thinking about the future.

Well you need to stop, Hayden. Because once he knows. he's going to leave, my subconscious scolds me. I can't argue because I know it might be true.

"Auntie Hayden, what's wrong? You look sad." Penelope strolls over, bringing me back from my thoughts. I bend down to her height and tell her "Nothing. I'm not sad. We're going to have a fun day at the aquarium, aren't we?"

"Yes!" Penelope jumps up and down.

"Although there is someone I have to introduce you to. He's a friend of mine and he's going to come too, if that's okay with you."

Penelope beams. "That's okay with me."

* * * *

I hear a knock on the door, and I know it's going to be Travis. I turn to Penelope. "Now Penelope, you have to be nice to Travis and use your manners. You need to be on your best behavior and act like a big girl."

"I am a big girl!" Penelope exclaims.

I walk over to open the door, but Penelope blows by me, cutting me off.

"I'll do it," she states.

Because Penelope has been shuffled around so many times and has had numerous people look after her throughout her life, she's not the shy type. She's basically the complete opposite. She's quite the chatterbox. I'm just hoping she won't say anything too embarrassing, because you never know with kids. She opens the door and Travis walks in. He's holding his car keys and wearing shorts with a grey t-shirt.

Penelope wastes no time introducing herself. "Hi Travis, my name's Penelope." She sticks out her hand. So formal. If Cori were here I'd make a joke about how a five-year old can remember a stranger's name better than she can.

Travis bends down to her eye level. "Hi, Penelope. Are you ready to have fun today?"

Oh, my goodness. He is already so good with her. I can just tell. And that is *such* a turn on. Guys who are good with kids. Bonus.

"Yup, but we better make sure we make the dolphin show. Dolphins are my favourite." She points to her shirt with dolphins on it.

Travis nods. "Well, I think we can make that work."

Penny jumps up and down. "Yay!"

Travis sticks his hand up, and Penelope gives him a high five. Oh, my goodness. That was so cute. Definitely swoon-worthy. Travis looks up to me. "You ready to go?"

I blink. "Yes, I just need to grab my bag." I look at Penelope. "Go grab your backpack." Penelope bolts out of the entranceway to go grab her backpack. I whisper to Travis "So, are *you* really ready for this? Now is the time to bail out. Penelope can be a lot."

"Do I look like I'm ready to run?" He glances at me.

I take a moment to scan him over. "Nope, you look pretty sturdy to me. Do you want me to drive?"

"No, I can drive." He looks confused. "Unless there's a reason you don't want me to drive? I'll drive slower if that's what you're hinting at. I wouldn't drive recklessly with a five-year old in the car."

Oh no, that's not what I meant when I asked if he wanted me to drive. I feel bad now. I try to look remorseful. "No, it's totally fine. That's not what I meant. I just know some guys wouldn't appreciate a messy five-year old in their car."

He gives me a look that tells me he thinks I know a lot of weird guys. In a gentle tone, he replies with "No, I don't have a problem with her in my car. I'm not weird like that."

Well that's a relief. Maybe I'm not giving the guy enough credit. Am I being too hard on him? I hope he doesn't think that. It's just that Kyle would...

Damn, that's my problem. I keep comparing him to Kyle and I need to stop doing that. It's just hard when I am so used to second guessing myself. I guess old habits die hard, and all that jazz.

Penelope comes running, with her backpack securely on her back. "Ready!"

"Okay, but put your shoes on."

Penelope looks down at her feet. "Oh, I almost forgot." She sits down and puts her sandals on. As Penelope is busy, I move closer towards Travis and whisper in his ear "Sorry. I just don't want you to feel uncomfortable about today and... stuff."

He turns and whispers in my ear "You would never make me feel uncomfortable."

Yeah right. As soon as he finds out about my condition, that will for sure change.

* * * *

It's another sunny day, so there are tons of people at the aquarium. I guess that's what happens when you decide to go to an aquarium on a Saturday in June. Penelope is having a blast, and since I'm studying marine biology I use the knowledge I have to teach her facts about the plants and animals. I think I even impressed Travis with some of my facts. Travis tries to join in and teach Penelope facts, but I ruin his thunder by calling him out for reading the signs beside the exhibits that have information and facts on the animals. Travis is a complete gentleman and doesn't rush us at all. I, of course, bring my camera and snap photos of Penelope by the exhibits. We take a couple of selfies together as well, as Travis refuses to let me take his picture. At the dolphin show, I think Penelope is going to combust from excitement. I have to hide my camera during the show because there is no way I'm letting it get splashed on.

After the dolphin show Penny asks "Hayden, what's your favourite animal? My favourite animal is a dolphin."

I stop to think about it. "Well I love dogs, but the tree frogs here are really cool too."

I catch a glance up at Travis and he starts to speak. "Oh. I thought birds were your favourite animal?" He winks at me.

I try to give Travis my best unimpressed look. "Ha-ha. No, birds are definitely *not* my favourite animal."

As we are looking at sea horses, I explain to Penelope, "And it's really cool because the daddy sea horses are the ones that carry the babies in their pouches, not the mommy sea horses."

Penelope's eyes light up. "Oh, cool." Out of nowhere Penelope turns to Travis and tells him "Did you know that I don't have a mom or dad."

Oh, shit!

Well this escalated quickly. This is so awkward. Penelope doesn't look upset. She said it in a monotone voice, just ... stated it, like it was a fact. I guess, because she doesn't remember Mikayla and never met her dad, the fact she doesn't have biological parents is indeed just a fact to her, as that's what she's always been told. I look to Travis to make sure he is not cringing. He looks a little taken back, but is definitely not cringing. He leans towards Penelope and says "I'm sorry to hear that. But is seems like you have a lot of aunts who love you."

Oh wow. That was the most perfect thing to say. He validated and then redirected her at the end.

Perfect.

I don't even know what I would have said to that comment. Travis looks at me and I mouth a 'thank you' at him, and ne nods.

Penelope gushes. "I do have a lot of aunts. Did you know that Hayden's my aunt? Every time I see her she always asks me who my favourite aunt is, and I always have to tell her it's her."

Wow. Thanks Penelope. Way to not embarrass me. I guess I deserve that, as I do make her say that. Just when I think I can't be more embarrassed, Penelope manages to dissipate that thought.

"Also, when I grow up, I'm going to be taller than Hayden. Probably not as tall as you, but definitely taller than Hayden. Everyone always says Hayden is so short."

Travis thinks this is hilarious, but I cut Penelope off. "Okay, thanks for sharing Penelope. Enough about me, I think I saw starfish nearby." This gets her excited and she keeps walking.

"Do we get to add that to the list?" he mutters.

I wince. "Yup. Because apparently the new cool thing to do is embarrass me. But you handled that parent situation with Penelope well. Sorry, I know it was super awkward. You can never predict what kids are going to say. I think she's just confused because she goes to school with other kids, and most of them have parents, and I think she's just realizing she doesn't have biological parents."

"No, I get it. It all must be confusing for her. I was telling the truth when I mentioned she's lucky to have an aunt like you. Especially an aunt who takes her to cool places like the aquarium and knows just about everything about every sea animal. "

I wink. "That's why I'm the favourite."

* * * *

After the aquarium, Travis takes both Penelope and I out for dinner. I remind Penelope to be on her best behavior, because there is nothing worse than being out at a restaurant with a screaming child. Everybody around you stares, whispers, and things get awkward really quickly. I guess it would be the ultimate test for Travis if Penny did throw a fit. If he could handle a screaming child, then he could handle almost everything. *Almost.* Travis and I decide on a kid-friendly restaurant just in case.

The hostess escorts us to our table, and we begin to take our seats. Travis walks over and pulls out the seat for me to sit. I blush and take a seat. Even if pulling out seats for a woman is old school, I sure appreciate when guys do it. It means the guy is thinking about you and wants to show he cares. After a couple minutes of looking at the menu, I ask Penelope what she wants.

"I'll probably have the ice cream sundae. It looks really good." She holds up her menu and shows me the picture of the sundae under the dessert part of the menu.

Travis chuckles, but I'm not impressed. "Penny, that's not dinner food. What do you want for dinner?"

"Well..." She looks back down at the menu. "The macaroni and cheese looks good."

"Okay, that's better. You can order that."

After we place our orders, Penelope decides she wants to interrogate Travis. "So, Travis, what grade are you in?"

I look at Travis and burst out laughing. He's laughing too. "Honey, Travis is already finished school. He goes to work at his job."

Penelope thinks about what I've said, but I'm not sure she fully understands, because her next questions is just as ridiculous. "Do you get play time at work?"

Travis chuckles. "Umm, not exactly. Although I get a break to eat my lunch."

Penelope has a confused look on her face. "Well, that seems boring."

"Penelope!" I scold. "That's rude. What do you say?"

She looks over at Travis. "Sorry, Travis."

He acknowledges her apology. "That's okay."

Even after scolding Penelope she decides she's not done asking questions. She looks at Travis with serious eyes. "Are you going to marry Hayden? Do you love her?"

I cringe. "Okay Penelope, that's enough of asking questions."

The waitress comes over with our food. What wonderful timing! Luckily Penelope is now focused on eating her dinner, so she stops asking questions. The rest of the meal goes by without any more rude or awkward moments. I really do have to give credit to Travis. He put up with a lot today. When the check comes, I go to grab it, but Travis beats me and refuses to let me even split the bill.

* * * *

After Travis parks the car, I invite him over to finish up our night with a movie, to which he agrees. He hasn't had enough of us? After some of those comments at the restaurant I'm even surprised he said yes to coming over. And Penelope, asking him if he was going to marry me, or if he loved me? I think that makes the top spot on my most embarrassing moments list. That might have even been worse than the bird incident. And I thought nothing could be worse than that. I unlock the front door, put my and Penelope's backpacks away, and tell her to go upstairs and put on her pajamas.

Penelope picks out some kid movie for Travis and me to suffer through. However, I'm learning that kids' movies and shows purposely put in jokes for the adults. It's as if they understand our pain, and they want to make it a little less painful.

On the other hand, I'm also nervous to see how Travis expects the night to go. I know he knows Penelope will eventually have to go to bed. Then what? Any other of my boyfriends I wouldn't hesitant to further our relationship at this stage. Maybe not sleep with them, but definitely do other stuff. Now with me being HIV positive, I can't partake in sexual activity without disclosing my status. And with Travis, I'm definitely not ready for that. It's too early. He'll definitely run. Then I'll have to worry about him telling other people. I think that would be the worst way for my friends and family to find out, from somebody else. I can't have that happen. Maybe I can pull the 'I want to take our relationship slow' card. Although how long will that last? He's twenty-six. He's not in high school, he probably won't be able to wait. Or *want* to wait.

If he's a good guy, he'll wait for you. My mother's voice pops into my head. I remember her telling me that when I began high school.

Maybe if I tell him I want to take it slow, he'll suggest we have an open relationship, and get the sex from someone else. No. That would suck. I don't want to share Travis.

Travis is a good-looking guy. He could find another girl almost instantly who would be willing to give him everything. I know there's been huge progress on limiting the incidences of transmission of HIV through sex. Dr. Shields always tells me that if I take my anti-retroviral medications properly and keep my viral load down to the point at which it becomes 'undetectable' in my bloodstream and other body fluids, then it is highly unlikely I will transmit it to my partner. The last couple of times I've seen Dr. Shields she has told me my viral load is well managed. Even with this reassurance, I tell myself there's always that possibility. And how awful would I feel if I ever found out he contracted it from me. I would be faced with so much guilt. Travis doesn't know me well enough, or trust me enough for that matter, to be willing to take on that risk. No matter how unlikely Dr. Shields says it is. There's also the fact I have to get to the point where I tell Travis the chances are unlikely. Some people wouldn't even let me get to that point without freaking out.

Kyle didn't.

All the education that's involved. Plus, Travis would have to trust me. Trust I am going to my doctor's appointment regularly. Trust I am taking my medications on time every day. He wouldn't want to deal with that extra stress.

Focus, Hayden. You're not there yet. You're not at that stage. Plus, Travis hasn't showed any signs he wouldn't be understanding. He's been nothing but great.

"Hayden, are you going to put the movie on, or do you need me to do it?" Penelope brings me back to the present. Of course, in these days a five-year-old would know how to put on a movie by themselves. I still remember having to rewind my VHSs when I was her age.

"Nope, I'll do it." I grab the remote and put the movie on. Just as I am going to sit next to Travis on the couch, Penelope zooms by, and decides she wants to sit in the middle, next to Travis and me.

The little cock blocker.

Whoops. Probably not the nicest thing to refer to my little five-year old niece as a cock blocker. Even in my own head. Sorry, how about 'oh no I'm so upset that she wanted to sit next to both Travis and me'. Better?

When the movie's finished, I couldn't be more relieved. On a scale of one to ten, with ten being the most painful, I would have to give the movie a solid eight. The movie soundtrack wasn't even that good, and the songs were not catchy. I make Penelope say goodnight to Travis. Penelope gives Travis a hug, which I think he doesn't expect at first, but he relaxes into the hug.

"Thank you for dinner. I hope we can hang out again." she tells him.

Travis responds with a "me too."

I'm not sure if he's being serious, but after Penelope goes to sleep I'll be happy to investigate.

I take Penelope upstairs, make sure she brushes her teeth, and tuck her in to Cori's bed, as Cori is staying over at Erik's house again. "Sweet dreams, Penny." I lean down and kiss her on the cheek.

"I really like Travis. He is so tall. Not as tall as Cooper, but close."

I look at her admiringly. "Yeah, he is really tall. You like him though?"

She nods.

"Want to hear a secret?" I ask her.

She nods again.

"I really like him too. Now be a good girl and go to sleep." I pull the covers up over her and turn the light off as I leave the room.

As I make my way downstairs, I notice Travis is still on the couch, flicking through channels on the television. He stops and looks at me as soon as he sees me enter the room. "Did you want something to drink? A beer? A water? Anything?" I ask.

"No thanks, I'm good."

I walk over, and now with Penelope gone I can sit as close to him as I'd like, so I do. I turn slightly to face him. "So, what did you think of the movie?" I can't help but laugh.

"Oh, it was really good. Definitely will win an Oscar." he says sarcastically.

"Kids movies were not as bad when we were kids were they?"

He shakes his head. "No. C'mon, we had *The Lion King* and *Toy Story*. You can't compete with that."

That is definitely true. Movies were better when I was a kid. "That's true."

I want to thank him for being so good today, but I don't want it to come out awkwardly. Although after today, I really shouldn't feel embarrassed around him. I have Penelope to thank for that.

"So, listen. I really want to thank you for being so good with Penelope. I know today was not an ideal date, but you were such a good sport." I look down and notice I'm fidgeting my hands. "And paying for dinner, you didn't really didn't need to do that. Penelope and I are really glad you came with us though. She was telling me upstairs how much she liked you."

Travis notices me continue to fidget with my hands, so he grasps my hands and intertwines them with his and places them on his lap.

"Well, if we're being honest, I normally don't often hang out with kids. It's not by choice, it's just that I don't know a lot of kids."

I'm a bit taken back and surprised with this revelation, because how he acted with Penelope was so natural. He continues on.

"However, I was surprised with how much I enjoyed myself. I like hanging out with you, Hayden." That last sentence he whispered so quietly, I almost didn't hear him.

I gaze at him. "I like hanging out with you too." I lean forward and press my lips to his. His lips are soft at first, but as the kiss deepens our kiss becomes more urgent. I reach up, and cup his cheek reverently with my left hand. He's closely shaven, but his skin is softer than I expect it to be. I reach up with my right hand to cup his other cheek. I gently lean back and pull him closer towards me. He gets what I am doing, leans forward and guides me backwards down onto the couch, so my back is touching it and he's leaning over me. He uses his arms to support himself over me, and I grip onto them, feeling his defined muscles. After a couple minutes, he retracts one of his arms supporting himself, and leans over to shift his weight to his other arm. Since I'm wearing a skirt, he takes this opportunity to slowly run this free hand from my knee up my thigh. He stops at my upper thigh, and strokes back down my thigh to my knee. He keeps this pattern up for a few seconds, and I know in a few strokes where his hand is going to continue to travel to. I immediately start to tense up, as I can't let him go any farther without telling him about my status. Am I ready? This feels good, but I still haven't come up with what I am going to tell him. Just as he feels me tense, and I know he's going to break the kiss, we are interrupted by a wide-eyed Penelope.

"Eew-ww, are you guys kissing?" she asks.

Damn it!

This isn't good. Travis immediately fixes my skirt and gets off me. I sit up on the couch, and notice Penelope is now covering her eyes with her hands.

"That is so gross!" she shrieks.

I can already hear the lecture I know I'm going to get from Brennley. Although, her and Cooper have been together a long time. Penelope has had to walk in on them doing something. Maybe Brennley will be good about it. Also, Travis and I did know Penelope was just upstairs, so we knew it was a possibility that she may come down. It was just a risk we were willing to take, I guess. I walk over to Penelope and remove her hands from her face.

"Look honey, I'm sorry you had to see that. Travis was just fixing my shirt because I spilled on it."

Wow. That wasn't a good excuse. I don't think she'll buy it.

She proves me right when she states "No, you guys were kissing!"

Oh no, I don't know how to get out of this one. I decide to just redirect the conversation. "Anyway, what are you doing awake? Why aren't you sleeping?"

"I couldn't sleep. I miss my own bed. Cori's isn't as comfortable."

I turn to Travis and give him sympathetic eyes. He reads me well and states "I'd better get going, I have to work tomorrow." He is so understanding.

See? He *can* be understanding, my subconscious claims.

"'Bye, Travis. I'll call you tomorrow?"

He looks hopeful. "Sounds good. Talk to you tomorrow." He leaves without even giving me a hug. I guess he doesn't want to re-traumatize Penelope.

As soon as I hear the door close, I glance back at Penelope. "How about tonight, you sleep in my bed with me?"

Penelope becomes excited. "Like a sleepover!"

I giggle. "Like a sleepover."

I take Penelope upstairs with me and she climbs into my bed. I head to the washroom to brush my teeth. I touch my lips and reflect on the fact that just minutes ago Travis's lips were on mine. That thought makes me smile. I'm really starting to like him. It's in that moment I decide, maybe I can tell him. Then we can progress our relationship in the way I want it to. I have no idea what he's going to say. I decide to give up on my internal conflict for the night and get some rest. Figuring out what to say is tomorrow's problem.

I head back to my room and climb into bed beside Penelope. Her eyes are closed but I know she is just pretending to be asleep. I pull the covers up and over us. As I glance at Penelope it reminds me of when I was a kid. When I used to have a nightmare, or just couldn't sleep I would head over to Lauren's room and climb in her bed. She never would tell me to go away and go back to my own bed. She always let me sleep in her bed with her. Man, I miss those days. Lately Lauren and I haven't been on the same page, but I'm thinking about reaching out to her. Although she can be a bit much at times, she has always been quite understanding. Maybe I should tell her about my HIV. That way she can give me advice on how to break the news to Travis. However, a small part of me still worries about how she will react. Will she be disappointed? Will she be nonjudgmental, considering she has made some poor life choices? If we get into a fight and she knows, will she spill the beans to our parents? Hold it against me? I have to stop thinking about the hypothetical's.

Tomorrow's problem I reiterate to myself. Tomorrow's problem.

Chapter Six: Hayden

Early Sunday afternoon, Brennley comes to pick up Penelope. Because I know Penelope will probably tell her, I tell her of the incident Penelope witnessed between Travis and me. Brennley laughs and said as long as Penelope didn't catch us doing more than kissing that it's okay and will blow over. I couldn't help but ask Brennley if the same has ever happened to her and Cooper, but Brennley says Penelope has never caught them doing anything. I didn't believe it either. I would have lost a bet. Either Cooper and Brennley are sneaky as fuck, or she is purposely lying to me to make me feel bad about what happened. I look at the time and realize I have to get ready and register for my fall courses.

After I register for my classes, and almost cry when I see how much tuition has gone up, my cell phone rings. My caller ID reads it's my mother calling me. Oh boy.

"Hello, mother." I answer.

"How did you know it was me?" she asks.

I roll my eyes, even though I know she can't see me. "We've been over this mom. I have caller ID that tells me it's you calling."

"Oh right. I think I remember you telling me that. Anyway, I am calling because I want you and Lauren to come over tonight for dinner. Your father's still away for work, and I miss my girls. I haven't seen you two in forever. You rarely visit, and you only talk on the phone for a short time."

I internally groan. Don't get me wrong, I love my mom unconditionally. But in the same way I love Lauren: in small doses. I thought moving out would help our relationship, but I feel like in some ways it has made it worse. I feel since I've moved out, she has become more overbearing. She constantly calls to check in. What makes it worse is that my dad travels for work, so it's just her at home. I think she calls out of boredom. I know, I'm just being hard on her. She worries about me.

"Yeah, I can come over for dinner. Do you need me to bring anything?"

"Nope. I have everything. Just come for seven. Maybe pick up Lauren though, because if you don't she'll probably be an hour late."

We sometimes tell Lauren to show up to places an hour early, so she'll make it to wherever she is going on time.

"Okay, will do. See you later."

"Love you, Hayden."

"Love you too, mom."

* * * *

On the way to pick up Lauren, my mind goes back and forth, debating whether or not I should tell Lauren about my HIV. Or maybe I could tell both my mom and Lauren at the same time over dinner. It would give me the perfect opportunity to fully explain myself. That, or...maybe I should just tell Lauren. I figure, maybe on the way home when I drop her off we could discuss it. Then if things turn out poorly, I could always bail.

I text Lauren to let her know I'm outside waiting in the car for her. A couple of minutes later, she comes down from her apartment and hops into the passenger seat. "Hey loser."

Wow, sisterly love.

I look at Lauren, and she is all dolled up. Full face of makeup with her hair loosely curled. She's wearing jeans with a white shirt underneath a tight fitted leather jacket. To match, she is wearing black heels. I look down at myself. I'm wearing yoga pants, with a sweater, and my hair is pulled into a ponytail. She must have plans to go out after? Makes me feel underdressed, although we are just visiting our mom.

I don't have a fast enough retort to her loser comment so I just mumble out a 'hi'.

I pull out from the parking lot and turn left onto the main street.

"So, what do you think mom wants to talk about?"

I glance over at Lauren, and then my eyes drift back onto the road. "What do you mean, what does she want? She just misses us."

That's why she called isn't it? It didn't sound like she had an ulterior motive.

"Well, her tone of voice on the phone made it sound like she had something serious to tell us."

Well they must have had a different conversation completely. I never got that impression. I nervously bite my lip. Maybe my mom does want to talk to us about something important. Every time she does tell us something important, she sits both Lauren and I down at the same time.

"Well I guess we'll see, won't we?"

* * * *

My mom, Lauren, and I are sitting around our dining room table. Lauren and I look very similar to our mom, especially in the face. However, mom has short blonde hair, and blue eyes instead of green. Lauren and I got our green eyes from our dad.

My mom made us comfort food—homemade chicken nuggets, mashed potatoes and gravy, and cooked carrots.

Yum.

For some reason everything always tastes better when mom makes it. The comment Lauren made in the car has left me feeling at unease. It's silent as the three of us eat. I can't help but break the silence.

"So, Mom, Lauren said there is something you need to tell us?"

My mom finishes chewing and puts down her utensils.

Oh no. So, Lauren was right. It is something serious.

"Well, I guess there's no point in beating around the bush. You guys know that dad has been working a lot, and it's been really hard on me. Actually, on both of us. We haven't been spending much time together. It feels as though we've drifted..."

Oh, I get it. So, dad is either switching jobs, or he's retiring. I mean my parents are in their late fifties, so retirement is definitely a possibility. And if he retires that means that he won't be away, and they can spend basically every day together if they want.

My mom continues on. "This is hard to say, but your father and I have discussed this a lot over the last couple of years. We've been to couples' therapy multiple times, but I don't think we can save our relationship. He's just not the same person I fell in love with..."

Wait, what? I had *no* idea my parents were having issues, never mind that they were doing therapy? This is coming out of left field.

I gasp. "Mom, what are you saying?"

My mom briefly looks away, and then back down at her dinner plate. "Your father and I are getting a divorce."

"*What!*" Lauren and I shriek at the same time.

No way! This is not happening. I don't understand. How could I have not seen the signs? Why did I not know my parents were having problems?

Because you were too busy focusing on your own issues, my subconscious scolds.

This feels unreal. I can't imagine my parents getting divorced. They've been married for my whole life. To see them not together would just be weird. Oh, my goodness. If they start dating other people... No. I can't picture that.

Lauren smacks a fist on the table. "You guys can't get a divorce! You guys are too *old!* C'mon, you guys have been together for basically forever. Why give up now? Mom, at this age you aren't going to do much better. Where will you both live? One of you will have to find a new place."

Lauren is angry. Actually, angry is an understatement. Although I don't blame her. I don't agree with everything she said. She's just acting out of hurt. She doesn't mean it. She's confused. I am too. I think it would be different if we'd known this was coming.

Lauren ups her volume. "I find it hard to believe you tried. If you guys were really having problems, why didn't you tell us?" Lauren looks appalled. "This is bullshit! You can't just drop this bomb that neither Hayden nor I was expecting! Not now!"

I want to stop Lauren, but it's like my mind can't process that this is actually happening. My parents divorcing? They can't.

Lauren's voice becomes shaky as she continues. "Did you guys even think about how this would affect Hayden and I? You guys were supposed to be role models for us. If you guys can't make it work, how the hell am I supposed to believe I can make it work with someone!"

Well, that's going to hurt. I look at my mom. I don't want her to cry. My mom doesn't cry often, so when she does, it feels like my heart is going to combust. I won't be able to look at her if she does cry. It will make me cry.

My mom takes a deep breath, but her voice comes out strong when she says, "Lauren it's not like that. Your father and I didn't want to push our problems onto our children. It's not your job to fix our problems or handle them. Your father and I are adults. We wanted to be sure this was the right decision for us, before we told you girls."

I'm surprised my mom's voice is coming out as strong as it is. She doesn't look like she is going to cry. Maybe she rehearsed what she was going to say before we came over? That, or she will cry after, when we both leave, which will make me worry all night.

Lauren stands up and crosses her arms. "Now what? This is the part where you try to convince me to take your side? I want to hear how dad feels about this. I don't believe he would give up this easily. This had to have been *your* choice."

I cringe. Oh, Lauren. You don't mean that.

My mom looks hurt, like Lauren slapped her across the face. "Lauren, you are an adult. I was trying to talk to you like one. I get your hurt, but I will not be spoken to like that."

I'm conflicted. I'm glad my mom is sticking up for herself and demanding respect. But I also can feel Lauren's pain. This confession from my mom hurts. It feels like Lauren and I were almost being lied to these last couple of years.

Lauren decides to ignore my mom and fire back. "You know what? I don't want to hear anything else. You're making a mistake, mom. This is what divides families, not bring them closer together. You and dad are being selfish. C'mon, Hayden, let's go."

I'm actually feeling relieved Lauren wants to go. Maybe she'll calm down and come to her senses. I give my mom a tight smile, mouth a "sorry", and stand up to clear my plate to the kitchen. I slip on my shoes and follow Lauren out the door to my car. Well I guess tonight won't be the night I tell Lauren and my mom about my HIV. Is it bad that a part of me is relieved?

* * * *

On the way home, Lauren and I stop at a local coffee shop to grab hot chocolates. Since it's a nice fairly warm, but not too warm night outside we walk around the park that is nearby. Lauren is the first to indulgence in the divorce topic.

"Can you believe Mom and Dad? I can't believe they are getting divorced. This came out of nowhere."

I take a sip of my hot chocolate. "Well I think mom was trying to explain that she didn't want to stress us out with their problems."

Lauren looks shocked. "Why do you always take their side?"

I'm appalled. That's not what I expected her to say. I'm sort of pissed off when I say "I'm not taking sides. I'm just trying to figure this out. *I* didn't know what was going on either."

Lauren lets out a breath. "Look, sorry. I didn't mean that. It's just I don't understand. I don't want them to get divorced. I just never thought it would happen. I mean they've always been together."

I nod. "I know. I feel the same way, but we have to trust they are doing what's best. They will still get along regardless if they're together or not."

Lauren kicks a rock on the pathway. "But it feels like they're just giving up. Remember when we were kids, and learning how to ride our bikes without training wheels? I kept falling over and wiping out. I threatened to quit numerous times, but dad kept telling me over and over again 'don't give up, you got to keep trying'."

I smile to myself, recalling watching her wipe out. Even though I was younger, I was able to ride a bike without training wheels before Lauren. I also might have laughed every time she wiped out. Well, I laughed after I knew she wasn't hurt. I do have some sort of heart.

"But Lauren, maybe they did try. We'll never know the extent, but that doesn't mean they didn't try."

"Why are you so calm about this?"

I arch my brows. "Well firstly, one of us has to be. Secondly, I don't know. I guess I just trust they know what they're doing. I mean they do have more life experience than we do. I don't think the decision was easy for them to make."

Lauren walks over and throws her empty cup into a garbage can. "I just don't want to feel like our family is broken."

I grab Lauren's hand, and we hold hands as we walk. "It's not. Mom and dad will be civil. Plus, you have me. I'm not going anywhere. You will always be my family. Mom and Dad are still our family. It will just be a little different, but we'll adapt. You *and* me. We'll figure this out together." I give Lauren a tight squeeze and let go of her.

Lauren looks at me admirably. "When did my baby sister become so smart?"

I give her a funny look. "What are you talking about? I've always been the smart one. And the favourite."

Lauren gives me a shove, and I struggle to reclaim my balance. "Are you kidding me? I'm Dad's favourite! I got away with everything when he was around."

"Well if you are dad's favourite, then I'm mom's favourite. Especially after tonight."

Lauren looks ashamed. "I know I should call her and apologize."

I agree. "Yeah, you should."

Lauren and I keep walking for a couple of minutes in comfortable silence.

"Hey Hayden, which parent are we going to celebrate thanksgiving with?"

I automatically respond. "Mom, of course. Dad can't cook worth shit." I laugh.

Lauren laughs as well. "Maybe that's all the more reason we should celebrate it with him. He's going to starve without mom. I don't think he's ever had to cook a dinner by himself. "

Oh man, I didn't think of that. My dad is an awful cook. I don't even think he can use a microwave.

I cringe. "No, it will be awful because he's going to pop up unannounced at our places right at dinner time, and say 'what's for dinner?'"

Lauren's jaw drops. "Hayden, don't even joke about that."

"A part of me is not though, that's the sad thing."

"Well, after that thought, I need a drink. A real drink."

I could definitely go for a drink after this night. "You read my mind."

Chapter Seven: Hayden

The week ends up flying by. After telling Cori and Brennley about my parents they suggest doing a girls' night on Saturday. I appreciate the gesture, but decline. I just want to be left by myself. Travis also texts and asks if I want to go out Saturday night. I politely decline. After learning about my parents, it makes me a little more hesitant to jump into a relationship with Travis. The separation will be good. I have so much to think about with my parents that I don't want the extra stress of a relationship.

On Saturday night, I decide to be super lame. I finish up some homework and get in my warm bed at eight. Cori sends me a text, saying to text her if I need anything. After rolling around and not being able to fall asleep, I decide to call Lauren. She answers on the first ring, and we chat about nothing for an hour. After hanging up with Lauren, I'm so emotionally exhausted that I fall asleep within minutes.

* * * *

Sunday morning, Cori and I decide to watch a movie while eating breakfast in our pajamas. After the movie Cori goes upstairs, and I hear a knock on the door. I wonder who it is. I wasn't expecting anyone. I have this quick internal conflict whether I should open the door or not, as I'm still in my pajamas. Quickly, I grab my pink robe, put it on, and open the door. It's Travis outside my door. My heart immediately flutters. Well, my body is definitely excited to see him. My brain, however, is cursing that I should have got ready this morning, so I would look more presentable.

"Hi." My smile is so big, I can feel my cheeks hurting. I look him up and down, and I notice he's got one hand behind his back. Is he hiding something?

"Hey. Sorry for showing up unannounced. I was at the mall this morning running errands and look what I randomly came across." He pulls out the hand that was behind his back and shows me a DVD of *The Lion King*.

"I just thought after that horrible kid movie we had to endure the other weekend, you could give Penelope an actually good movie to watch. That way you won't have to suffer again."

Oh, my goodness. How sweet is he? Not only did he buy a kids' movie, but he came over to hand deliver it to me. I can't believe he remembered our conversation. I smile like a kid on their birthday.

"Travis, that's really sweet of you. Penelope is going to love it. And so do I. Best. Childhood. Movie. Ever." I squeeze him tightly in a hug.

He whispers in my ear. "Is everything okay?"

I break away from the hug. "Yeah, why would it not?"

He looks apprehensive. "Well, you were vague about why you couldn't come out last night. I was just a little worried. I wanted to check in on you."

He was worried about me?

Why do I keep saying I need to distance myself from him?

"Well I guess since we're friends, I can tell you. I found out last weekend that my parents are divorcing."

Travis looks at me with concerned eyes. "I wish you'd told me earlier. I wouldn't have gone out last night. How are you taking it?"

I don't know if it's the way he said it, or if I haven't really given myself time to really accept the fact my parents are divorcing, but I sudden feel it. The loss of it. Like my family is being torn. I reflect on all the times my parents appeared happy when they were together. My heart is racing, and I feel like the floor is slipping under me. Is it the uncertainty of how my parents' divorce is going to play out, or am I just feeling anxious that I'm getting emotional in front of Travis? Suddenly, I feel tears creep up in my eyes.

"Aw. Hayden, it's okay." Travis pulls me into another hug, but this time I don't let go. I need something to hold onto.

I absolutely *hate* crying in front of people. I hate being vulnerable. Period. But right now? Having *his* arms wrapped around me makes me feel secure. Makes me feel safe. It makes me feel as though the situation with my parents is going to be okay. I keep telling myself I have to be strong for both Lauren and me. But with Travis, I feel like a weight has been temporarily lifted off my shoulders. I tuck my head in his chest and take a few deep breaths as he strokes the back of my head.

I don't know how long we stand there together. Could be a couple of minutes, could be an hour. When I feel better, I pull back slightly, so I can look Travis in the eyes. He takes his thumbs and wipes away the rest of my tears.

"Thank you, Travis. That actually made me feel a lot better."

He gives me a soft smile. "Good, I'm glad. I'm here for you, Hayden. Whenever you need." He brushes his thumb on my cheek.

"Do you have plans for the rest of the day?" I ask.

He shakes his head. "No, I don't."

I tilt my head, but don't move away from him. "Well if you wanted to, you could stay and watch a movie with me? I promise it will be a million times better than that awful one we had to suffer through."

He smiles that smile where his dimples show through. "Yeah I'd like that. But no chick flicks."

I chuckle. "No chick flicks."

* * * *

Travis

Hayden and I are seated on her couch, with her sitting on my lap. I've got my arms wrapped around her, and I'll admit it feels nice. I feel content. On the other hand, I feel horrible for her. I couldn't imagine my parent's divorcing. It must be devastating for her. I remember her telling me how she is close to both her parents. I hope she won't have to be put in the middle. I hope her parents will separate amicably. She's going to face a lot of adjustments.

It makes sense why she bailed last night. I should have figured something was up. And seeing her cry today? Just about killed me.

I can't help but think about Tristan. I hope he knows what he's getting himself into. This getting married without really knowing his girlfriend. Anything could happen. You never can predict how relationships are going to end.

Hayden stirs slightly, and I realize she's fallen asleep. I lean down and press my lips gently on her temple. She relaxes, and her breathing becomes easy and even. I wonder if she's had any sleep this past week. Probably not. I stretch out my legs onto the coffee table, and the next thing I know, sleep consumes me.

* * * *

Hayden

The next day on Monday night I'd decided to make tacos for dinner for Cori and me. Just as I'm turning off the stove element, Cori walks in the door. She's dressed in skinny jeans and a blue t-shirt. Her curly hair is pulled up in a ponytail, so she must have come from the lab.

"Mmm, smells divine. You're an angel."

"Well you can thank me by doing the dishes after." I finish setting the table and we sit and start assembling our tacos. I realize I never followed up with her regarding her issues with Erik. "So, how are you and Erik?"

"Actually, we're a lot better. I decided to accept that every relationship moves at a different pace, and every relationship has issues. I think it took the pressure off. Plus, we've been spending more time together, just the two of us, as opposed to going out every night. I feel like now that I am twenty-four, I'm almost getting tired of going out. I don't do hung-over well anymore. Is that sad?"

"Well you know when you go out you don't have to drink to the point of getting hung over," I point out.

"Wow. Okay, *mom*. Anyway, talking about relationships. You and Travis looked nice and cozy on the couch yesterday. Like two love birds."

I groan. "Please do *not* use the term birds when referring to Travis and me."

Cori laughs. "I totally forgot. But now you've reminded me, I'm always going to use that term when describing you both."

Gee, thanks Cori.

"We totally lost track of time. We ended up taking a four-hour nap."

"So, how's that going? Are you guys officially together?"

I finish taking a bite of my taco. "Well, we haven't really put a label on it. We decided we would just see how it goes."

Cori looks disappointed. "Hayden, you have to be careful with that. If you don't put a label on it, that's where miscommunication happens. Then one of you gets mad if the other hooks up with someone else, but you can't really get mad because you weren't exclusive. You know how it is. It's unclear and messy."

She is right. Relationships get messy, and people get hurt when the status of the relationship is unclear. I have a mouthful of taco so I just nod.

Cori puts down her taco. "Do you want to be in a relationship with Travis?"

I wipe my face with a napkin. Tacos are amazing, but definitely messy. Wiping my face gives me a chance to think of a response.

"Yes, and no. I really like Travis, but I don't know. He seems too perfect. Like there's nothing wrong with him. It worries me."

"Are you sure it's that? Maybe you're trying to find something wrong with him, so you don't feel bad about not pursing him. Why are you so scared? You never were like this with guys before. Is it because of what happened with your parents?"

Man, sometimes you got to hate best friends. Especially when they can read you like no one else. But it's really not what happened with my parents that's holding me back. It's about trusting Travis. I'm just scared, if I do trust him and things don't work out, it will back fire on me somehow. Just the unknown is making me nervous.

Do I lie to Cori or tell her the truth? I guess I can tell her a half truth. "No, it's nothing to do with what's happening with my parents."

"Then what is it? Is it still about Kyle?"

Is it about Kyle? I mean I know his reaction was nowhere near ideal, but I'm starting to think the problem is not just Kyle. Should I just tell Cori why I'm conflicted? I've been avoiding this conversation for two years. She is my best friend. I know she'll be understanding. I just don't want her to be disappointed in me. She's never afraid to speak her mind and be honest with me. Am I ready to hear what her honest opinion of my situation is?

No not yet. I decided to go for a generic statement. "It's just hard to trust people."

Her eyes light up with understanding. "I know it is, but just think of how rewarding and exciting it is when you do."

* * * *

July passes quickly. On the first of July, Cooper and Brennley hold a barbeque for Canada day. Travis and Jesse even come. They've become part of our group now. It was a nice hot day, and at night I got to watch the fireworks while curled up in Travis's arms.

The following two weeks of July, Travis went by himself to Portland to meet up with his cousins. Something about one of his brothers needing to be close to home in case his wife has their baby early, and another brother having lots of wedding planning to do. Travis was going to stay here, but I almost forced him to go.

The last week of July didn't work out for Travis and me. He was stuck working a lot of the weekends while his co-workers went on vacation, while I struggled to finish up my school work and cram in studying for finals which start in the beginning of August. That, while trying to maintain my summer job at the Aquarium.

Our relationship is a bit 'on hold', I guess you could say. Yes, we kiss when we see each other, but we've been doing lots of group activities, and focusing on work and school, so we haven't had much one on one time, which I am somewhat glad for. It's given me time to think more about our relationship, and what I'm going to say if I want to further it. I think he doesn't want to pressure me, with what happened with my parents.

Even with our busy schedules, we still manage to squeeze in moments together. One day I stopped by his work and brought us lunch. He really enjoyed that. One other day, he spent five whole hours going through my biology cue cards with me, so I would be ready for my final exam. Some Saturday mornings we meet up and go on a run together. It's the little things about Travis that make me most attracted to him. He remembers everything I tell him, and always wants to hear how my day was.

Lauren and I have actually become closer. We talk on the phone at least twice a week and make more of an effort to see each other in person. We meet up for coffee, go on hikes, or spend Sundays binge watching our favourite television shows. Lauren is very supportive of Travis. She demands I 'ride him like an elevator'. Whatever that means. Lauren is weird. She also demands I have his babies as soon as possible, which I politely decline to do.

I've talked to my mom a few times. Apparently, Lauren apologized to her, which is a relief. I told mom I would support her, no matter what. She seems to be doing well, but she was always the strong one in the family. I've spoken to my dad a few times as well. He apologized for not making it work with mom, but promised Lauren and I that we would always be his little girls, and he would be there for us no matter what. My parents are selling their house, and each moving into their own apartments. It will take some time getting used to, but if they are happy, then that's all that matters to me.

By the second week of August, I am officially finished my summer semester. I get a couple weeks off until I go back to school at the beginning of September. Travis texts me and wants to celebrate with me for finishing up the semester. He decides he wants to make me dinner at his place. I tell him he is only allowed to make me dinner if I am able to come over and help him. He says he doesn't need me to pick up anything at the store, so I head over to his place for five.

As I walk up to his apartment door, realization hits me— I've never been to his place before. He's been to mine a handful of times, but I've never been to his. I knock on his door. He opens the door with a wide grin on his face. We say hello and he embraces me into a hug. I show him the bottle of wine I brought, as I tell him I can't go over to someone's house empty handed.

Since I didn't really know if tonight was a date or not I was unsure of what to wear. Cori suggested to dress up, because it's better to be over dressed than underdressed. I decided on a turquoise summer dress, tightly fitting at the waist and flowing out at the bottom. I decided it makes my curves stand out in all the right places. The neck line is rounded and low, but not too low where I'd have to pull my top up all night. I decided to curl my hair to dress up my look. Travis hasn't stopped looking at me since I've showed up, so I'm assuming he likes what he sees.

He looks me up and down before he speaks. "I hope you like pasta, because it's one of the few things I can actually make."

"Yes, pasta is one of my favourite foods, so I definitely approve. What would you like me to do?"

He walks over to his cupboard and pulls out a cutting board. "Well, if you don't mind chopping up an onion and some peppers, that would be great."

I give him a coy smile. He's wearing jeans that fit low on his hips, with a nice white shirt. The white shirt definitely works with the tan he has going on.

"I definitely can manage that. Where are your knives?"

I face the counter to see if I can find the knives. A second later, Travis comes up behind me. I feel his warm breath on my neck. He murmurs "You look nice," in my ear. He then gingerly moves my hair to one side over my shoulders, so my hair is falling down my chest. He places a quick, light, soft kiss on my neck. I tilt my head back to give him more access, and he plants another kiss, this time an open mouth kiss on my neck. I immediately get goose bumps. It seems the temperature has increased in the last couple seconds, and I don't think it's because the stove top is on. He rubs my arms gently and reaches around me to pull out a knife from the drawer besides us.

He passes me the knife, blade pointing down, so I can grab the handle. "Here you go. This knife should work." He then moves away from me to return to the stove top to stir the sauce. What a tease.

If I wasn't so hungry, I'd be a bit flustered. Who am I kidding? I'm definitely flustered. "Thanks. I'll get started."

I chop up an onion while he mixes a variety of spices into the sauce. A couple of minutes of silence pass. It's not awkward—it's a comfortable silence. But I am curious about one thing.

"Where did you learn how to cook?"

He shrugs. "I learned a couple of things from both my parents here and there."

"Do you cook a lot?"

He grins mischievously. "Not as much as I should. A couple of times a week after work, I usually pick up takeout food."

I laugh. "Hey, at least you're honest about it. Should I feel special that you are cooking for me then?"

He smiles shyly. "I actually have never cooked for a girl. You're the first."

I'm genuinely surprised. "Really?"

He nods. "Really."

"Then I definitely feel special."

He looks at me, and my chest tightens. He then continues to stir the sauce. "You should."

I blush. After I finish chopping up the onions and peppers, I add them to Travis's sauce mix. We then start discussing our week, and he tells me all about his trip in Portland. After about twenty minutes of conversation, he asks me, "You want to try the sauce?"

I walk over closer to him until I am only a foot away from him. "Sure."

He scoops up some of the tomato sauce with the wooden spoon he was using to stir the sauce. He turns towards me and places his hand underneath the spoon in case some spills. I notice the sauce is steaming, and I don't want to burn my mouth, so when I lean forward to take a bite, I decide to blow on the sauce first to cool it down. I blow a little too hard because the next thing I know red sauce goes flying up directly on his face. He flinches and moves back with his mouth wide open, shocked.

"Oh, my goodness, I am so sorry." It doesn't come out sincere though because I am laughing while I'm saying it.

He laughs too and says, "I can't believe that happened. Is this payback for me seeing you with bird shit on your face? You have to try to get something to splatter onto mine?"

"No! I promise it was an accident!"

I can't even speak after that. I'm hunched over laughing so hard my abdominal muscles begin to start to hurt. Travis is bent forward as well, laughing just as hard as I am. After a few seconds, I'm able to pull myself together enough to grab a napkin.

"Here, let me clean you up." I wipe up the splats of sauce on his face and kiss the spots after. "Better?"

He grins devilishly. "Yeah, better." He leans down and kisses me right on the lips. The kiss doesn't last long because in the corner of my eye I can see the pot of noodles almost boiling over. He pulls back and turns the element down.

"Well in a couple minutes the noodles should be done. I'll just mix the salad and we should be ready to eat. "

After everything is ready, we sit down at his kitchen table. He brings two wine glasses over and he opens the bottle of red wine I brought. I can't help but ask, "Do you live alone?"

He takes a sip of his wine, and I can't stop myself from staring at those lips. "Yes, I do. I used to room with Jesse, but for the last seven months I've had this place to myself. He was able to get a one-bedroom apartment for a good deal, so we decided it was time to part ways."

"Do you miss him?"

He takes a couple of seconds to respond as I see him thinking it over in his head. He finishes chewing. "Yes, and no. I liked having him here, but he did piss me off at times. Do you and Cori get along well?"

I finish my bite of salad. "Yes, we surprisingly do. We don't feel the need to have to always hang out together. We're fine being home and doing our own thing, and giving each other space, so it's nice." I take a sip of my wine. I remember it's August and there was something I've been meaning to ask him.

"Oh, and I meant to ask you. I think I mentioned it before, but at the end of August, my friends and I go up to Brennley's cabin to do some camping. I talked to Brennley, and I wanted to know if you and Jesse would like to come? It's not for a long time, just for the long weekend. I don't know if you'd be able to get time off work or if you work that weekend, but I'd love you to come."

"Yes, I'd like that. I can take a look at my schedule, and if I'm working see if I can swap shifts with someone."

I grin. "That would be great. It's a lot of fun."

We finish up our dinner, and he takes my plate and his and drops them into the sink. I stand up from my seat and follow him. I have no problem helping him with the dishes. He turns around and grabs my hands. "Where are you going?"

I look at him innocently. "I was coming over to help you with the dishes."

He groans. "No, you definitely will *not* be doing the dishes."

I free my hand from his, and gently place my palm on his cheek. "I can help. I ate the dinner too. I have no problem helping. Plus, if we both do it, it'll be done faster."

He looks down and shakes his head. "Nope, I won't allow it."

I bat my eyes at him. "Please. It will make me feel better. I'll feel bad if I don't help, and you don't want that, do you?"

He rolls his eyes. "Okay, you win. I'll wash, and you dry."

I bite my lip, and then release it. "Deal."

As he's washing the dishes, and I'm drying, I can't take my eyes off him. I don't think I've been this physically attracted to a guy before. Every couple of seconds I find an excuse to touch him. When he hands me dishes, it's like I can't pull my hands away from him. It's as if our hands are a magnet that need to connect together. The further we pull apart, the stronger the pull is. My hands brush his for longer and longer each time he passes me a dish. I feel like a kindergartener, waiting to be scolded for not being able to keep her hands to herself.

Travis washes a knife and passes it to me. I take it and start to dry it. I become preoccupied with his hair. I stare at his hair and desperately want to run my fingers through it. I know how it feels, and I want to feel it again. All of a sudden, I feel a sting of pain on my finger. I look down.

Oh shoot!

I've cut myself with the knife. My finger starts to bleed, and soon all I can see is a pool of redness over my finger.

"Shit!" I exclaim out loud.

Travis looks over and drops a plate into the sink. "Oh fuck, are you okay?"

I use the dishtowel and wrap my finger around it, trying to place a moderate amount of pressure on it to stop the bleeding.

Ouch.

It actually hurts a lot. It's stinging really badly. But I don't want Travis to think I'm a baby, so I try to keep my feelings in check.

Travis reaches out his hand. "Here, let me see it."

I flinch, and immediately jump back so he can't touch me. "No! No! Don't touch!" I panic.

"Okay, okay. Calm down. I have a first aid kit in my bathroom. I'll go get it. You really should sit down. " He tries to walk over to me, I assume to guide me to sit on the kitchen chair. I can't let him touch me. "No, don't come near me. I can manage."

"Hayden, it's okay." He tries to use a soothing voice. "It's just a cut. I'll grab the kit and we can assess the damage. It might not be that deep."

I take a seat, and he goes to grab the kit. Shit. He probably thinks I'm overreacting. It's just—I'm HIV positive. For all I know he has an open area on his hand, and if my blood gets in that area I could transmit it to him. I know I'm overreacting and being dramatic, but I don't care. I don't want him near my blood. I don't want to take any chances. And if he finds out after that I'm HIV positive and he's dealt with my blood, he'll be destroyed, and he'll hate me. I can't let him help me. I know when he comes back he is definitely going to try to help me. He's a gentleman. He'll probably take my finger over the sink, wash the wound, assess the damage and bandage it up. If I need stitches, I know he'll rush me over to the hospital. No question. Then when we're at the hospital I'll have to let the staff know I'm HIV positive, and then he'll find out. He'll be mad I didn't tell him.

My mind is running too fast. I'm panicked. I'm scared. My finger is throbbing so badly. I want to cry. What am I going to do? I can tell Travis I'm just not good with blood. That's believable. A lot of people get queasy and uneasy around blood. I could be a mature adult and just tell him the truth.

No, it's too soon.

I decide to take the childish way out and get up to leave. As soon as I stand up, Travis comes back into the kitchen.

His eyes are gentle and sincere when he says, "Here sit down, and let's take a look."

I embarrassingly start to cry. "No, no. Please, just let me do it."

"Okay, okay. Here, I'll put the kit on the table." he says solemnly.

I get up and run my finger through the cold water in his sink. I can feel Travis's eyes on me. My cut is not as deep as I thought it would be. I don't think I'll need stitches. After most of the blood drains down the sink, I take a sponge and wash the inside of the sink with my good hand, to make sure there is no blood residue left. I use the dishtowel that I'm still holding to dry my finger. I walk back over to the table and I grab a bandage from the kit and secure it on my finger.

Travis looks like he doesn't know what to say. I'm worried he won't look at me the same.

"Do you want me to take the dishtowel? I'll throw it in the laundry room."

I shake my head. Most of my tears have dried. "No, I'll take it home. I can buy you a new one."

"Hayden, don't be silly. You don't need to buy me another one. It's just a dishtowel. I've got lots."

I look directly into his hazel eyes. I can see my reflection in them, and I look weak. "Would you be mad at me if I told you I want to go home."

He doesn't appear taken back, but there is understanding in his eyes. "No, but I'd like to drive you home."

"I drove over. I don't want to leave my car here."

"I can drive you home in your car, and I'll walk back."

I gasp. "You can't do that. It's a long walk."

He smirks. "It's not that far. It won't take me long. I promise."

I really want to go home, so I agree.

Travis drives me home in silence. I would pay to know what he's thinking. He's probably never going to want to see me again. He parks my car, and we climb out. He passes me my keys.

"Thanks for the ride. Sorry about tonight."

"Take care, Hayden."

He turns and starts walking in the direction of his house. *Take care Hayden?*

Was that meant as a goodbye? A goodbye in the fact that he doesn't want to see me again? Maybe I'm right. All I know is, this night was a test of our relationship. He knows something is up. Him just knowing I have a secret is enough to scare him away.

Chapter Eight: Travis

I don't know what was up with Hayden. We were having a great night, and then she panicked out of the blue. The way she flinched when I tried to help her or go near her. She looked deeply hurt. What was that about? What made the whole situation worse was, she wouldn't let me help her. I felt useless. I play out different scenarios in my head. The only two explanations for what happened were either that she doesn't do well with blood, or she's hiding something. But what? It's like every time we get closer, something happens, and she immediately retracts. It's difficult because even know I've known her for a short time, I've really grown to care for Hayden. She's smart, witty, and fun to be around. And I can't deny she's definitely attractive. The dress she wore last night? That left little to the imagination. I could barely concentrate.

So, what's her problem? I hope she'll confide in me, so we can move past whatever is bugging her. I am a patient guy, but I will not stand being lied to.

"What do you think of this one?" Tristan asks.

Trevor and I are out with Tristan, shopping to find suits to wear to the wedding. I know. It's cutting it pretty close. Tristan's other two friends, who are also groomsmen, comment on the suit, while Trevor and I acknowledge that it doesn't matter what our opinion is, Tristan can choose whatever he wants. He was never one to follow the crowd. As Tristan goes to try on another suit, Trevor turns to me.

"So, are you bringing a plus one to the wedding?"

I lie to him. "I don't know; I haven't really thought about it."

"Well maybe you should bring one, so mom stays off your ass."

I groan. "Yeah, she already gave me the speech the night Tristan announced his engagement."

Trevor, the asshole laughs. "Rough, man. But in all seriousness, is there anyone you're seeing?"

Since Trevor has been with his wife for years, he gets it, so I don't mind confiding in him. "Well, there was this girl I was sort of seeing."

He looks confused. "What do you mean, sort of?"

"Well after last night, I don't think she wants to see me again."

He gives me a stern look. "What did you do?"

I immediately get defensive. Probably because I honestly don't think I did anything wrong. At least not intentionally. I think her behavior might have had to do with her parents. I don't feel it's my place to tell Trevor that piece of information though. "Don't look at me like that. Why do you assume it was me who screwed up?"

He smirks. "Because it normally is."

I punch him in the shoulder. "Fuck off."

He looks at me seriously. "What actually happened?"

I look down at the floor. "I honestly don't know. We were having a great night, and when we were doing dishes she cut her finger on a knife accidently and freaked out when I tried to help her. She left soon after that. But I don't understand. Before that, everything was fine."

Before Trevor can reply, Tristan comes out of the change room. "What do you guys think of this one?"

The suit is a classic black. Nothing fancy but it fits him well. I'm honest when I answer him. "I like that one."

"Yeah, I think I am going to go with this one. " He pulls out his phone. "I just need to take a picture and send it to Addison to see if she approves."

I'm confused. "I thought you weren't supposed to see each other until the big day?"

"That's her, not me, dumbass." Tristan responds.

Is it though? I'm pretty sure I'm right, but since I haven't got married I don't know. I look at Trevor, and Trevor just shakes his head. Smart guy. He chooses to stay out of this discussion completely. Maybe that should be my new tactic to handle Tristan. When Tristan goes back to change back into his clothes, Trevor and I carry on with our conversation.

"Honestly, Travis, just apologize. Even if you didn't do anything wrong. There's no point in picking fights over stupid things. The more you read into things, the more complicated and worse it gets. You'll never find out by yourself why she got upset. Girls are way too complex. At the end of the day, girls just want to know that you care about them. And you can show them you care by apologizing."

"When did you become so philosophical?"

He gives me a hard look. "Since I've been doing everything in my power to avoid sleeping on the couch these last few months. I found out apologizing goes a long way. I wish I knew that sooner. Unless this girl isn't worth pursuing... Then, just move on."

I mutter. "No, she definitely is worth it."

He looks at me with hopeful eyes. "Then show her."

* * * *

Hayden

I've been nervous about telling him, but I think he'll understand. Hope he understands. So far, he's been sweet. I know I want to further my relationship with him, but I have to tell him first. It's only fair. Once he finds out, this weight that's keeping me down will finally be lifted. The barrier between us will be lifted. He can't fault me for this one mistake. I'm sure he's made some unfortunate decisions he wishes he could take back as well. Love is about trusting each other, and accepting each other, flaws and all.

It's six o'clock, and he promised he was going to be here at six-thirty. Here, meaning my apartment. Cori is staying at her dad's this weekend, so I won't have to worry about Kyle and I being interrupted. I begin pacing back and forth in my living room, swinging my arms back and forth as I move. Why does time sometimes feel like it is barely moving, when other times you blink, and it's been hours?

I've played out different scenarios in my head, and I think the one I've decided on is the best way to tell him. I've practiced what I'm going to say to Kyle over and over. Last night, I even dreamed that after I told him, he reassured me it didn't matter that I have HIV. What matters to him is that I'm still Hayden, and I love him unconditionally.

Trust

My throat suddenly feels dry. I stop my pacing and grab a cup of water from my kitchen. I down the whole cup, faster than I realize. I can feel the sweat building on the back of my neck. I run my hand under the cold water in the sink and place it on the back of my neck to cool myself down. It feels better.

He will understand, won't he? I push that negative away. My mom told me it was important to look at the positives in life. Funny to think of that saying now. She also told me to not worry about things until they actual occur. 'Your imagination can get you into a lot of trouble' she would tell me.

A knock on the door finally brings me back into present time. That must be Kyle.

As I open the door, I see him standing there. His blond hair is gelled to the side, and his blue eyes are almost clear-looking. He's dressed in jeans and a black button down. He looks handsome. And to add icing to the cake, he is holding a bouquet of flowers. Pink Carnation flowers. My favourite. How did he know that? He must have asked Cori.

"These are for you." He hands me the flowers.

I grab them from him and inhale the scent of them. "These are lovely. Thank you."

I open the door wider, and he enters my apartment. I go fill up a vase full of water to put my flowers in, letting him know he may make himself at home. I quickly check on the stuffed chicken I have cooking in the oven. It's almost done. I can almost taste the flavor in my mouth. Definitely going to be spicy enough.

When I come back into the living room, Kyle is sitting on the couch, with his arm stretched across the back of it. I smile and walk over to sit next to him.

"Dinner will be just a couple more minutes." I put the flowers on the table. "They really are beautiful. You didn't have to do that."

He smiles back at me and brings me closer to him. "Well, I knew bringing you flowers would put a smile like that on your face, so I couldn't resist."

I lean forward, and softly kiss his lips. When I lean back ending the kiss, he reaches out and brings me back to his lips. He deepens the kiss and I can't help but let out a small moan. Just as our tongues get involved, I hear the oven timer go off. Man, what timing.

I stand up and straighten the red strapless dress I decided to wear. I thought that since it might be our first time tonight, I should go all out, which means pulling out this beauty.

"Let me check on that."

When I check on the dinner, it appears ready. I take it out of the oven and put it on a cooling rack. I already pre-set the table, so I tell Kyle to come on over and grab his plate. When we finish grabbing our food we sit at the kitchen table. Kyle reaches over and grabs one of my hands. He rubs his thumb against my hand as he says "Thank you for making dinner. This looks amazing."

I blush. I don't do compliments well. I'll feel good if I can impress him with my cooking. Especially considering I am only twenty-three years old. Most of my twenty-three-year old friends basically only know how to make macaroni and cheese. Not even homemade, right from the box macaroni and cheese.

Kyle cuts up his stuffed chicken, and I watch him cautiously as he takes a bite. I desperately want to know what he thinks.

"Mmm, this is really good. I'm impressed. Where did you learn to cook?"

I'm so excited, I'm almost giddy that he likes my cooking. "My mom taught me how to cook. She's an amazing cook, so she taught me all her tricks."

"Well it definitely paid off, because this is delicious."

After finishing dinner, we head back to the couch in the living room. I feel a little nervous about telling him, but a part of me just wants to get it over with. It's better to tell the truth and not have secrets. If he's going to find out eventually, it's better now, than later.

We face each other on the loveseat, and I grab both of his hands and place them in my lap. "So, I know I told you I have something really important to talk about."

He rolls his eyes playfully. "How could I forget? It's been driving me crazy all day. The only reason I'm not panicking is because we haven't had sex yet, so the news can't be that you're pregnant. Anything besides that I can handle."

My expression must display shock, because he looks at me funny as he says "What?"

"Do you not want kids one day?"

He chuckles. "Of course, I want kids, someday. Just at least a few years down the road. Closer to my thirties. I'd like to at least finish post-secondary first."

Wow. I'm relieved, because one day I would like to have children. "Well, I'm glad to hear we're on the same boat. Let's definitely finish school first."

"Anyway, you were saying..."

"Oh right. I'm sorry, you distracted me."

"It's okay. You distract me all the time. Especially right now in this dress." He takes his hand and slowly starts stroking my thigh.

I push his hand away. "Okay, well stop distracting me! I'm trying to talk to you about something serious."

He retracts his hand. "Sorry, you have my full attention, now."

I take a deep breath. "Before I start, I want you to be open-minded and non-judgmental. Remember that during this time I was only twenty-one, and I made some less than ideal decisions, you could say."

Kyle nods his head. "Okay."

"And you have to let me tell the whole story okay? Wait until I am finished before you cut in and ask questions."

His facial expression looks cool and relaxed. He nods again. "Okay, deal."

Since I know he's not going to interrupt me, I tell him the story of how I contracted HIV. When I finish, I notice his mouth hanging open.

"Is this some sort of joke?" he asks.

I shake my head. "No unfortunately, it's the truth. I am in fact HIV positive."

"What? I though only homosexuals and drug addicts got HIV?"

Wow. Way to Stereotype. That's exactly what I was afraid of. "No, anyone can contract HIV. There are a few ways to transmit it. One being through unprotected sex which is, unfortunately, how I contracted it. I told you I was young, and I made some really bad choices I fully regret. But it's too late. I can't take it back now."

He lets go of my hands. "I'm confused. So, this isn't some sort of sick joke. You really have HIV?"

My shoulders sink. "Yes, I do."

He runs his fingers through his hair. "You're fucking with me. I don't believe you. You don't look like someone who would have HIV."

I gasp. "And what does someone who has HIV look like exactly? Didn't you listen to what I said. Anyone can contract HIV. Do you think if you could tell someone had HIV, I would have slept with the person who gave it to me?"

Kyle stands up. "This is the strangest conversation I've had. You do realize that there is no cure for HIV? It's not like some of the sexually transmitted diseases that you can treat and get rid of. HIV is for life."

I stand up too. "You don't think I already know that?" I'm angry now. "That's why we're having this conversation. Before you get sexually involved with me. I'm trying to do the right thing here by telling you. This isn't exactly an easy conversation for me to have. Do you know how many different times I tried to tell you? Or the different ways I came up with for telling you? I love you Kyle, and I want us to work. I don't want my HIV ruining my shot at finding love. I thought you'd be understanding."

He takes a step back from me. "Wait, you said before we started getting involved. We've made out and touched plenty of times." He looks at me with a disgusted look. "Should I be getting tested? Is there a chance I might have got HIV from you?"

I move forward, trying to close the distance between us, but he steps back further. He looks at me as if I'm a disease.

"No, you don't have to get tested. HIV is not transmitted through saliva and we haven't made physical contact where you should be worried about contracting it. Do you think I'm stupid? That's why we are having this conversation now. But you don't have to worry. I already talk to my doctor—"

He gaps. "You talked to your doctor about this. About us? Is she expecting me to come to your next appointment and ask questions? Talk about safe sex? How many people know, Hayden?"

I'm on the verge of tears, but I tell myself 'stay strong'. This is definitely not the reaction I thought he would have. "Of course, I had to talk to my doctor about becoming sexually active. This HIV is new to me. I need to know how to be able to protect myself and you."

"Well, I think the best way to protect me, is definitely to not fuck me. If I don't fuck you, then I can't get HIV."

How can he say something so cruel? I'm trying to be a mature adult and do this the right way. I never in a million years thought Kyle would say these things to me. I thought I knew him better than this.

I go on. "No one, but you, knows I have HIV. I'd like to keep it that way. Look, I can tell you are scared—"

"Scared? You think I'm scared? I'm pissed. And to be brutally honest, a bit disgusted."

I'm shocked. "How can you say that to me? I thought you were better than this. More understanding than this."

He crosses his arms. "Well I thought you were better than being a thoughtless whore who sleeps with the city's trash."

Wow. I think it would have hurt less if he punched me in the face five times in a row. After that comment, tears creep up in my eyes.

"How could you say that? You know me."

He pulls at his hair. "Well obviously, I don't know you Hayden. And obviously, you don't know me. How could you think I would be okay with this?"

I wipe my tears away, but they still threaten to come down. "You didn't let me finish. If I take my medications, the chances of you contracting HIV—"

"Whoa. Let me stop you there. I don't care what the chances are of me contracting HIV. There's no way in hell, I'm sleeping with you, knowing you have HIV."

"You don't mean that."

He laughs. He actually laughs. "You're damn right I mean that. I can't even look at you without thinking about it."

"I know you're mad, but please don't tell anyone. I don't want people to know."

He gives me a funny look. "You think I'd tell people. Are you crazy? I'd be a laughing stock. There's no way in hell I'd tell anyone. That would be way too embarrassing."

Well at least he won't tell anyone. Well, he says he won't tell anyone.

"I'm leaving. This is too much. Don't bother to call me, Hayden. We're through. Have a nice life." He slips on his shoes and slams the door on the way out.

As soon as I hear his car drive off, I lean back against the wall and fall to the floor. I'm shaking all over. I cradle my face in my hands and sob uncontrollably.

The way he looked at me? The way he told me he wouldn't tell anybody because he was embarrassed by me? Why did I think he would understand? I think that hurt almost as much as finding out I'm HIV positive. Telling me I'm a whore, like I don't already regret what happened every day of my life. How can he judge me like that? He's slept with a ton of girls before. Way more people than I have.

I cry and cry until I don't think there are any tears left in my body. I'm so exhausted. My throat feels raw and my eyes sting. I can't move. I end up curling up on the floor, letting the cool tile hit my puffy face, hoping that tomorrow I'll wake up and this will all be a dream.

I wake up moaning from my dream. I'm completely covered in sweat and shaking. 'It was just a dream', I keep telling myself, knowing very well it wasn't a dream. It actually happened. Kyle did say every one of those hurtful things.

Cori blasts through my door and climbs on my bed. "Hayden, are you okay? What's wrong?"

I mumble a soft "bad dream".

She embraces me in a tight tug, and strokes my hair, like I'm her child.

"It's okay, Hayden. It was only a dream."

Although it wasn't *just* a dream. And that's what scares me the most. Even though I like to think Travis will be different, there's always a chance he'll react the same way Kyle did. What if he does? I don't want him to look at me the way Kyle did. Like I'm some disgusting disease he can't go near.

Trust

'Your imagination can get you into a lot of trouble'.
Well so can reality.

Chapter Nine: Hayden

The next morning, I wake up with a severe headache. I don't feel well rested, and I just cringe thinking I have to go to work. I would feel bad about calling in sick to work, as my job is only for the summer, so I feel I have to make a greater effort to show up. Also, if I want to work at the aquarium after I finish schooling, then I need to make a good reputation for myself.

I walk down to the kitchen, where I see Cori sitting at the table, sipping coffee out of a mug and looking down at her cell phone. She's in pink pajama shorts, with a white tank top on, and her hair pulled up into a messy bun. She's also wearing her black rimmed glasses, which I love. Cori mainly wears contacts because she hates her glasses, so I feel lucky to be one of the few to get to see her in glasses, because she totally rocks them.

When I enter the kitchen, Cori looks up from her phone, and puts it off to the side of the table. "Hey, I made coffee."

Oh my goodness. The things I would do to get my hands on a cup of coffee right now. "Thanks." I walk over to the coffee pot and pour myself a cup of coffee. I then join Cori at the kitchen table.

"How are you feeling?"

The great thing about having Cori as a best friend is I don't have to feel embarrassed around her, so I don't have to feel bad about last night's unfortunate nightmare. "I feel like I got set on fire, then set on fire again, and then hit by a bus."

Cori adjusts her glasses that have slipped down her nose. "Well, that's quite the visual. Do you want to talk about it?"

I take a sip of my coffee. "No, not really."

Cori nods, and goes back to texting something on her phone. I feel bad. She won't pressure me to talk about what's bothering me which I appreciate, but I feel bad because lately she has been honest about confiding in me about Erik. I feel like I need to give her something, so I tell her. "I'm just still shocked about my parents divorcing. I know I don't live with them anymore, but it's just weird you know? I'm worried about how our family dynamic is going to change." That was half the truth of what is bothering me.

Cori puts her phone back down. "Well that's understandable. But your parents are good people, so they will be good people together or separately. I doubt they'll put you in awkward situations. Worst case scenario, you can spend the holidays with me and my dad."

"Thanks. But hopefully my family will work something out." I make a rash decision to share more. "I also think I'm going to friend-zone Travis."

"What? Really? But you looked so cute together napping the other week. Why?"

Do I really have a good reason to friend-zone him?

No.

"I think I just need to work on myself a little more before jumping into another relationship." This is me being honest. If I work out the issues I have with myself, then maybe I'll be able to move forward gracefully with Travis.

Cori looks at me skeptically. "I don't mean to hurt your feelings, but are you sure you're not just making this decision because of what went down with your parents?"

If I didn't know what the issue was really, I would say she's thinking logically.

"No, it has nothing to do with them. I still want to be friends with Travis. I still want him to come to Brennley's cabin."

"Okay, well, do whatever is right for you."

I stand up and put my coffee mug in the dishwasher. "I will. Thanks for the coffee. I have to get ready for work."

* * * *

Wednesday night I receive a text message from Travis asking to meet up. I feel like I owe him an explanation for Saturday night, so I agree to meet him at a local coffee shop. When I arrive, he's already there, so we order our coffees and sit in the corner of the shop, away from other customers. Travis looks good. His hair is still a little wet. He must have showered before coming here. His hair is pushed to one side. And he smells delicious. I can't help but lean forward to inhale that wondrous scent. Now I know why animals use scent to attract mates. It's powerful. Something I've never smelt before. Something only Travis contains. Because I'm being weird and preoccupied with Travis's scent, before I can start to apologize and explain myself, Travis speaks.

"So, I'm sorry about Saturday. I didn't mean to freak you out or make you uncomfortable so much that you wanted to leave. Can I ask what made you so upset?"

Oh, my goodness. He is apologizing to *me*? I don't understand. He didn't do anything wrong. I'm the one who made the night awkward. I'm the one who freaked out. He really is too good for me. That's why I have to end this.

I close my eyes for a second and blow out a breath.

"Travis, you didn't do anything wrong. I'm the one who should be apologizing to you. I'm really sorry for Saturday night. I acted childishly. It's not an excuse, but I don't do well with blood. When I see it or look at it, I get lightheaded and nauseous. I felt helpless and just panicked. Then I was embarrassed that I'd panicked in front of you. For some reason, I get extremely nervous around you. You're just so calm, and collected, and I'm a mess. I really want you to like me, but the truth is, I got out of a relationship not too long ago. Long story short, it didn't well. My ex-boyfriend hurt me in a way I didn't think he could. He broke a lot of my confidence, and I just haven't been the same since. I'm not normally as insecure as I am around you. I think that's what bothers me the most."

Travis reaches across the table and grabs one of the hands. Using his thumb, he starts stroking my hand. It feels nice.

"I wish you would have told me this, Saturday."

I swallow the lump that has formed in my throat. Why is he so understanding? That makes this situation so much worse.

"I was embarrassed. The stress of the breakup with my ex was hard on me, and with the addition of learning my parents are divorcing, it's been harder on me than I'd care to admit." This is the truth. "I think I just need some time to regroup. I'm not used to depending on other people, so it stresses me out when I find myself leaning on other people. I'm twenty-four. I should be able to take care of myself. The day I broke down in front of you at my house? That's not me. I'm not vulnerable. I *can* take care of myself. I'm not some damsel in distress, that needs constant reassurance everything is going to work out. I fix my own problems. "

Travis lifts up my hand and kisses the back of it. "Maybe that's your problem, Hayden. You rely on yourself so much, it's beginning to break you down. Asking for help doesn't make you weak. And I never got the impression you couldn't take care of yourself. That's actually what I do like about you. The way you care about everyone in your life: your parents, Cori, Brennley, Lauren, Penelope. You don't always have to put up this tough front. The way you just opened up to me now. I want you to be able to do that. "

He always knows the right things to say without sounding too corny. I'd be stupid to let a guy like him go. Guys are not usually like this. What is it about him that's makes it so easy to talk to him? We have this unusual connection. He's this old soul. I feel like I've known him my whole life. It's like my body recognizes him. My heart wants to beat out of my chest to say hello. But with every hello, comes a goodbye...

"I know I'm changing the subject, but I wanted to know if you would be my date for my brother's wedding this weekend? I know we haven't dated that long, and it's last minute, but I would love for you to come and meet my family. I promise it won't be awkward."

Meeting his family? Attending his brother's wedding? Could you imagine if it doesn't work out between us? Years down the road he'll have to look at these photos at his brother's wedding with this random girl? I decide I have to break this off now. I open my mouth to politely decline but what comes out instead is a "Yes, I would love to go."

What did I just do? I'm such a tease. I'm being *that* girl. The girl who leads him on and suddenly shatters his heart to tiny pieces.

If I thought I was going to die a 'good' girl, that's all changed now.

* * * *

Thursday night, I skip group to go dress shopping with Cori. Cori finds this beautiful green dress that matches my eyes. With my blonde hair we both agree I look a little bit like Tinkerbell from *Peter Pan*. It shapes my body nicely, and flows out at the end, and I decide it's perfect for a wedding.

Early Saturday morning, Cori styles my hair. She braids my hair on both sides of my head and draws them back, so they tuck nicely into a low elegant bun. Cori does my makeup and even adds false eyelashes to complete the look. After she finishes spraying my hair with hairspray for the tenth time, she stands back to gloat at her work. "You look absolutely gorgeous! Travis won't be able to keep his eyes, or hands, off you."

I blush. "Thanks."

Cori was confused at first when I told her I was going to Travis's brother's wedding. I mean the last time we spoke, I told her I was going to friend-zone him. But she didn't ask many questions. She likes Travis, so I think she is happy I didn't do it. There's a knock at the front door and I know it's going to be him. I grab my purse that I left hanging over the couch and answer it.

Travis is on the other side of the door and looks exceptionally handsome. He's wearing a black suit, with a white dress shirt and black tie. His hair is slicked back and styled just a bit, and he's freshly shaved.

"You look absolutely stunning." He bends down and kisses my cheek.

"Thanks. You don't look half bad yourself."

"You ready to get going?"

"Yup." I shout a 'goodbye' to Cori and close the front door. Travis and I begin walking down the hall. As soon as we turn a corner, he pulls on my arm, and pushes me back up against the hallway wall. He places each arm on either side of my head and leans down to start kissing me. He catches me off guard initially, but I soon relax into the kiss. His kisses me with a strong need. He's never been like this. I don't want to say rough, but intense. I like it. Our tongues come out to play and I lift my hand to grab onto his flexed bicep. He pulls back, and we are both slightly out of breath. He leans his forehead against mine, and I can feel his breath on my nose. "What was that for?" I ask.

He grins. "I just had to kiss you. You look amazing."

I grin back at him. "Well as much as I love what we're doing, I'd feel really bad if we were late for your brother's wedding. Especially since you are in the wedding party."

"You're right. Let's go." He holds my hand, lifts it up to kiss it, and we walk to his car hand in hand.

* * * *

We arrive to the church early; Travis is in the wedding party, so he has to. We walk down the hall and run into an older guy who looks very similar to Travis, and a woman who looks very pregnant.

"Hey man, how's it going?"

The older guy and Travis quickly give each other one of those bro hugs.

"Savannah, you look lovely." Travis leans down and kisses Savannah on the cheek.

"Hayden, this is my oldest brother Trevor, and his wife Savannah. And in here," he points to Savannah's stomach, "is my niece or nephew. We won't know until the beginning of September."

"Hi, I'm Hayden. It's nice to meet you both." I hold my hand out. "And congratulations on the baby. You must be really excited."

Trevor puts his arm around Savannah. "We are excited. Travis has mentioned you before. I'm glad you could make it."

I turn to Travis. "You've mentioned me?"

He gives me a coy smile. "I might have mentioned you to Trevor, but that's it."

"Well, it was quite obvious he was into some girl or other. You can't find him without a smile on his face these days."

Travis groans. "Thanks, Savannah."

She winks. "No problem. Anyway, I have to go find the bride. I have something blue she might like. I'll catch you guys later. It was nice meeting you, Hayden."

"It was nice meeting you, too."

Savannah and Trevor continue to walk down the hall.

"You told them about me?"

"I swear I didn't tell them. Trevor figured it out. And of course, he told Savannah. None of my other family knows. I promise."

I straighten his tie. "I'm not mad. I'm kind of glad. It's nice to know you're not embarrassed of me."

Not like Kyle was.

"Why would I be embarrassed by you?" He leans down and whispers in my ear, "My date is amazingly hot. *Nothing* to be embarrassed about."

I lean up and kiss him on the lips.

"Oh, my god, is that Travis?"

I break apart from the kiss and turn. An older woman in her late fifties comes storming over to us. Following her is a man with salt and pepper hair. She has dark medium length hair, and eyes almost hazel. Almost hazel eyes. Sort of like Travis's...

"Mom?" Travis says.

Oh, my goodness. It is Travis's mom. Wow, way to go Hayden. You haven't even met Travis's mom and the first time you do, is get caught kissing her son. Luckily it was all very PG.

Her eyes light up. "Who is this?"

Travis rolls his eyes. "Mom, this is my date, Hayden. Hayden, this is my mom, Andy. And behind her is my dad, Robert."

"Hi, Hayden. It's nice to meet you." Andy squeezes me into a hug so tight it almost hurts.

"Okay, Mom, please don't hurt my date. Have you seen Tristan?"

Andy lets go of me, and I straighten my dress. "Well, Trevor dropped him off. I think he's in one of the rooms down the hall that way." She points down a hallway opposite us.

Travis nods. "Okay. Well, I'd better go check in with him. Let him know I'm here."

"Okay, we'll see you guys later. Nice to meet you, Hayden."

I smile back at her. "It was nice to meet you, too."

As Travis and I continue walking down the hall, he shakes his head. "Sorry about my mom. She gets excited when she goes to weddings."

I squeeze his hand. "You can tell she really cares about you. It's nice."

"Are you going to be okay sitting in the church without me? I put you next to my cousin, who is the most normal out of the bunch."

I playfully hit his arm. "That wasn't nice. I bet your cousins are lovely."

He winks at me. "Not all of them. Anyway, any trouble and you know where to find me. I'll be up front a few feet away from the groom."

I wink back at him. "Oh, I'll be looking all right."

He leans down and gives me a quick kiss. "You can't say stuff like that to me when we're in church."

I give his bum a gentle squeeze. He grabs my hands. "Or do that."

I frown. "Well that's no fun."

* * * *

The wedding ceremony is short and sweet. There are only about seventy-five people who attend the wedding, so it's nice and intimate. Travis looks good as he stands up with his brothers. Tristan's wife looks absolutely stunning in her dress. It's low cut, lacy, and has a long train on it. It fits her well. Her bridesmaids look gorgeous, all wearing a deep red color.

At the reception, Travis introduces me to his grandparents. They are both in their early nineties and adorable. A little hard of hearing, but definitely adorable. His grandmother has almost the same eyes as Travis and his mom. Next, I get to meet the bride and groom. Tristan gives me a welcoming hug, while his new wife is a bit more standoffish. Travis warns me that's just the way Addison is. It has nothing to do with me. I get to meet some of Travis's cousins, including the few he went to visit in Portland. All his cousins are extremely tall. Height runs in his family. I thought Travis was tall. Turns out, at six-three he is not only the youngest brother, but the shortest. Both Trevor and Tristan are six-five. Travis's dad is six-four. Even his mom is tall at five-foot nine.

At the end of the dinner, Travis's mom comes over to talk to me. "You look lovely tonight."

"Thanks. You look too young to be a mom of a married man," I replied.

"You're too kind." She blushes. "How did you and Travis meet?"

Oh boy. I could go with the embarrassing truth, but that would take way too much explaining.

"We met through a mutual friend, Cooper. Travis used to play baseball with him, and he's one of my best friend's boyfriends."

Andy's eyes glow. "I think I remember him."

"You have a great son. You taught him how to treat a woman right. You should be proud."

Andy turns her head and looks at Travis sitting at the head table. "Yeah, he's a good guy. He has a good heart, if he would only put himself out there and open up."

I think about all the talks Travis and I have. He opens up to me all the time. I didn't even take him for being more on the conservative side. Knowing this now makes me feel special and valued.

"He seems to adore you. When I caught you together earlier, I couldn't believe it was him. He isn't much into PDA, but apparently, you're an exception. He glows now."

I don't know what to say to that comment. I just smile.

After dinner, Travis comes to sit next to me, so I don't feel left out. He forces me to come onto the dance floor to dance with him. I put my arms around him and we dance in time with the music. Of course, it is a family function, so we're all very PG when we dance, and his hands are appropriately placed.

When a slow song come on, Travis pulls me closer to him, so he is looking directly at me. I have my arms wrapped around his neck and his arms are wrapped around my waist. "I'm really glad you came today. Thanks for coming."

I look up at him admiringly. "Thanks for inviting me. I'm glad I came. It was nice meeting your family. All of them are wonderful."

"Ah-h they're okay I guess."

I smack him on the shoulder.

"I'm just kidding. They are wonderful."

"Well, considering my parents just got divorced you should feel extra lucky to see your parents still in love after all these years. And hope that Tristan and Addison will have a similar future."

He looks regretful. "Oh man, what was I thinking. Inviting you to a wedding? This is probably the last place you want to be. I'm so sorry."

I shake my head furiously. "No. Absolutely not. I wasn't even thinking about that. I was making a point about the positives of weddings. It's my fault, I brought up my parents. *I* didn't mean to ruin the mood. Just because my parents divorced doesn't mean I don't believe in true love, because I do."

His eyes glow. "You do?"

I smile shyly. "Of course, I do. Love makes living worthwhile, don't you think?"

"Yeah you have a point."

"I really want to kiss you right now, but I think it would be inappropriate to do it in front of your family, especially your young cousins. "

He nods over to the door. "We could always leave."

I gasp. "No, we can't. We can't leave your brother's wedding early."

"Well it was worth a try."

* * * *

After the reception, Travis walks me back to his car to take me home. It's dark, but not too dark as it's late August. As we're walking in the parking lot, a shadow appears in my peripheral vision. I turn to look and notice someone who looks familiar. As he appears nearer, I recognize my ex, Kyle. What's he doing here? I quickly turn my head. I don't want to talk to him. Hopefully he doesn't notice me.

"Hayden, is that you?"

Shit. It appears he's noticed me. He's the last person I want to run in to. Travis and I both come to a halt. I hope this won't be awkward. I decide I should probably be polite. Make this nice and quick.

"Hey, Kyle. What are you doing here?"

He runs a hand through his blond hair. "Oh, I'm actually picking up my girlfriend. She's the cousin of the bride." He looks me over, and notices I'm dressed up. "I'm guessing you were at the wedding?"

I grasp Travis's hand. "Yes, I was. I know the groom's side of the family." I just met most of them tonight, but I don't have to tell him that.

"Is he your boyfriend?" Kyle nudges his head towards Travis.

Okay, so we're going to make this awkward. I don't really know what to say. Travis and I have been seeing each other, but we still haven't put a label on our relationship. I think we both assumed we were together. Before I can answer, Travis beats me to it.

"Yeah, I'm her boyfriend."

I squeeze Travis's hand, and he squeezes it back. I think he notices how uncomfortable I am.

"Does he know about your...umm...situation?"

Wow. How rude. That is none of his business. How dare he ask me that. Just because he couldn't handle it, doesn't give him the right to judge if other people *can* handle it. And to ask right in front of Travis? I can't believe I actually dated this guy. I can't believe I used to think so highly of him.

I give Kyle a disgusted look. "That's none of your business." I turn to Travis. "C'mon Travis, let's go."

As Travis and I start walking away, I hear Kyle yell, "Well I hope he's a *positive* influence in your life."

I let go of Travis's hand, and clench my fists. I turn to storm off to confront Kyle. I can't believe he said that. I know exactly what he was referring to. I am so angry right now I wouldn't be surprised if steam was coming out of my ears. Travis grabs my arm and spins me around.

"Hayden, don't go after him. He's not worth it."

I narrow my eyes. "No, you don't understand what he was referring to."

Travis grabs holds on to my shoulders, so I have to look him directly in the eyes. "I know what it's like being angry with an ex and trust me it's not worth it. He wants you to go after him. The best thing you can do, is show him that he doesn't affect you. That he isn't worth your time, or feelings."

I squeeze my eyes shut, and then re-open them. "How did you know he is my ex?"

He tilts his head. "It wasn't that hard to figure out. The body language and tension in the air said it all. C'mon, let me take you home."

I take a few calming breaths. "Okay."

As we're driving room, Travis turns down the radio. "I take it that's the ex-boyfriend where things didn't end well."

I look out the passenger side window. "Yup, that's the one."

"Do you want to tell me what he was talking about?"

I turn and fidget with my dress. "No, not really."

He quickly looks at me, and then looks back onto the road. "Well, it was bad enough to get you rattled."

I lean back in the seat. "I really *don't* want to talk about it."

Travis waits a couple beats before talking.

"Okay, well I haven't told very many people this, but I feel like I should be honest with you. I had this girlfriend in high school. Her name was Courtney. I really liked her. Most of the guys in high school wanted to experiment, and you know, sleep around. Me, I didn't. There was just something about Courtney I was really attracted to. When I was with her, I didn't think about other girls. She was it for me. We dated all through high school and the beginning of our first year of college. She lived on-campus, and I didn't because I wanted to save up for a place once I graduated. I guess there was a lot of temptation, and she ended up cheating on me numerous times. I had a bad feeling when we were together, but she always denied cheating on me. She would say things like 'you're it for me' and 'you're the one I want to be with and have a future with'. Months later, I caught her cheating on me at a party. She didn't expect me to show up at this party. " Travis lets out a breath and continues on.

"To be honest, it really hurt me. Here I thought, this girl I really liked loved me, when she clearly didn't. It was after that, when she told me she liked me, but never really loved me. It was hard. It was embarrassing. I was so mad because I had wasted so much time with someone who didn't care about me, as much as I cared about them. What was worse about the situation is, I let her feelings about me affect me for months after the break up. So much so, that I swore I would never date again. The point of the story is that we all have exes, and relationships we aren't proud of, or are disappointed with how they ended. Everyone can get hurt. It's up to you to decide what you do with that hurt."

That was really insightful. "Wow you really have a way with words. And perception."

He shrugs. "My dad is a psychologist, so even though I hoped it wouldn't, I think it rubbed off on me. Nothing is worse than getting a lecture from your parents, but when one of them is a psychologist, it's even worse. You can't tell any of my guys friends how insightful I am. They'll rag on me for the rest of my life."

I make the motion of zipping my lips with my fingers. "Your secret's safe with me."

Travis slows the car down to a red light. "So, talk about secrets, are you going to let me know what your secret is?"

I gulp. "I will, but not today."

He groans. "Why not? I told you my ex-girlfriend story. I don't just tell everyone that story. Your secret can't be that bad. If you are eventually going to tell me, why not just tell me now."

I don't know what to say to that. I know he's partially right, but if he knew my secret, he would understand why I want just a little more time before I tell him. I want to tell him, and I will. I just need a little more time to be one hundred percent sure I can trust him and want to move forward with our relationship. I was being honest with Cori when I said that maybe I should take some time for myself.

Especially seeing Kyle tonight; it brought back all these fixed feelings. Those haunting memories. How he looked at me when I told him. How he reacted to me. How he wouldn't even let me finish and explain the whole story. How he jumped to ridiculous conclusions. The fear I had that he would tell everyone. Time. I just need a little more time.

Travis breaks me from my thoughts. He looks over at me and when he speaks, it's almost a whisper. "Is it because you don't trust me?"

Is it? I want to trust him. I do. I've only known him for three months. How can I possibly predict how long our relationship is going to last? I decide to be honest.

"I want to trust you. I'm getting to the point where I can trust you. I just need a little more time. *Please* understand," I beg.

Travis glances back onto the road. "So basically, you *don't* trust me. Then why the hell did I bring you to meet my family? I trusted you enough to meet them. My brother's wedding is a huge milestone for our family. I wouldn't bring just any girl there."

I panic. It was a nice gesture for him to bring me and introduce me to his family. "I am so glad I got to meet your family. They are all lovely. But just because you've reached the point in fully trusting me, doesn't mean I automatically fall into that same category of fully trusting you. I'm working on it. Just because we haven't reached the same page yet, doesn't mean we won't."

Travis refuses to look at me. He mumbles out a "whatever".

"Please, don't be mad at me," I beg. "I really like you, Travis."

Travis pulls up in a spot in my parking lot. "Hayden, I've done the keep secrets from my boyfriend game with Courtney. I am not doing it again."

It feels like I've been stabbed in the heart. "So, what does this mean?"

He looks out the driver's side window. "It means we're done for now. When you finally decide you can be one hundred percent honest with me, then we can talk. But for now, I refuse to play these stupid games. I'm getting too old for this shit."

It takes everything in me to be able to speak the next few words. "I guess that's fair enough. I don't like it, but I understand. Thanks for the ride, and thanks for taking me to the wedding."

Travis doesn't say anything back. He won't even look at me. I climb out of the car and close the passenger door. I walk up to my apartment, and run to my room, avoiding Cori. I slip my dress off and pull a large t-shirt over me. I climb in my bed, and sob into my pillow.

I can't even be mad at Travis, because I know the reason we broke up is my fault. I won't open up to him. I'm the one who wanted to friend-zone him.

But after meeting his family, I changed my mind. I didn't want to friend-zone him. I wanted to move forward with him.

I hate these conflicting thoughts and feelings. I just needed some space to think about how I was going to tell him. I just didn't want to tell him, after all the anger I felt running into Kyle.

But now it's too late, and I have no one to blame but myself.

Chapter Ten: Hayden

The next morning as Cori and I are drinking our coffees at the kitchen table, I tell her Travis and I broke up. When you aren't officially together, can you call it a break up? Well even though we didn't have any labels, it felt like we were in a relationship, so I am calling it a break up.

Cori is shocked when I tell her.

"Hayden, I'm so confused. One moment you and Travis are together, and the next day you're wanting to break up with him. This has gone on for the last few months. I can't keep up with this endless cycle. I thought we were friends because you weren't into drama."

Is that what this is? Drama? I moan.

"I'm not into drama. I guess I keep leading him on, and then backing away when things seem to get too real. I don't know. Why does it seem impossible to trust guys?"

Cori picks up the newspaper that's on the table and wraps it into a cylinder shape. Then hits me on the head with it.

Bitch.

"Hey, what was that for?"

"Snap out of it, Hayden. I hate to be the one to tell you this, but life isn't easy. You don't get just the perks life has to offer. Everyone's in the same boat as you. You have to learn how to trust people. Life is about learning."

I throw my hands up in the air. "Why is everyone so philosophical lately? It seems like everyone has the answers to life, except me."

"Learn to deal. And stop feeling sorry for yourself. If you want things to change, you've got to change them yourself. Not wait for life to do it for you."

I decide to be cynical. "Well it sure works that way for Lauren."

Cori gets up and pats my head. "Well, you're not Lauren." She rinses her coffee mug in the sink and puts it into the dishwasher. "Is Travis still coming to Brennley's cabin?"

119

I hadn't even thought of that. "I don't know. From what he's told me, he's been spending lots of time with Cooper. Maybe I shouldn't go. It will make things awkward."

Cori gives me the mom look, which is surprising since her mom left her when she was young. She has it mastered though. "You are two mature adults. You'll figure out how to deal, and not ruin the weekend for everyone else."

I salute her. "Yes, Ma'am."

* * * *

"I can't believe I agreed to go this weekend." I groan.

Why did I agree to go to Brennley's cabin this weekend? And why would Travis still want to come, knowing I'm going to be there too? Is this to prove a point? That I wasn't a big deal, and he was able to get over me in less than a week?

Erik is currently driving us to the cabin. The car's load consists of Erik, Cori, and me, and our friends who were at the bar: Dominick and Cassie.

In case I forgot to describe them, Dominick has dark brown hair and dark eyes, with a massive muscular chest. He basically goes to the gym every day. He's also quite shy so he barely talks. Cassie has dark hair and dark eyes as well. She's half Pilipino, and super gorgeous. Her hair is literally perfect. It's dark, straight, and super glossy and shiny. She should really be on a shampoo commercial.

"It's going to fun!" Cassie announces.

I groan again. "That's what we say every year, except something bad always ends up happening."

Cori smirks. "Remember last year, when those teenagers tried to steal our booze?"

I laugh. "Yeah, except Cooper chased after them and totally tackled them football style. That's what happens when you try to run away from a guy whose run track all his life."

"If you are going to try to steal, at least do it well." Erik states, and we all nod in agreement.

* * * *

We finally arrive at Brennley's cabin. Her cabin only has three bedrooms, so we rotate who sleeps in the cabin every year, and the rest of us bring camping tents and camp in her backyard. This year Kelsey and Keegan get one room and Dominick and Cassie get the other. Obviously Brennley and Cooper don't rotate and get the master bedroom every year. The property is quite big so there's lots of room. The backyard is connected to the woods, which is why one year the bear managed to find us and steal our food. There is also a back patio with a hot tub. The patio has stairs which leads down to a gravel area with a fire pit, which we use often. Brennley doesn't have too many neighbors; there's lots of space between them, so noise is usually not an issue, as we do tend to be quite loud. Especially when some of us drink.

The rest of the gang is here, and we're all sitting outside on chairs surrounding the fire pit. Besides the five of us who were in the car, the others who've shown up are Brennley, Cooper, Jesse, Travis, and another couple of friends, Kelsey and Keegan. Both Kelsey and Keegan have blonde hair and blue eyes. They're both going to school to become dentists. Keegan has a scar just above his eyebrow from a wicked biking accident he was in when he was eight. Though he always tells people he was in a fight with some other guy and the other guy pulled out a knife on him. Every time he tells the story it always changes slightly.

Cooper and Keegan begin to start chopping up wood for a fire for later tonight. I make eye contact with Travis and give a shy smile, but he just looks away. I guess he wants to make this weekend as awkward as he can.

All of a sudden, this red head walks out of the cabin. I recognize her a bit, but I just can't remember where I've seen her before. I think her name is Julie, or Jordan or...

Cooper looks up. "Hey everybody, this is my cousin, Jade."

Right! Jade That's right. I was close. I got the J part right, didn't I? And yes, that's Cooper's cousin. I definitely knew that. Man, I haven't seen her in years. The last time she came up with us had to be about five years ago. She was fun last time we hung out. I mean we didn't become best friends, but we didn't not get along. Her hair's also more red than I remember. She's wearing super short jean shorts that barely cover her bum, and a red tank top.

"Hey, guys! How's it going?"

Everyone mumbles a 'hey' to her. She then walks by Travis and bends down in front of him to hold out her hand. "I don't think we've met before. I'm Jade."

He looks her over. Man, is he checking her out? I guess it's hard when she basically sticks her boobs in his face. We aren't together, so I guess he can check out whoever he wants. I turn to look at everyone else and notice Erik and Dominick not so subtly checking Jade out as well. Assholes. Although, I'll admit, Jade is hot. But does she have to be wearing the shortest shorts that exist? No. Does she have to push up her boobs when she walks? No.

"No, we haven't met. I'm Travis and this is my friend, Jesse." He points over to Jesse.

Jade gives him a flirty smile. "Nice to meet you. I like that name. Travis. I guess this weekend is going to be fun after all."

Umm, barf? Did I say Jade and I didn't not get along? If this is how the weekend goes, I might change that sentiment. Jade comes over and sits beside me on the open chair. "Hey, Hayden, nice to see you again." She cracks open a beer.

I smile sweetly. "Nice to see you again."

Jade leans over and whispers in my ear. "Is that Travis guy single? He's super cute."

I internally groan. I've decided Cooper needs new cousins. Stat. First his guy cousins can't make the baseball tournament and it becomes mandatory that I go. And now this cousin starts the weekend off by flirting with Travis? Fuck me.

* * * *

After the group that has to sleep in tents sets them, we decide to throw on bathing suits and fill up coolers, so we can head down to the lake. I know you're wondering where I get to sleep. I opted to have my own tent. As much as sharing with Cori and Erik would be fun (sarcasm intended), I'll definitely pass. To make sleeping arrangements even more fun, Travis invited Jade to sleep in his tent with him, while Jesse opted to have his own tent. So, this weekend is already looking up (sarcasm intended again).

Is Travis attractive? Yes

Is it my fault Travis and I aren't together? Yes.

Did I have a bad feeling that it hadn't taken him long to move on with another girl? Yes.

Will I have a good time this weekend? Yes.

Am I supportive of Travis and Jade's new budding relationship? Afraid not.

Will I behave and act like a grownup? I'll try, but no promises.

The guys are playing some weird sports game in the lake. At least that's what I think they are doing. They are throwing around a spongy football shaped looking thing? So, a sport, right?

We girls opted to set up our towels, so we could drink and tan in the sun. Did I say girls? All the girls...except, who? You guessed it. My new bestie Jade. She decided she wanted to join the guys in their football/sport excursion. She's wearing the skimpiest bikini I've ever seen. It's also white, so no doubt it will go see-through in the water. She's laughing and trying to steal the ball from the guys, but they're so much taller than her. They extend their arms and hold it over their head, while she giggles and jumps up and down desperately trying to steal the ball. Pathetic.

Sorry did I think that? At least I didn't say it out loud. I told myself I was going to be nice this weekend.

Suddenly, Cooper throws the ball to Travis. Jade jumps on his back and attempts to retrieve the ball. Jade and Travis both laugh, and how they both end up falling over into the water, I'm not sure. They pop back from out of the water still giggling. I turn to Brennley who is lying on her front on a towel.

"Why did Cooper decide to invite Jade?"

Brennley lifts up her sunglasses to look at me. "I don't know. She's had a rough year, so Cooper thought it might be nice to invite her. She's our age, so we thought she'd fit in well. Plus, she came a couple years ago."

I don't really know what to say so I just mumble, "I see."

Brennley begins sitting up on her towel. "She's flirty with everyone. Not just Travis. It's just her personality. You have nothing to worry about."

Do I? I don't remember her being this flirty last time. Although, was I really paying attention?

"Why are you jealous? You kept telling me repeatedly you wanted to work on yourself and wanted to break up with Travis." Cori states.

I groan. It's becoming a new bad habit. "I know. I deserve this. It doesn't matter to me. I was just curious about Jade, that's all."

Brennley laughs. The traitor. "Yeah okay. If you are already getting this jealous now, then it means you really do like him."

I look over to Cassie. She's sitting beside the cooler. "Hey, Cassie? Can you throw me over a beer?"

Cori coughs out a not so subtle, 'denial', while I catch the beer Cassie has thrown to me.

I close my eyes and try to relax as I sip on my beer. In the background, all I can hear is Jade yelling "Oh my god, I think I lost my bathing suit top!"

Are you fucking serious?

* * * *

After the lake, we all head back to the cabin. I'm sunburned on my shoulders and face, which is frustrating because I wore a ton of sunscreen. Pale person problems. The guys take off for a hike, while we girls get started on dinner. Friday night is girls' designated night to cook dinner, and the guys get to make dinner on Saturday night. We've decided to cook steak, potatoes, and vegetables using the fire pit, and to make some fresh salads. While the rest of the girls are outside, Jade and I are prepping the salad inside. As I'm washing a piece of lettuce, Jade blurts out, "So I heard you had a thing with Travis?"

I try to play confused. "What? Who told you that?"

"Brennley."

"Oh. Well, like I told you before, Travis is single. We used to have a thing I guess, but it's over now."

She bats her lashes. "So, you wouldn't mind if I said I kind of have a thing for him."

What am I supposed to say? No, you can't. He's not my boyfriend but I forbid you to see him.

"No. You can do or like whoever you want."

"So, it won't be weird, if I make a move this weekend?"

Umm, absolutely it would. I'll throw her into the lake. I give her a fake smile, hoping she'll think it's genuine. "No, it's fine."

Jade gives me a hug, and I want to tell her to get the fuck off me, but I don't.

"Thanks, Hayden."

Is there really a reason to hate Jade? I mean she did ask. *Of course, there is, it's Travis, he's mine.*

When did I turn into a cavewoman?

* * * *

After dinner, we all squeeze into the living room in Brennley's cabin. Brennley has decided we all should play *Pictionary*. She's even set up an art easel with big blank white sheets on it. We've changed some of the rules. But of course, we play in partners. All the couples group up. Then it's awkward, because the four of us who're left are Travis, Jesse, Jade, and I. Jade jumps at the chance and partners up with Travis, while I am left partnered up with Jesse. Jesse notices my discomfort of Jade and Travis, so he nudges me and says, "We have to win now."

I grin. "Definitely. Game on."

But is winning *Pictionary* actually what I want to win or claim as a prize?

Cooper and Brennley are up first. Cooper goes up to draw, while Brennley has to guess what he's drawing. Within five seconds, no joke, Brennley has guessed the word, 'pineapple'. Is pineapple one of the first words you would guess when someone draws a circle? No, so I have no idea how they got that right. Pineapples are oval, not circular—just to clarify.

"That's bullshit! Cooper and Brennley should not be able to play! They've dated so long, they basically have telepathic abilities," Cori argues.

"I agree! We have no chance." Cassie insists.

I decide to become competitive for the first time in my life; I think it throws Cori and Brennley off. I stand up and walk over to the easel. "Nope, Jesse and I are winning this. Keegan, hit me with a card." Keegan passes me the deck of cards. I look at the card. The word I have to draw is 'flat'.

I look at Jesse. How am I going to draw this? Should I draw a bumpy line, and then a straight one and cross the bumpy one out so he guesses flat? No that would be too hard. Think guys, Hayden. How would guys see the word flat? If Jesse had to draw the word flat, how would he draw it? Oh, my goodness. I chuckle to myself. I have an idea.

"I'm starting the timer, go!" Keegan calls out.

I begin drawing a woman. Jesse guesses things like "girl", "woman", "female." I shake my head and keep drawing. I draw another woman beside the original woman. One of the women I draw to have gigantic boobs. The other woman, I draw very tiny boobs. I know, offensive, right? Sorry, just trying to win a game. The woman with the small boobs, I make an 'x' on her boobs. Jesse then calls out "flat!"

I laugh. "Yes, that's right!"

I run over and give Jesse a high five. "Dream team." I tell him.

I look over at Travis and he frowns. He looks mad. Why is he mad at me? I haven't done anything wrong so far *this* weekend. I look away. Now I really feel uncomfortable. I stand up. "You want another beer, Jesse?"

"Yes, thanks Hayden."

I get up to go to the kitchen to grab two beers out of the fridge. I close the fridge door, and when I turn around I almost smoke Travis.

"I'm sorry, I didn't see you there."

Travis gives me a cold look. If his eyes looked any more intense they'd be shooting lasers out of them at me. "What are you doing?" he asks.

I'm a little on edge. I feel a little trapped. "Umm, I'm grabbing a beer for Jesse and me."

"That's not what I meant. What are you doing with Jesse?"

What's his problem?

I glare at him. "I'm not doing anything *with* him. All we're doing is playing a board game. Unlike you, I'm trying to have a good time. If I knew you were going to make this awkward, I wouldn't have showed this weekend."

"Yeah, *okay*." He turns and walks back to the living room before I can answer.

Seriously what is his problem?

* * * *

After Brennley and Cooper kick our asses at *Pictionary,* we have a fire outside, and shortly later we head to bed. I head to my tent, positioned between Cori and Erik's, and Travis and Jade's tent. As I lie down, cocooned in my sleeping bag, I hear noises coming from the tent on the left side of mine. Of course, it would be Travis and Jade's tent. A few seconds later I hear the sounds of them kissing. Oh my goodness. They are *those* kinds of kissers. Super loud and obnoxious kissers.

After a couple minutes of hearing them, I decide, I've had enough. I unzip my tent, and head out to sit on one of the chairs by the fire pit, far enough away that I won't hear Travis and Jade. I can't imagine what they are doing. They are probably going to have sex. Sex. Something *I* couldn't give Travis. Tears prick my eyes, but I squeeze my eyes shut hoping the tears won't fall. As soon as I sit on a chair, I hear a quiet whisper. "Hayden?"

I turn and see Jesse. He walks over and sits on the chair beside me. Man, If I didn't like Travis so much, I'd definitely be into Jesse. He's really attractive and has really nice eyes.

I'm shocked to see him outside though. "What are you doing out here?"

He shrugs. "I couldn't sleep. You?"

"I couldn't sleep."

He gives me the 'yeah right' look. "I'm guessing you heard Travis and Jade?"

I frown at him.

"Look, I know Travis isn't an angel, but I know he won't have sex with Jade. He likes you a lot. He's mad and frustrated because he wants to be with you. He's just trying to make you jealous, and I can see it's working."

"Yeah, well he's the one who told me he doesn't want to play games. And look what he's doing! He's playing games! He's twenty-six, not sixteen."

Jesse nods. "I agree. But I've also never seen him like a girl the way he likes you. He talks about you. I can tell he cares about you. Look, you didn't hear this from me, but Travis had this girlfriend in high school. Her name was Courtney, and according to his brother, he really liked this girl. Thought he was going to marry her one day. They dated all throughout high school, but after she went to college, she ended up cheating on him. It broke him. More than he'll admit. That's why he doesn't put himself out there. I think he's scared of really liking a girl and getting hurt like that again. Or having the girl not reciprocate the same feelings. He will give you one hundred percent of himself to you, as long as you do the same. When you don't confide in him, he thinks you don't care. Secrets broke his last relationship, so he's worried it's the same with you."

I don't tell Jesse I've already heard this story from Travis himself. I'm just glad I didn't have to see him hurt like that after his breakup. He deserves better. Better than me.

I shake my head. "He won't be able to handle my secret. My last boyfriend didn't."

Jesse gives a sympathetic smile. "I don't think you're giving him enough credit."

"But it's too late now."

"Says who?"

"Me. Travis."

"That's the thing though Hayden. At this point, it's not too late."

I don't know about that.

* * * *

The next morning, Brennley stalks into my tent and wakes me up by saying. "Hey, Hayden, emergency question."

I groan. Told you it's becoming a habit. I turn over, but don't open my eyes. "What is it?"

"Do you have a tampon? My period started early, and I don't have one. The nearest store is hours away."

I think over her question. Unlike Brennley, I'm always prepared. "Yes, I do. In my purse at the corner of the tent."

"Great, thanks." I immediately roll over to try to fall back asleep. I hear Brennley fishing through my purse. A couple minutes later I hear her zip up my tent and her shoes crunching on the gravel as she makes her way back to the cabin.

* * * *

Saturday, we head back to the lake. Erik decides to show off by attempting to do a back flip off the dock at the lake. He ends up not completing the rotation, and belly-flopping. We all wince, and grimace, as we hear that horrible smacking sound when he hits the water. I'm a terrible person because after I grimace, I can't help but let out a guffaw. It was hilarious. I mean I laughed after realizing he was okay, so I am not completely horrible. I feel better once everyone else joins me by laughing. The chain of guffaws and Cooper's comment of "That's going to sting" result in Erik giving us the finger. Totally worth it. It couldn't have happened to a more deserving person.

Okay, maybe I am a terrible person. At least I can admit it, to myself.

After a couple of rounds of beach volleyball, we alternate swimming in the lake and tanning and drinking. I don't help but notice Jade sitting directly on Travis's lap. I decide to ignore Travis, and he decides to ignore me. I decide it's way easier to not be jealous than to be jealous.

Brennley and I decide to use an air mattress to float in the lake. Not without drinks in hand of course. It's relaxing. It's another hot day, and I find myself enjoying the day. Brennley nervously keeps fixing her hair. As soon as she puts it in a ponytail she yanks it out and redoes it.

"Is everything okay, Brennley?"

"Umm, I'm not sure."

"Okay, am I supposed to know what that means?"

"Are you okay, Hayden? Like, really okay?"

What the hell is she talking about?

"Umm yes I'm fine. Sorry, I was being jealous about Travis, but I promise we're over it. I'm not going to play games and act childish anymore."

Brennley looks away. "Not what I was talking about."

What is she talking about? I'm super confused and definitely not in the mood to argue with another person on this trip.

"Oh, for fuck's sake Brennley, just spit it out!"

"Well now's obviously *not* the time. "

I groan. "I'm just confused, and you keep beating around the bush. What's going on?"

Brennley jumps off the air mattress. "We'll talk about this later when we get home, Hayden."

Okay?

Cassie decides to jump onto the air mattress to replace Brennley's spot. "What's wrong with Brennley?"

"I have no idea. I don't understand what she was trying to tell me. I told her I'd try to get along with Travis for the rest of the trip, but besides that I have no idea what she would be needing to tell me."

Cassie looks over towards Brennley, who is now sitting in Cooper's lap. I follow her gaze. "I guess it's not something to do with Cooper."

Cassie takes a sip of her drink. "I don't know, but that was sure weird."

Finally, someone agrees *with* me, as opposed to being *against* me. "Right?"

Later in the afternoon, the guys decide to go fishing, so us girls decide to make sangria. Brennley comes up to me to apologize. She contributes her weird behavior to menstruating, which makes sense. I've had my fair share of outbursts when trapped in the menstruation dungeon. I forgive her, and the tension between us fades away.

I've also decided I don't hate Jade. She whips out a few wine bottles (which happen to be my favourite), and she offers to share, so I decide to not hate her. I mean we're not besties, but I can appreciate a person who likes good wine. I think the two of us just have good taste in wine; and guys.

After a few drinks, the girls are drunk. Even I'm drunk. I usually don't drink, or if we go out I have a drink or two, but because I feel safe with everyone who's here I decide to let loose. We exchange hilarious and embarrassing sex stories, and crazy stories about our ex-boyfriends. After a few hours of catch up we decide to have a dance party. After minutes of dancing to some of our favourite songs, I decide to change the song to R. Kelly's *Ignition*. Everyone gets excited and sings along to the song.

As we're halfway through the song, the guys come back into the cabin, and laugh when they see us goofing off and dancing embarrassingly. Brennley suggestively dances over to Cooper and pulls him over to come join us. The guys laugh, and they all drop their stuff to join our dance party. It's fun to see everyone letting loose. After a couple of songs, the guys leave to get started on dinner, while us girls continue to dance.

After our delicious burgers and hotdogs, the drinking continues, and the guys join us in the same drunkenness. We're all sitting around the living room, when Cori decides we should play another game. "Let's play truth and dare."

I give my signature groan. "No. That's so high school."

She pouts. "So? It's fun. We can change the rules. It will be fun."

Why do I have a feeling it won't be fun? Oh right—because truth and dare never ends well.

"I dare you to lick peanut butter off the toilet seat," Cassie dares Keegan.

Ew-w. This is why we shouldn't play this game. We're too old to play stupid games like this. But apparently everyone agreed to it. I guess it's true, some people never ever grow up. Or maybe it's because we usually always have to act serious and mature, like adults, so when we are given the opportunity to act like kids, we take it.

"Okay, I'll do it."

We all follow Keegan to the bathroom and watch him lick peanut butter off the toilet seat.

"Ew-w, everyone out. I'm seriously going to throw up." Kelsey pushes the guys out of the way and pukes in the toilet.

See? This is why this game is not fun!

Kelsey rinses her mouth and decides to come back into the living room where we continue the game.

"Okay, my turn. " Cori looks at Brennley. "Brennley, truth or dare?"

"Dare."

"I dare you to do five vodka shots in a row *in* thirty seconds."

Brennley agrees, but Cooper on the other hand is not for it. "Hold up. No way. Brennley, you'll puke, and I'll be the one who has to take care of you. You shouldn't do it."

Brennley challenges Cooper. "Watch me."

Obviously, Brennley has had too much to drink. She does manage to complete the dare in twenty-six seconds. I'm actually surprised. Would I recommend doing that? Absolutely not.

Don't try this at home kiddos.

But because I am also drunk, I did cheer her on. Am I a bad friend? The jury's still out on that one.

Brennley drunkenly walk over to Cori. "Cori, truth or dare?"

Cori shakes her head and points out, "You can't ask me that, it's not my turn. I just dared you."

Brennley gives her the 'so what' look. "I don't care. I'm vetoing the rules. Truth or dare?"

Cori decides it's pointless to argue with a drunk Brennley. "Okay, I'm going with truth this time."

Brennley puts her hand on her chin and thinks it over. "Tell us about your first kiss."

Cori looks at Erik, puts down her drink, as she recalls the story. "I had my first kiss when I was thirteen or fourteen. It wasn't the best kiss. We were both inexperienced. He actually looked like one of the guys from *One Direction,* now that I think of it."

Erik turns to her. "Which one?"

"I don't know all their names. There's a lot of them." Cori picks up her drink and takes a sip.

Kelsey jumps in. "Yeah, I think there's six of them, right?"

Six is a lot isn't it? "No, I think there's only five of them." I answer.

Cooper speaks up. "No, there are actually four of them. There used to be five, but only four now since one of the guys left the group."

Everyone is silent and looks at Cooper. "How do you know this?" Dominick asks.

Cooper is quick to respond. "Because Penelope listens to them."

Brennley giggles. "Don't lie, Cooper. You have a few of their songs on your iPod."

Cooper gets defensive. "No, I don't."

Brennley giggles again. "Okay, whatever you say."

All of us laugh.

"So, did we decide on which one of them looked like the guy you have your first kiss with?" Kelsey asks.

Cori waves her hand. "I'm going to go with the one who left the group."

"Oh, the Zack guy." Cassie nods.

"His name is Zayn." Cooper corrects.

Dominick covers his face with his hand and shakes his head. "Dude, you aren't helping your case."

Kelsey chuckles. "Actually, that Harry guy is pretty good looking."

Keegan looks at Cooper. "So, Cooper, which one do you think is the best looking?"

Cooper flips him the finger.

Cori decides to put her iPod on shuffle, so we can have background music as we play. Lots of our dares end up turning into dance dares. As Dominick is finishing up a drunken version of the worm for his dare, Jade sits on Travis's lap. Jade's had way too much wine to drink. We had to cut her off about five minutes ago. She looks at Travis. "Me and Hayden are best friends now. We love the same wine. She is my new wine buddy!" I turn and salute her with my wine glass. See, that should tell you how drunk I am.

Dominick finishes, and it's his turn to come up with a dare. "Okay, wine buddies, I dare you both to make out."

Jade stands up and challenges Dominick. Because she's been drinking it comes out more of a slur. "Yeah, you don't think we'll actually do it, but joke's on you because we will."

Because I've been drinking clearly too much, and feeling too good, I join in.

"Yeah, we'll do it, so joke is on you." I stand up and start to giggle. Like actually giggle. Then Jade turns to me and next thing I know we start making out *in front* of everyone.

The room goes silent. I think we shocked them into silence. A few seconds later I hear the guys cheering and whistling.

How did this happen? If you were to ask me yesterday if I'd be making out with Jade, I wouldn't have believed it. But it did. As we pull away, I fall off balance, and an arm grabs me to steady me. It turns out to be Travis. His eyes are wide. I don't think he can even comprehend what just happened.

"Hayden, are you okay? I think you need to stop drinking."

I whisper in Travis's ear before I go down to sit on the couch. "Well, know that I know what she kisses like, I know I'm the better kisser."

Travis doesn't say anything. He just sits back on the couch, and Jade joins him on his lap. I look at Cori and she mouths 'oh my god'. After a couple minutes, the song in the background ends and switches to a new song. The new song just happens to be *I Kissed a Girl* by Katy Perry. Of course, that would happen. Everybody looks at Jade and me and we all burst out laughing. I glare at Cori, but she throws her hands up, and states "I swear I didn't know that song was going to come on. I don't have a controller. My iPod is on shuffle."

After truth and dare we decide to play the board game *Twister*. I have never laughed so hard in my life. My abs actually hurt from laughing too much. Dominick has a hard time staying up. He keeps falling over and crushing Cassie on the ground who just laughs. Keegan thinks everything is funny and laughs at every comment. Cooper is having trouble playing the actual game because he's way too tall. Cori is way too into the game and won't let anyone else spin the colour board.

I would fill you in on the rest, but embarrassing enough, my memory is a bit foggy after that.

The next morning my alarm for my anti-retroviral medication goes off and stirs me awake. Where am I? Right my tent. I did make it out here. Where is my medication?

Damn.

Where did I put it?

I panic for a couple seconds, when I remember I have them in my purse. I reach over and find my purse and pull them out. I use an old water bottle I find in my tent and down them. I recall the events of last night. Why did I drink that much? My throbbing head is asking the same question. This is why I swore I wouldn't drink heavily again. After *that* night I promised it wouldn't happen, and look what happened? I lean back on my sleeping bag, and feel the tears coming. Why do I keep making poor choices?

After I get changed into presentable clothes, I unzip my tent. Mm-m, something smells good. What is that? Is that bacon? As I walk over to the fire pit, I see Keegan, Kelsey, Cori, and Erik eating what appears to be pancakes and bacon.

"What am I going to have to do to get a piece of that?" I exclaim.

Erik finishes his bite. "Make out with Jade again." Cori reaches over and hits him in the shoulder.

I smile snidely. "Sorry, that was a onetime deal."

Cori points to the cabin. "Dominick and Cassie are making breakfast. Go inside, they made tons. Thought we could use it after last night."

Yes, that's an understatement. I walk into the cabin and see Dominick frying bacon, and Cassie flipping pancakes. Dominick sees me and passes me a piece of bacon. I take a bite. Deliciousness.

"Dominick, my friend, you are my new favourite person to roam this earth."

He smiles.

Cassie looks hurt. "What about me? I'm making the pancakes!"

I give Cassie a side hug. "You too. "

Cassie lifts her brows. "So, you and Jade?"

I cough and almost choke on my bacon. "I don't even want to talk about it."

Before we leave the cabin to head back home, I tell Cori I'm just going for a quick walk down by the lake. I bring my camera and snap some photos as I go. When I finally reach the lake, I look up from my camera and spot Travis sitting on a rock. It reminds me of the first time we kissed on the rocks on the hike we went on. As I walk closer to Travis, he turns when he hears my footsteps.

"Hey," I say softly. "Do you mind if I sit down?"

Travis starts to get up. "No, I was just leaving."

I grab him by the arm and pull him back down, as I sit down. "I want to talk to you."

His jaw clenches. "I don't have much to say."

To lighten up the mood, I risk a joke. "Well most people had a lot to say this morning about what they saw Jade and I doing last night."

He lets out a quick laugh, and I can almost see some of the tension leaving his body. Now I know I can continue on to what I had planned to tell him.

"Look, I just want to apologize for this weekend. I didn't mean to make you feel uncomfortable. I'll admit, seeing you with Jade, and hearing you with Jade, made me a little jealous. It's a new emotion for me. I don't feel jealous often. But the truth is, I was jealous because I really do care about you Travis. However, I'm not going to apologize for wanting to take my time trusting you. When I commit to a serious relationship, it's a big deal for me. It's not that I'm incapable of trusting people, I'm just a little more timid around the idea. A little more hesitant. I guess when we first talked about what we wanted, or where the status of our relationship was heading, I should have been more honest with you. I should have told you I wanted to take things slow. That might have solved a lot of our issues."

He looks down at his hands. I think he's feeling shy. I can tell he's thinking over what I just told him.

"You don't have to say anything to me. I just wanted you to know that." I start to stand, and this time it's he who pulls me back down.

"Wait. I appreciate you apologizing, but I feel bad because it should be me who is apologizing. When I met you, I got excited. We had this immediate connection. An awkward connection, but still a connection."

I cover my face with my hands and he pulls my hands down. "But I'm glad we did meet. I guess because I knew I really liked you, I thought you would feel exactly the same things as me, exactly at the same time. As fast as I did."

"I didn't."

He gives me a reassuring smile. "I know. I figured that after you ran away from me for like the tenth time."

I gasp. "I didn't run away from you that many times!"

He squeezes my hands. "I know, I'm exaggerating. Anyway, the point is that I decided I can wait for you, if you still want me to. You were right when you said something along the lines of 'it doesn't matter when you trust me, as long, as you end up trusting me."

I don't think that was an exact quote, but I'll take it. Then I think about the sounds I heard coming from his and Jade's tent that night. I immediately stand up and this time he doesn't pull me back down. I dust my shorts off

"What about Jade? Don't think I'll forget what I saw you guys doing or heard you guys doing."

Travis flinches, but stands up. "Look, it was juvenile, and stupid. But I was trying to make you jealous. I was mad that you wouldn't trust me. I was mad that you didn't want me."

It's not because I *didn't* want him. It's because I wanted him to wait for me.

"Why would you think, me seeing you with another attractive girl would immediately make me think 'yeah maybe I should take him back'? It basically has the opposite effect on me."

We both stay silent for a few minutes. The question in my head is killing me, so I ask him, "Did you sleep with her?"

He immediately shakes his head. "No, I swear I didn't. We just made out, that's all."

I know I shouldn't ask questions I don't want the answers to, but I still ask, "Did you like kissing her?"

He has a mischievous look on his face. "Not as much as I liked seeing you kiss her."

Man, this is definitely not the time to joke. I get that he thinks that, because it worked on him, it will work on me, but I'm too angry to joke around right now. I storm away, but Travis is fast and catches up easily.

"Hayden, slow down. I'm sorry. I thought it would lighten up the tension. I don't want there to be tension between us."

I really don't either. I slow down and come to a stop. "Okay, you have a point. Where do we go from here now? I don't want it to be awkward between us."

"Well first, I want you to know I don't like Jade. It's nothing like kissing you. Nothing. She doesn't mean anything to me.

Secondly, you said you want to take things slow. How about we try that?"

After this last few weeks, I really don't know if I can handle any more drama. Cori was right when she made that comment about liking me because I don't do drama. "How about we start hanging out as friends? If that works out, maybe we can talk about moving forward?"

He nods, but doesn't look too happy. "If that's what you want."

I lie. "It's what I want."

Chapter Eleven: Travis

Over the next week, Hayden and I share a few texts, but we don't hang out. I do however, officially become an Uncle. Savannah had a baby boy named Noah on the third of September. When I go to the hospital to meet my nephew, I can already tell he's going to be just as tall as Trevor. Apparently, he was a little over nine pounds, so he's quite a big baby. I had to take pictures on my cell phone and send them to Tristan who is currently on a Mediterranean honeymoon with Addison. Trevor and Savannah ask about Hayden, and I lie to them, telling them it's going great—because I don't want to ruin their current blissful joy of just having a baby. I do text Hayden a picture of Noah. She immediately texts back smiley faces, stating how adorable he is.

I want to ask Hayden to hang out, but I decide she has to be the one to make the first move. She keeps stating she needs time. I'm trying to be a patient guy, but how much time does she need? I miss her, but I don't want to come off desperate and clingy. I talk about how I hate girls who're like that, and now I'm turning into one. I remember when I was a kid my mom would tell me guys know the moment they meet a girl if they are going to marry her, but girls take way longer to come to that conclusion. Talking about my mom, she keeps asking about Hayden which makes this situation that much worse. She keeps wanting me to invite Hayden over for dinner. I keep making excuses, but if we don't work things out soon, my mom will pick up on it.

* * * *

Hayden

After the camping weekend, I feel completely physically, mentally, and emotionally exhausted. I am somewhat confused by all the events that occurred. Travis texts me during the week, but we don't meet up. I was serious about needing space and time to collect my thoughts.

On Thursday night at group we reviewed the different ways HIV can be transmitted, and how to protect ourselves, and others around us. It was a good review. Ever since I found out I was HIV positive, I've forced myself to learn everything I can about it. It's important to be well informed. At the end of group, I feel some of the stress leave me. I guess it does help, knowing I'm not the only one who is HIV positive. I'm not the only one who has the same fears. It gives me a safe place to talk about my concerns and worries. Every week gets better, and I find myself contributing more to the discussions

It's a weird feeling lying to my friends and family. In some ways I know I don't have to tell them about my HIV, so I tell myself I'm not lying to them. It's having privacy, and they are respecting my privacy.

Some days, I feel somewhat distressed that I haven't told them. Since my family and friends can't 'see' my illness, when I see them it's easy to pretend it doesn't exist. I can carry on like normal. It's this dirty little secret that only I know. It's a troubling thought, but a part of me is glad I can keep this secret from them. That I am *that good* at keeping it. They absolutely have no idea. Why would they though? We don't want to think the worst of our friends and family. On the other hand, I feel the complete opposite. I feel guilty.

I feel I'm in the middle of a poker game. I've been dealt a really awful hand of cards, but I can't let everyone around me know it's bad. I have to keep up this act to convince them I have a good hand, when I actually don't.

The hardest part of having this illness for me is the mixed emotions it brings. Some days I want to be able to share the news with my friends and family. I *hate* the loneliness. Other days, I don't. I *appreciate* the loneliness. Since I bounce back too often, and my mind confuses itself on a regular basis, I always resort to not telling them. I do this because I know there could be a potential day I tell them.

I hold onto that thought. Because once I do tell them, I can never take that knowledge away from them. I can't change my mind and rewind my life to when they didn't know. But I can always look forward to the day I choose to tell them. Is that messed up or what?

Trust

On Friday night I receive a text message from Brennley, asking to meet up on Saturday morning. I recall the awkward conversation we had over the weekend, and the weird way she acted. I wonder what it's about. Brennley is always open and honest, so what she wants to discuss must be important. I invite her to come over for breakfast, and she agrees.

Saturday morning, I wake up feeling a bit off. I can't describe why or how I feel a bit off, I just do. My stomach is unsettled, and I'm feeling nervous. A part of me is worried about what Brennley wants to talk about. It's like the feeling of watching a horror movie. You know something bad is going to happen, you just don't know what.

I walk down the stairs and meet Cori in the kitchen. Cori is starting to make a pot of coffee. I told her yesterday that Brennley was coming over for breakfast.

"Brennley is going to be here in a few minutes. I was thinking about making omelets for breakfast? You down?"

Cori leans back against the kitchen counter. "Yeah, I'd love one."

As I begin to get eggs out of the fridge, Brennley knocks on the door and walks in and comes to the kitchen. She has makeup on, and is in jean shorts, and a blue halter top. I look at Cori and I, still in our pajamas, with no makeup on. Although I did brush my teeth.

"Why are you dressed up? The point of doing breakfast at my house is so we could eat in our pajamas." I clearly state.

Brennley waves her hand and puts her purse down beside the table. "I have to run errands later, so I thought I would just get ready now, so I wouldn't have to do it later."

Valid. But honestly, I try to wear pajamas as often as I can.

Cori pours herself a cup of newly fresh coffee she's made and turns to leave the kitchen.

"Where are you going? I'm making your omelet right now."

Cori turns back around and shrugs. "You guys have important stuff to talk about."

"Well, you can stay here. We're all friends. Whatever Brennley and I talk about, I would share with you later anyway."

Brennley gives me a worried look. "Maybe you should decide after we talk if you want Cori to know what I have to say. It's about you."

What could she possible need to ask me? Cori is my best friend. She knows almost everything about me. I flip an omelet and look back at Brennley.

"No, I want Cori to stay. I don't care if she knows whatever you have to tell me. Sit down, Cori. Your omelet's ready anyway."

Cori comes back and sits at the table. She throws her hair up in a ponytail. "Mm-m, this looks delicious. Thanks, Hayden."

I grin. "No problem. Just give me a couple more minutes and I'll join you both at the table and we can talk."

After I finish making omelets the three of us sit at the kitchen table and start eating. Brennley looks uneasy, so I decide to break the ice.

"So, what did you want to talk to me about?"

Brennley puts down her fork and pulls her hair to one side over the shoulder. She looks nervous. "Umm, this is going to be hard for me to say." She looks at Cori.

I also put my fork down. "Okay. You're really worrying me Brennley. Just say whatever you need to say. You won't hurt my feelings, if that's what your worried about. If it's about Travis and Jade, I already know."

She shakes her head. "No, it's not about Travis."

I tilt my head. "Okay then, what it is it about?"

Brennley fidgets with her hands. "Do you remember this past weekend when I asked you for a tampon? You said I could borrow one, so I got one from your purse."

I think back. "I vaguely remember." At the time I had just been woken up, so I wasn't fully awake, but I do recall her asking for a tampon.

Brennley puts her hands on the table, almost clutching the edge. "Will you be honest with me when I ask you this next question?"

Does she really need to ask? "Yes, of course."

Brennley gulps. She takes a quick breath, and exhales. "When I was going through your purse to find a tampon, I came across something."

Okay. I'm not sure where this is going. I don't have anything to hide in my purse. At least I don't think I do.

Brennley runs a hand through her hair. "Look Hayden. I'm going to school to become a pharmacist. I know most medications. I didn't purposely mean to see, but I accidently pulled out medication containers with your name on it. I wasn't snooping, but because I'm becoming a pharmacist I recognized the names of the medications."

Oh, shit!

This isn't good. She knows, damn it. I can't even lie to her and tell her I take the medications for a different reason. She knows what the medications are for. I completely forgot I had my medications in my purse when I gave her permission to go in it to grab the tampon. I mean, I wasn't thinking. I was half asleep.

I don't know what to say. She's caught me off guard. I stay silent.

"The medications are anti-retroviral medications. They are used to treat HIV."

Cori gasps, completely shocked. Cori looks at me, but I turn my head. I can't look at her. "Do you have HIV?" She asks.

I stand up to clear my plate. I've lost my appetite. What am I supposed to say?

"Those aren't mine."

Brennley stands up. "Hayden, I saw your name on them."

I get defensive. This is my worst-case scenario. I wanted to be the one to tell them on my own accord, so Brennley finding out this way? It's awful.

"Maybe I took them out under my name for someone else, did you ever think of that? Maybe someone who's ashamed of having to go to the pharmacy to buy them, worried they will be judged? Did you ever think of that?" Okay, that was a horrible lie, but I'm feeling cornered.

Brennley blows out a breath and scratches her head. "No, I didn't. I wasn't accusing you of anything. I was just stating what I saw."

I'm angry, but only because they found out like this. "Well, don't jump to conclusions."

I look over at Cori and I can see tears forming in her blue eyes. "Hayden, just be honest with us. Whose medications are those?"

I squeeze my eyes shut. I will not cry. "No one's!" I shout.

I look over and see tears now forming in Brennley's eyes. I can't do this. There are too many emotions floating throughout this room. I'm sad, hurt, angry, devastated, frustrated, and feeling very, very guilty.

"They aren't mine," I sob. My shoulders begin to shake. Cori comes over and lifts my hands away from my face and wraps me in a hug.

"Hayden, it's okay if they are yours, just be honest with us. We don't care if they are yours."

You know the feeling you get when you are about to cry, and someone asks you if you are alright, and it's them saying that, that makes you ultimately cry? That's what I'm feeling right now. I release Cori's grip on me and gently push her away. I turn and walk to the other side of the kitchen. I turn to face them. I wipe the tears that have spilled down my cheeks. I shake out my hands. My heart is hammering in my chest. My chest feels tight, like an elephant is sitting on it. I feel a bit dizzy, like the room is moving and I'm having trouble seeing straight. I take a deep breath until both of them come back into focus.

I decide it's time for the truth to come out. Although when I tell them I can't look at them. I'm scared to see their reaction.

"Alright, I give up. Those pills are mine." I cry. "Because I am, in fact, HIV positive." The tears continue to come down like waterfalls.

Both Brennley and Cori walk up to me and give me a hug. All three of us are crying. I'm feeling unsteady. My feet give out, and the three of us sink to the kitchen floor.

We eventually make it off the kitchen floor and sit together on the couch in the living room, after we all had a good cry. We sit together in silence besides our occasional muffles. Brennley decides to bite the bullet and speak first.

"Can I ask how long? And how this happened?"

I nod. "Roughly two years. It took a couple months for me to find out. I honestly just thought I had a bad cold."

I then muster the strength to tell them the whole story of how I contracted HIV, and how Kyle reacted when I told him.

Cori has anger in her eyes. "That asshole! I knew I didn't like him. I want to go over to his house and kick his ass. How dare he! I've seen some of the girls he has slept with. He has no right to judge you."

I muffle out a laugh and wipe my eyes with a tissue. "I wanted to hurt him so bad, but at the time I just couldn't. I was in shock. I couldn't believe he could be that cruel."

"Well, you better hope I don't run into him, because the next time I see him I am definitely going to go off on him."

I half smile. That's why I love Cori. "Don't bother. I ran into him the other day at Travis's brother's wedding. He made a smart-ass comment and I almost went to beat his ass. Travis luckily pulled me away before I could. I was so mad though."

Brennley gasps. "Does Travis know?"

I let out a sob. "No, and that's the problem. Why we've had so many issues. Every time I want to tell him, I bail. Because of the way Kyle reacted, it scares me that Travis will react the same way. I know I have to tell him if I want to sleep with him, but I'm worried he won't once I tell him."

"I don't know that much about HIV, but the medications have come a long way. Don't they reduce the risk of transmitting HIV significantly if you take them properly?" Brennley asks.

I nod. "Kyle didn't even let me get that far though. I said HIV and he freaked out. He wouldn't listen."

"That's shitty, Hayden. Forget Kyle though. He doesn't deserve you. Travis seems like a good and open-minded guy. Do you really think he'll react the same way as Kyle?" Brennley asks.

I grab another tissue. "I don't know. You should have seen the way Kyle looked at me though. He wouldn't come near me. He looked at me like I was a walking disease."

Cori clenches her fist. "This makes me want to go off on him even more." Her face then relaxes a bit when she sees my reaction. "You didn't deserve that response from him Hayden. You're an amazing person and if Kyle couldn't look past that, then he didn't deserve you. Don't let it get you down Hayden. You made a poor judgment choice, but you can't punish yourself forever. Don't let it define you."

I cringe. "It's hard though, because it's changed my life significantly."

"It's a part of your life, but it's not your life. You are more than your disease." Cori points out.

"Aren't you guys mad at me? I lied to you guys for two years. I wanted to tell you, I swear I did, but I just couldn't. I didn't want you to bombard me with questions and be disappointed in me."

Cori grabs my hand and gives it a quick squeeze. "I could never hate you, Hayden. You've always been there for me. Just because I don't agree with every decision you make, doesn't mean I'd hate you. I'm not disappointed. I'm more hurt that you felt like you couldn't tell me. That you felt you needed to hide it from me. We are best friends. We tell each other everything."

And doesn't that make me feel like a million bucks.

"I'm sorry. I know I should have been able to tell you both, but I didn't know how to start the conversation. I was embarrassed by my mistake."

"We all make mistakes we regret and aren't proud of. But that's what friends are for. To be there for you when you do make mistakes, with no judgment, and help you through them." Brennley adds.

"But I totally lost Travis because of it. He knows I have a secret and because he thinks I don't trust him he broke up with me. I told him I would eventually tell him, and I just needed some more time. I guess his ex-girlfriend kept secrets from him, and I remind him of her. I just need to make sure I can trust him before I tell him."

Brennley looks at me with understanding eyes. "That's completely understandable. You need to feel safe and be able to trust him. If he can't wait, then forget about him."

I sob. "I can't, because I already love him."

"Oh, Hayden. " Cori sighs.

I jerk from her touch. "There's also something else."

"What?" Cori asks.

I decide to just put the whole truth out there. "Thursday nights, I don't have class. I go to an HIV support group."

Brennley's eyes widen. "That's actually really good, Hayden. Support is always good."

"It's been my only place these last two years."

"But now you have another safe place. You have us. Unless... do your parents know?" Cori asks.

I shake my head. "Nope. And I can't tell them. They are going to be so disappointed in me. I especially don't want to tell my dad how I contracted it."

Cori winces. "Do you think that's best, if they don't know?"

I gasp. "Of course, it's best if they don't know. I don't have to tell them if I don't want to."

Cori nods. "Okay, it's up to you. We'll support you either way."

I gulp. "Thanks."

"Everything is going to be okay. Life has a funny way of working out." Brennley reassures me.

"I hope you're right, Brennley."

I really do.

Chapter Twelve: Hayden

It's been a couple of weeks since I told Brennley and Cori. They've both been amazing the whole time. I should have known they would be understanding. We've been hanging more often than usual. We've stayed in most nights, but it's been nice, and comforting. I started school and am still in the stage where I'm figuring out my classes and what my instructor expects from me. I'm also getting used to my new schedule. By the end of September, it's been a little chillier at night. I remind myself to make sure I keep checking when the flu shot comes out, so I can get my flu shot as soon as possible. Because I am HIV positive, Dr. Shields recommends I get it, to prevent me from getting really sick.

I haven't seen Travis these last couple of weeks, and we have barely texted. I miss him. More than I thought I would. I decide maybe I should make the first move. I decide that maybe we can go to a movie. That will be good, because if it's awkward at least we will be distracted by watching the movie. I pull out my phone and shoot him a text asking if he wants to catch a movie Friday night. He replies within a couple minutes and agrees to go to a movie. I can't help the smile that creeps on my face. I'm excited to see him. Even just hanging out as friends. I text him back a smile emoticon and turn my phone on to silent as I head to my next class.

It's Friday night and I'm waiting for Travis to pick me up. I'm wearing skinny jeans, and a pink sweater, with boots. My hair is down, and I even had time to straighten it. There's a knock on the door and I grab my keys and purse, anticipating it will be Travis. When I open the door, he greets me with a huge grin. The one I love. The one that shows both his dimples. He is dressed casually in jeans and a dark gray t-shirt. He leans forward to give me a hug, and I try to not let him affect me, but I can't help but inhale his scent as I hug him back. He gives me a quick kiss on the cheek.

"Ready to go?" he asks.

"Yup."

We walk down to his car, and he opens the passenger door for me. It's a nice gesture. I climb in the seat, as he makes his way around the car to the driver's side. The ride over is mainly silent. It's not a comfortable silence, but it's not an awkward silence either. I gently comb my fingers through my hair for something to do. I rack my brain to think of something normal to say. "How have you been?"

He keeps his eyes on the road. "I'm been okay. Been busy working. You know, the usual."

I nod in understanding. I comb my fingers through my side bangs. They are not cooperating today.

"What about you?" he asks.

"I've been okay. I started a new semester a couple weeks ago."

"How much longer do you have?"

"Hopefully not too much longer, and then I'll have my masters. I still haven't decided if I want to get my PhD or not."

He half smiles. "Well you have lots of time to decide." He looks over at me, and I feel a bit self-conscious. "Your eyes look super green today."

"Yeah, they always change different shades of green depending on the lighting." I simply say. "Although yours change all the time too. Sometimes they appear brown, and other times they look more hazel."

"That's interesting. I've always thought of them as just brown."

I recall meeting his mom and grandma. "You have the same colour eyes as your mom and grandma."

He runs a hand through his hair. "That's what everybody says."

"Because it's true."

Travis pulls up into a parking space. We both get out of the car, and I suddenly feel unsure. Should I grab his hand? Should I not? He looks a bit uneasy, and I notice he hesitates and then sticks his hands in his jean pockets. He must be having the same debate in his head as I am.

I don't force the issue on him. We quietly walk up to the front counter, where he refuses to let me pay for the movie tickets or popcorn. I decide I don't want to make a scene in public, so I let him pay. We are early for the movie, so we head to the far back row. There are only a few other people in the theatre, sitting up closer to the front.

"I totally had my first kiss at this movie theatre." I blurt out.

I don't know why I felt the need for that to come out of my mouth.

Travis reaches over and grabs a handful of popcorn from the bag I'm holding. He looks a bit surprised.

"Really?"

I nod. "Yeah, pretty cliché, hey? Although nowadays you can't afford to make out at the movie theatres. Movies cost too much."

He laughs.

"What? It's true."

"I'm not saying it's not true. It's just funny."

"Where was your first kiss?"

He bunches his brows. "I guess I get to join the cliché department because I had my first kiss playing spin the bottle at my buddy's thirteenth birthday party."

I almost spit popcorn out of my mouth. "You actually played that game? I thought people only played that game on TV and in movies."

He leans back, shocked. "What, are you saying you didn't?"

I never did. "Yeah, I never played it. I played the typical truth and dare, but never spin the bottle."

He chuckles as he puts another handful of popcorn in his mouth.

"Why are you laughing at me?"

He shrugs his shoulders. "You can't say you haven't really played spin the bottle. You kind of played a combo of spin the bottle and truth and dare during the weekend we went camping."

I groan. "You're never going to let me forget that are you?"

"No, I liked it."

I roll my eyes. "Of course, you did."

"They never put enough butter on the popcorn. It's all on the top but by the time you reach the middle of the bag there's none left." Travis grabs another handful of popcorn, sticks it in his mouth and wipes his hands on his jeans.

"It's probably better they don't put on too much butter. It's healthier." I argue.

He gives me the 'really' look. "I don't eat popcorn because I'm trying to be healthy."

I smirk. "I guess that's a valid point. Are you going to complain the whole night?"

"Nope. Nothing to complain about when I'm hanging out with you."

I roll my eyes. "That was super cheesy."

"Actually, you know what would make this popcorn better? If it was cheese flavor."

I feel like we're at that stage in a relationship where you can be completely one hundred percent weird with each other. The beginning of a relationship, you kind of have to always be on your best behavior. After a little while, once you've decided this person likes you enough that they probably won't run once you show them your real side, that's the best part. Weirdness makes them one of a kind. Travis just happens to have a love-hate relationship with popcorn. Now I know that.

I cover my eyes with one hand. "How old are you again?"

The screen lights up and the previews start. Travis lifts this index finger to his mouth. "Shh, the movie is starting."

After the movie, Travis and I decide to go out for ice cream. At the ice cream parlor, I tease him. "So, are you going to get cheese or extra butter flavored ice cream?"

He sticks out his tongue. "Ew-w, no; that' s gross."

"I was being sarcastic."

"I know."

We grab our ice cream cones and sit at a corner booth. "I actually have this really good stuffed chicken recipe that contains lots of butter and lots of cheese. It's amazing."

Stuffed chicken.

It reminds me of the night I told Kyle about my HIV. I made him stuffed chicken for dinner.

"I'll have to make it for you one night...I mean if we decide to hangout again."

I'm too busy thinking of the night I told Kyle, that I barely hear Travis.

Travis waves his hand in front on my face. "Hey, earth to Hayden. You there?"

I blink. "Yeah sorry, I zoned out for a second."

"What were you thinking of? You looked lost in thought."

I lie. "Nothing. I was just thinking of when I was a kid, on my birthday, both my parents would take me out for ice cream for my birthday dinner. I was never allowed to have dessert before dinner, but my birthday was always an exception." That was a true story. Not the one I was thinking of, but definitely a true story.

Travis reaches out with his free non-ice cream cone hand and squeezes one of mine. "I'm sorry."

I tuck my side bangs behind my ear. "No, I'm sorry. I didn't mean to ruin the mood."

"You didn't. I like when you share your thoughts with me."

He likes it?

I don't know what to say to that comment, but he decides to change the subject anyway. "Anyway, I know we're avoiding the talk, but I think it's best to decide now if we want to be friends or more? I'm fine being friends... Well. actually, I'm not. I want to be more than friends. I think I've made that clear numerous times, but you have to tell me now. It's better in the long run to decide this now, then get too deep, and not know how to get out."

He's definitely right. I mean he isn't Kyle.

"Will we be exclusive?" I ask.

"Yes, absolutely," he agrees.

"Can we take things slow?"

He nods. "Haven't we already been doing that?"

Yes, I suppose he's right. "There's also one condition. It's going to sound really weird and paranoid, and a little bit like I don't trust you, but I *need* you to do something for me."

He gives a playful smile. "Depends what it is."

I reach across and hit his shoulder. "That's totally something my dad would say."

"Do I remind you of your dad?"

I furiously shake my head. "No, definitely not. But that was borderline dad joke territory."

He laughs. "What?"

I wave my hand. "Never mind. Anyway, I need you to be serious when I ask you to do this next thing."

He squeezes my hand and lets it go. "Name it."

I swallow the lump in my throat. I am going to be brave. Brave. And responsible. Something I should have done before that *night.*

"It's not that I don't trust you, but before we sleep together, I need you to get tested so I know you're clean."

He raises his brows. "Wow, we're just talking about being exclusive and dating, and you are already thinking about sleeping with me. Who said it was guys who only think about sex?"

I hit him on the shoulder again. "Very funny. But I am being serious."

He exaggeratedly rolls his eyes playfully. "I guess I can do that for you. Although, just putting it out there, I am clean."

"I know. But it would just make me feel better. More comfortable for when the time comes."

He winks at me. "When the time comes or when you come?"

I gasp and hit him again on the shoulder and look around the parlor to make sure no one heard that. "You can't say things like that in a public place."

"You're the one who taught me how to be blunt."

"Well, I'm regretting it now. " I stand up from the booth. "Now let's get out of here."

"Coming."

All I can muster out is an unimpressed frown.

When Travis pulls into a parking space in my apartment complex, I don't get out of the car right away. "I had a really good time. "

He laughs. "Me, too."

I lift my hands out exasperated. "Why are you laughing?"

He groans. "I don't know."

"Well, goodbye." I take my seat belt off and turn to get out of the car, but he stops me by grabbing my elbow.

"Wait, before you go..." He pulls me closer to him and tilts his head as he leans down to press his lips against mine. He hasn't shaved his face in a couple days, so when I place my hand on his scruff, it feels different. Different, but nice. I open my lips and give him full access to my mouth. He runs his tongue along the roof of my mouth, exploring. He lets out a deep groan, and as he pulls his mouth away from me he bites my bottom lip gently.

"Okay, now you can go... And to answer your question, I was just laughing because I have this permanent smile on my face when I'm with you and I can just imagine how creepy it must look. I don't normally smile this much."

My eyes glisten. "Well, you should. I like your smile."

"Goodnight, Hayden."

"Goodnight, Travis."

I walk back up to my apartment with probably the same permanent smile he was wearing tonight.

Chapter Thirteen: Hayden

Over the next weekend, Travis is stuck working and I am swamped with a massive paper. I can't tell if it's because I've been staring at my laptop all weekend, but I am getting the worst throbbing headache ever. I run to the kitchen and take two Ibuprofens. I then tell myself I need to power through, and at least finish writing the content of the paper. Editing and formatting can wait until tomorrow, even though the paper is due tomorrow morning at seven sharp. I can always wake up at five thirty.

After I give myself a pat on the back for finishing up, I close my laptop and head to the couch in the living room. The muscles in my legs are really starting to ache. That, and the throbbing headache hasn't loosened up, even with taking the Ibuprofen. I tell myself I'm just feeling all the stress from school. It's getting to one of the most stressful points of the semester. It's the beginning of October, so it's midterm week. I've been staying up extra late to catch up on my readings that I avoided during the earlier part of the semester, which I tell myself every semester *not* to do.

My brain doesn't listen to me. It's like my body craves that adrenaline rush. *Will she complete all the readings on time to ace the exam? Or, will she be able to hammer out those last ten pages of her paper by midnight in under two hours when It's due?*

My body gets joy from that uncertainty. That *pressure*. It's messed up, I know. Since my mind is still focused on school work, in addition to the unrelenting headache, it takes me longer than usual to fall asleep.

I wake up from my nap, disoriented. My throat feels a bit scratchy and sore, but I don't have time to think about it. I have no idea how long I was out for. It could be thirty minutes, or it could be six hours. That's a scary thought. To think, I've been out for six hours. I look at my cell phone and realize it is six twenty-four in the morning. I went down for my nap yesterday at roughly seven forty. So much for a nap. I don't think what just happened classifies as a nap. I can't believe I slept for almost eleven hours! And my paper! I have half an hour to edit and format it. Shit!

I jump up from the couch and open my laptop. My computer decides it's the perfect time to do upgrades on my laptop.

Are you fucking kidding me?

It's like laptops have this sixth sense and know exactly when you need to use it for something important. When I just want to use Facebook, it works no problem. If it's school related, it decides it's a good time for updates. I think about using Cori's laptop, but I don't have my paper saved on it.

Shit, shit, shit.

I should have emailed the paper to myself. After a couple of minutes, my laptop finishes updating. The palms on my hands are sweating as I look and see the time. Six forty-one. Okay, Hayden, focus. You can do this. I quickly format my paper, and briefly scan my paper for grammar and spelling. I look at the time and realize I have to send my paper in if I want to make it on time. The brief scanning is going to have to do. I open the internet and at this point it decides to take its sweet time to load. I slam my fist on the table beside my laptop.

"Damn it! Load, internet!" I shout, as if the computer can actually hear my pleas.

The internet loads, and I tell myself the shouting worked. I quickly turn in my paper at six fifty-eight. I breathe out a sign of relief.

Man, that was *way* too close.

My throat still feels scratchy and dry. I walk to the kitchen to grab something to drink to soothe it. It's then that I put two and two together. Headache, throbbing muscles, sore throat. Am I getting sick? No, I can't get sick. I can't afford to. I can't miss midterms or any other classes. Not at this point in the semester.

I start going through the kitchen cupboards to see if we have any chicken noodle soup. That will fix this, right? I mean, that's what my mom always used to tell me as a kid. Last year when I got a brief cold, I had chicken noodle soup, and it worked. I scrounge through the cupboards, and success! I have some chicken noodle soup. As I am making it, I suddenly begin to feel really hot. I decide it's probably because I'm standing so close to the stove.

After I'm done making the soup, I sit at the kitchen table and slurp the soup. It sooths my throat a bit. After I'm done eating the soup, I suddenly become very nauseous. My stomach is doing somersaults. I run to the bathroom and vomit out all the chicken noodle soup I just ate. Well I guess that the soup *won't* help me after all. After I feel I can't possibly vomit out any more stuff, I rinse out my mouth and head upstairs to bed. I just need to rest. My legs almost give out before I hit my bed. I close my eyes, and for a second, I think I feel better as I don't feel as hot anymore. After a few minutes, I become cold and start to shiver and shake. I get under my bed covers and cocoon myself. Lying down doesn't seem to help, as I get a tickle in my throat and begin to cough. After a brief coughing attack, I use my pillow to position myself in a semi-upright position. It's then I finally fall asleep.

A loud knock on my bedroom door finally wakes me up. "Cori?" I ask, although my voice comes out raspy.

"No, it's Travis."

Oh, Travis. "Come in, although I don't think you'll want to."

I turn over as my bedroom door opens. "Why don't you want me to come in?"

I moan. "I'm dying."

Travis laughs at my exaggeration. "Why are you dying?" Travis walks over to my bed. I hold up a hand to stop him from coming closer. He halts. I use my other hand to wipe my hair from my face. "Don't come near me. I'm sick. I have a bad cold. Get out now while you can."

He chuckles but walks over and sits on the edge of my bed. He runs a hand down my back in a soothing way. "Do you need anything? Ginger ale, lozenges?"

Aw, he's so caring. "Actually, if you don't mind I'd love some lozenges. But I don't think I have any left. My throat is on fire." Talking was a mistake because another coughing attack claims me.

"Okay, why don't you rest, and I'll run to the store to get you some medicine?"

I shake my head, but then start coughing again. "No, you don't have to do that."

"I know I don't have to. I *want* to."

I'm too tired to argue, and every time I speak a coughing attack happens, so I just nod my head. He kisses me on the head. "I'll be back soon. Rest."

I nod my head again, and he leaves my bedroom. He quietly closes the door on the way out. I didn't even have a chance to ask him what he was doing here. I look over at my phone and see I have some missed calls and texts from him. Oh, he must have been worried about me. That thought warms me. It's a nice feeling knowing someone cares. That nice thought is soon replaced by a not-so-nice thought. I remember my HIV. When I had a cold last year, my body was able to fight it off, so I didn't need to worry. At my last appointment Dr. Shields said my levels looked good. Should I give her a call? I decide to wait it out to see if I get better. I'm so fatigued I can't even move right now.

You always take for granted when you aren't sick. Then when you get sick you realize how awful it is. I try to fall back asleep but every time I lie down I start coughing. My chest is beginning to hurt because I can't stop coughing. I even almost vomit when I notice the disgusting phlegm I cough out. I hate phlegm, it's so gross.

I don't get any sleep while Travis is gone due to my stupid cough. When he comes back he has a bagful of items. He shows me everything he's bought: ginger ale, chicken noodle soup, crackers, cough medicine, Ibuprofen, and lozenges.

"You are the best. Thanks." I say in hoarse voice as I reach for the cough medicine and lozenges.

"Your voice kind of sounds sexy like that. Very raspy." He says as he puts the rest of the items on my side table.

I groan. "I definitely *don't* feel sexy right now." I cough again. I grab a tissue from my side table and spit some more phlegm into it. *Definitely not* sexy. "I really appreciate you being here, but you should go. I don't want you to get sick."

His eyes narrow. "I'll take my chances. I don't want to leave you here by yourself."

I suck on my lozenge. "I'm not alone. Cori is down the hall if I need her." I begin to feel hot again, so I pull off my covers and take my sweat shirt off. Travis leaves the room, and I think he is gone, but a couple minutes later he comes back with a wet cloth. He sits on the side of my bed and leans down to place the cool cloth on my forehead. It feels nice. I mutter out a "Thanks." After a couple seconds he moves the cloth to the back of my neck. It also feels nice. "You're not leaving?" I ask him.

"No. I want to be close just in case you need something. I don't start work until later tomorrow anyway."

I yelp. "But what if I get you sick?"

He shrugs. "That's a risk I'm willing to take."

I force a half smile, but then start to shake. I hate fevers. Feeling hot one second and then freezing cold another. I put my sweatshirt back on and pull my covers back on. I must be visibly shaking, because Travis puts the cloth back on my side table and walks around to the other side of my bed, and climbs in. He moves closer to me, so my back is against his chest. He moves his hands up and down my arms trying to warm me up. I like it. He is my own personal furnace.

"Don't say I didn't warn you," I say, my voice coming out raspy again.

"I won't," he promises.

"What time is it?" I ask.

"Almost nine." he replies.

"Thank you for everything, Travis. Goodnight."

He pulls me tighter against him. "Goodnight, Hayden."

* * * *

Travis

The next morning, I wake up feeling like an oven. I look down and Hayden is lying half on top on me, her head on my chest and her left leg hooked over my legs. We probably have six blankets on us. I gently roll over, holding her close to me so she doesn't stir as I reach over to grab my cell phone from the bedside table. I look at the time. It's eight in the morning. As I roll back so I'm flat on my back, Hayden stirs.

"Hayden, you awake?"

She responds with a grunt. She doesn't even open her eyes. I slowly and gently slide her off me, so I can get out of the bed. I feel disgusting and sweaty and in definite need of a shower.

I decide to let her sleep some more and hope she doesn't mind if I use her shower.

After I'm done showering, I head down to her kitchen to make her some chicken noodle soup for breakfast, for when she wakes up. I run into Cori in the kitchen.

"Good morning," she says with a huge grin across her face. "I didn't know you were here."

I scratch my head. "Uh, yeah, sorry. Hayden isn't feeling well, so I decided to stay the night just in case she needed anything."

Cori's smile gets wider. "Aww, that's sweet of you." Her smile quickly disappears, and she has a puzzled look on her face. "Is Hayden okay?"

I move towards the kitchen cabinets to find a pot. "Uh yeah, I think she just has a cold."

Cori looks worried. "Are you sure it's just a cold?"

"Umm, yeah, I think so. She has a fever, cough, and sore throat, so I'm guessing it's a cold."

Cori crosses her arms. "Maybe I should go check on her."

I stop her, because I don't want her to wake Hayden up. "I already did. She's sleeping I think it's best if we let her rest."

Cori cringes. "It's not good if Hayden gets sick."

I finally find a pot to use. I turn on one of the elements on the stove. "I know. She told me she was worried about falling behind in school, especially since it's midterm week."

"Not only that." Cori quickly covers her mouth with her hand. "I mean...I think I'm just going to go check on her. She might say she's fine, but Hayden knows how to down-play things, so I just need to make sure she's okay with my own eyes."

I put the lid on top of the pot. "You worry about her, don't you?"

Cori gives me a tight smile. "Of course, I do. She's my best friend. I know you care about her too."

I open a package of the chicken noodle soup. "I do."

Cori heads upstairs and I continue to prepare the chicken noodle soup. Not long after Cori heads upstairs I hear her, shouting.

"Travis! Come quick! Something's wrong with Hayden!"

I don't even turn off the element. I run up the stairs taking three at a time. I storm into Hayden's room to find Cori trying to shake Hayden awake. Cori has tears in her eyes.

"She's not waking up!" she cries.

Cori moves aside as I approach Hayden. She's lying flat on her back with the covers half on her. I can tell she is breathing, because her chest is moving up and down. She appears pale. Paler than yesterday. Her eyes are closed. I lean down and grab a hold of her shoulders as I give her a gentle shake.

"Hayden, wake up."

She doesn't flinch. She doesn't respond at all. I start to worry, but don't show it as I don't want to worry Cori any more than she already is. I shake Hayden again and this time raise my voice. "Hayden. Babe, you need to wake up." No response.

Now I am really starting to worry. As I think about calling an ambulance, Hayden stirs a bit, and opens her eyes slowly.

"Travis?", she groans.

I cradle her head in my hands. "Hey, you weren't waking up. Are you okay?"

She blinks and tries to sit up. When she sits up, I reposition her, so her back is up against my chest and her head rests on my shoulder. "Yeah, I'm okay. I just really don't feel well." She sits up slightly and coughs again. After a couple of long seconds of coughing, she closes her eyes and rests her head back down against my shoulder.

I'm a little worried. I mean this is probably only a really bad flu, but maybe I should take her to the doctor just in case. I have a bad feeling in the pit of my stomach.

"Hayden, should I take you to your doctor's?"

She shakes her head. "I think it's okay. I just need to rest."

Cori looks at her and in a stern voice says, "Hayden, I think you should see your doctor. You never know what this could be from."

"I was fine last year when I had a cold. I honestly just need to rest." She tries to get up, but I pull her back down. "Where are you going?"

"I just need to go to the bathroom."

I release her, and she stands up. Cori stares her down. As Hayden is walking to the bathroom, I can hear her breathing getting worse. Cori looks at me.

"We need to take her to a doctor, *now.* I'm not joking Travis."

I hold up my hands. "I agree. I'll make her go." I grab my cell phone and call in sick to work. There is no way I'm going in to work today. I'll just worry about Hayden.

Hayden comes back into her room and walks over. Her breathing is definably more labored. She looks even more pale if that is even possible as she has porcelain pale skin to begin with. As she walks over to the bed, she abruptly stops and places her hand on her head.

"I feel dizzy."

I immediately stand and thank goodness I do because I barely have time to catch her as she falls forward and passes out in my arms. Cori screams, and becomes panicked.

"Travis! You need to get her to a hospital, now!"

I bend down and grab Hayden's legs, so I can lift her and carry her in my arms. "Don't worry, Cori. I'm taking her to emergency now." I'm surprised how calm my voice comes out, because inside, I am freaking out. How does this happen to a person who has a cold?

Cori begins to shake a bit. "I'm coming with you."

I readjust Hayden in my arms. "Maybe you should stay here. I can call Erik if you want. You're shaken up."

Cori furiously shakes her head. "No! I'm coming with you."

I want to argue for her to stay here, but I'm really worried about Hayden. With no time to waste, I agree. We head out to the parking lot to climb into my car. Cori gets in the back seat and I lower Hayden next to her, so she can hold and support her.

"I've got her," Cori reassures me. I let Hayden go and run into the driver's seat. I remember I never turned off the stove element. Shit!

I quickly run back into the apartment, turn off the stove, and book it back to my car. I pretty much speed on the way to the hospital, not caring if I get pulled over. When we are almost there, I can hear Hayden's voice.

"Cori?"

I look in the rear-view mirror and see Cori stroking Hayden's cheek. Cori tells Hayden, "It's okay Hayden. We're taking you to hospital."

I hear Hayden mumble out a "No, hospital."

Cori is stern as she tells her, "Yes we are. No arguments."

Hayden is more awake by the time we hit the emergency, but her breathing still doesn't sound good. I grab a wheelchair and bring it back for Hayden. I wheel her into the emergency and she tells the front desk why she is there. After what feels like forever, a woman in blue scrubs calls her name. I follow the woman as I wheel Hayden. Cori comes with us. When we reach a hospital bed, I help Hayden climb onto it. Her breathing is still a bit labored. The woman in scrubs takes her vitals, and tells Hayden she has a high temperature, and will need oxygen to help with her oxygen levels. The nurse positions oxygen tubing under Hayden's nose to assist with her slightly increased work of breathing. She leaves a finger probe on Hayden's index finger. The nurse leaves the room, stating a doctor will be in shortly. I grab Hayden's hand, the one without the finger probe, and give it a quick squeeze. I lean down and kiss her head.

Hayden looks at me and gives me a weak smile. "Travis?"

"Yeah, babe."

"I really love that you care enough about me to take care of me and take me to the hospital, but would you mind stepping out when the doctor comes? I'll get Cori to get you when the doctor is finished. I just don't want him to ask embarrassing female questions while you're in the room."

I guess they could ask her those types of questions. I'm a little hurt she wants me to leave, but I also get that she wants some privacy. I probably would too.

I lift up her hand and give it a kiss. "Sure. I'll be in the waiting room. Have Cori come grab me, if you need me."

She gives me another weak smile. "Thanks Travis. For everything."

I give her a weak smile back. "You're welcome. I just hope they can help get you better. Do you want me to call your parents?"

She shakes her head. "No, not yet. I don't want them to worry. If I need to, I will later. I'm sure it's nothing."

"Okay." I turn and leave to sit in the waiting room, surrounded by other families waiting with their loved ones. I stretch out my legs and left out a breath.

Damn. Hayden had me so worried. Especially when I couldn't wake her up. I think over worst case scenarios but shake those thoughts out of my head. Hayden's probably right. She probably just has a bad flu or is super dehydrated. I mean, she hasn't had many fluids. I run my hands through my hair. Hopefully everything will be okay.

* * * *

Hayden

To be honest, the reason I asked Travis to step out, was because I knew I would have to tell the doctor about my medical history. My medical history being the fact I'm HIV positive. I am going to tell Travis, but now is just, not the time. The emergency doctor is an older man with grey hair and glasses, who introduces himself as Dr. Wells. He is wearing blue scrubs and a white lab coat. He takes a listen to my lungs with his stethoscope, and asked me a bunch of questions such as "When did your symptoms start?", and "What medications are you currently taking?" Medical kind of questions.

Dr. Wells did ask me about my medical history and I told him about my HIV. He told me he thinks I have pneumonia, but he wants me to get a chest x-ray and some blood work done first. He is going to get in contact with Dr. Shields, so he can review my latest blood work just as a precaution. I asked him if he thought the pneumonia is related to my HIV. He didn't really answer my question. He told me I was more at risk of getting pneumonia because I have HIV, but he reassured me lots of people who don't have HIV also get pneumonia. He also reassured me it was a good thing, when I stated I'm vigilant at taking my anti-retroviral medications. After I answered all his questions, he let me know he thinks I am quite dehydrated, so he said a nurse would be in shortly to put in an IV and start me on some fluids.

Before the doctor left the room, I told him Cori is the only one who knows about my HIV, so if any other family members or friends come or need to be contacted I didn't want him to tell them. I didn't want to go into detail, letting him know Brennley knows too. It's just easier to say no one knows, just in case. He gave me a serious nod and let me know he wasn't permitted to let them know, due to confidentiality and privacy laws. I let out an exhale, relieved. Cori leaves to get Travis after she informs me she's texting Brennley to let her know. I don't want to worry Brennley, but Cori hushes me and texts her anyway.

Cori and Travis return, as a younger nurse finishes inserting an IV in my left hand and hooking me up to fluids. She tells me a porter would come soon to take me for my chest x-ray. Travis grabs an extra chair from the corner of the room and places it beside my bed where he takes a seat. Cori walks over to my other side and sits in the chair she was occupying earlier. Travis reaches down and kisses my hand not connected to the IV.

"So, is everything okay?" he asks.

I move my head up and down. "Yeah. The doctor thinks I have pneumonia. I have to get a chest x-ray and some blood work. The fluids..." I point to the IV, "are because he thinks I'm severely dehydrated which he thinks is why I may have passed out. He's going to let me know more, once he receives my test results."

Travis lets out a breath. "Well, that's good. Pneumonia is treatable, right?"

"I think so. Hopefully they can give me some antibiotics or something and I can go back home."

Travis points to my oxygen. "How's your breathing?"

"Better with the oxygen. But my chest hurts so bad every time I cough."

Travis rubs my arm. A few seconds later, a younger man comes in and states he's going to take me for the chest x-ray. I look at Travis. I really want him to stay. I know he has to go to work, but he's been so loving and caring. I could use his support.

"Do you need to go to work?"

He shakes his head. "No, I called in sick."

I groan. "You called in sick because of me?"

He shrugs. "It's not a big deal. You're more important than work."

I smile. "So, you're going to be here when I get back?"

He grins. "Absolutely. I'm not going anywhere."

After my chest x-ray and blood work, Dr. Wells comes by to tell me I do have pneumonia. He says he was able to contact Dr. Shields and is hopeful that I will respond well to the treatment for pneumonia, since my HIV has been responding well to my medications, and my HIV viral load looks good. It makes me feel reassured because I always worry when I get sick, because I never know how my immune system will be able to handle any infections because of my HIV. Dr. Wells said it was good that I came in to get treated, as the infection could have spread to my bloodstream. Dr. Wells says he wants to keep me overnight, just to be on the safe side, to make sure I am responding appropriately to treatment. He wants to continue me on IV fluids to keep me hydrated and see if by tomorrow my breathing improves and I can come off the oxygen.

They move me to a private room on one of the top floors of the hospital. Travis and Cori have been wonderful and haven't left. They offered to get me 'real food' as opposed to hospital food, but I decline, saying I don't really feel up to eating.

At about six in the evening, Brennley, Cooper, and Penelope come visit me in my hospital room.

"Auntie Hayden, we heard you were sick." Penelope comes up and runs over to my hospital bed. "Here I made you a card." She gives me a piece of pink construction paper that says, "feel better Aunt Hayden." Inside the card is a picture Penelope drew, of what I am assuming is her and me playing. There are hearts and flowers all over the card as well. Her card is super sweet.

"Thanks Penny, I love it. It will definitely make me feel better."

Brennley lets go of Cooper's hand and walks over to me. I notice she's carrying flowers. She hands the flowers to me. "Here, these are for you. How are you feeling?"

I smell the flowers. "These are lovely. Thanks, Brennley. I'm fine. The doctor says it's just pneumonia, but he's optimistic I'll response well to the medications he prescribed."

"Did he mention how he thinks you contracted the pneumonia? Do you think it has to do with...you know?" Brennley looks around the room to make sure no one clues in. Although her wording it like that actually makes it less subtle.

I start to shake my head, but a tickle develops in my throat and I get to enjoy another coughing attack. "I'm not sure. Although, the doctor says there are many types of pneumonia and anyone can contract it."

Cooper finally speaks. "Do you need us to get you anything? We can stop by your apartment if you want? Or pick you up some food?"

Just as I am about to respond, Penny pipes up. "We could buy you some popsicles."

Everyone laughs, although my throat is still on fire, so popsicles would actually make it feel better.

Cooper grins. "Yeah, if you really want we can buy you popsicles."

I giggle. "No, I'm good, but thanks for the offer."

Brennley looks at Cooper and then back at me. "Do you need me to call your parents? Do they know?"

Oh right, my parents. I don't want them to worry. My mom always overreacts. "Umm, no. I didn't tell them. I'll call them tomorrow. You know them, they'll just worry."

Brennley gives me a stern look. "Of course, they worry. They are your parents. They should know if you are in the hospital."

I fold. "Okay, I guess you can call them. But please, downplay it, because it isn't that big of a deal."

Cori gives me the 'are you serious' look? "You wouldn't wake up when Travis and I tried to wake you this morning, and you passed out at home. You had us both extremely worried. Don't downplay this."

Brennley looks shocked. "Hayden, you passed out? Are you sure everything is fine?"

I groan. Thanks Cori. "Brennley I swear. Everything is fine. The doctor thinks I passed out because I was a little dehydrated."

Brennley narrows her eyes. "Hayden, you need to take care of yourself."

I gasp. "I am!" My voice cracks and I start coughing again.

Travis steps in. "I think Hayden just needs to rest."

Brennley gives me a good look-over.

"You're right, Travis. I'll call your parents Hayden. Feel better, okay? Please call me tomorrow and update me on any changes."

"Yes, mom." I say sarcastically.

Brennley comes over to give me a hug. I hold a hand out. "No hugs. I don't want to get anyone else sick."

Brennley nods. "Yeah, you're right." She grabs Penny's hand. "Say 'bye' to Aunt Hayden."

"Bye, Aunt Hayden, I love you. Feel better." Penny blows me a kiss. I blow her a kiss back.

Just before they leave, Brennley leans down and gives Travis a hug. "Please, take care of my best friend."

I groan. Brennley gives me the bitch glare.

Travis just chuckles. "I will, don't worry."

Just as Brennley, Penelope, and Cooper leave, Cooper throws out, "Remember Hayden, if you need anything just call us, okay?"

Aw, Brennley did so well with the boyfriend game. Although Travis has become quite the catch. Travis has been nothing but amazing.

"Thanks, Cooper. I appreciate it."

As soon as the three of them leave the room, I turn to Travis. "Thanks for the save. I think because Brennley helps raise Penny, she likes to take on the role of being mother bear."

He smiles. "That's what I'm here for."

Chapter Fourteen: Hayden

About twenty minutes later, I try to get Travis and Cori to leave. Cori finally calls Erik to come pick her up, but Travis is adamant on staying the night. He says he's just going to sleep in the chair, which is ridiculous. Just after Cori leaves, a familiar face walks into my hospital room. It's Dr. Shields. She is all dressed up in a high-waisted black skirt with a black blouse, and black heels. I'm really glad to see her.

"Hey, Hayden. Dr. Wells called me at my office today. He informed me what happened. I was worried about you, so I decided to come check. How are you feeling?"

Did I say Dr. Shields is a good doctor? She's actually *the best* doctor. "I'm okay. Just a really bad cough, but I think the fever's going away.

"Well, that's good. Dr. Wells said he's just keeping you overnight for observation."

I nod. "Yeah, he wants to make sure I'm responding to treatment."

She gives me a polite smile and nudges her head to Travis. "Who's this?"

Oh right, I forgot for a second that Travis was in the room. "This is my boyfriend, Travis."

Dr. Shields holds out her hand. "Nice to meet you." Travis returns the handshake.

Travis looks at me and I realize he is probably wondering how I know Dr. Shields.

"Do you need anything from me?" Dr. Shields asks.

Oh, my goodness. One more person to ask me this. Boy, do I feel loved. "No, but thanks for asking."

After I reply, my mom bursts through my hospital room and comes over to squeeze me in an insanely tight hug.

"Oh, Hayden, I was so worried! Brennley called me to tell me what happened. Are you okay, honey? What did the doctor say?" My mom turns around and see Dr. Shields. "Hi, are you my daughter's doctor?"

Oh, know. What is Dr. Shields going to say? She knows I haven't told my parents. I cringe just thinking how she's going to get out of this.

Dr. Shields shakes her head. "No, I'm not her doctor."

I decide to jump in. "She works with Dr. Summers. She was notified I was in the hospital, so she decided to come check on me. Make sure everything is okay."

Dr. Summer's is my family doctor. I give myself props. I did well. My mom continues to look around the room. "Well, where is your doctor? I want to talk to them."

I groan, probably louder than I should. "Mom, I am an adult. The doctor isn't going to talk to you. He talked to me. He said I have pneumonia. I am being treated with medication. He is only keeping me overnight for observation. Everything's fine."

My mom relaxes her shoulders. "I'm sorry, Hayden. It's just that even though you are an adult, you're still my baby. I'm always going to worry about you. If something bad happened, I'd be devastated."

Dr. Shields points to the door. "Hayden, I'm going to go. Call me if you need anything."

"Thanks for coming, Dr. Shields. I really appreciate it."

She gives me a curt nod and leaves.

"I know, mom. But you are being a tad overbearing. I'm fine."

She gives me a playful smile. "Well, I wouldn't be your mom if I wasn't overbearing."

Travis chuckles, and my mom turns to look at him. "Hi, who are you?"

Oh, I realize I haven't told my mom about Travis. Probably because we were so on again, off again. Awkward. "Sorry mom, this is my boyfriend, Travis."

My mom lets out a loud gasp. "Hayden, how come you didn't tell me you were seeing anyone. You didn't tell me you were in the hospital. Why are you keeping so many things from me? I'm your mom. I want to know about these things."

Well mom, if you only knew what I *was* keeping from you.

"Travis and I haven't been dating for that long. I'm introducing you now."

My mom blushes. "Well, I am glad you found someone so handsome."

Oh, my goodness. Talk about embarrassing. I think moms have this special ability that, it doesn't matter how old you are, if they need to embarrass you they can do it at the drop of a hat.

Travis smirks at me.

"Mom, please stop."

Travis sticks out his hand to my mom. "Nice to meet you..."

"Michelle." she clarifies. I don't know if Travis had second thoughts and realized my mom probably wouldn't appreciate being called Mrs. Myers, as she is going through a divorce. The thought makes me sad. My mom won't have the same last name as me anymore. On the other hand, good catch, Travis. Not only handsome but smart too.

My mom looks back at me. "Your dad wishes you well. I told him I would come check on you and give him a full report. How come I haven't met Dr. Shields yet? I probably see Dr. Summers more than you."

Oh, shit. Not good. What do I say to that? "Oh, I don't know. I haven't seen her that many times, mom."

I guess my mom brushes the thought off because she doesn't force the issue, which is good. I hope she doesn't investigate this further or ask Dr. Summer's any questions about Dr. Shields. Then I'd be in trouble.

"Mom, I'm kind of tired. I don't mean to be rude, but I'd love to get some sleep."

"Oh, of course, honey." She walks over and gives me a kiss on my head. "Feel better, okay honey? Call me if you need me. I love you, sweetheart."

"I love you too, mom."

She turns and leaves the room. I lift the bed covers up. "See this is why I wanted to wait for you to meet my mom. I love her, but she can be a little much at times."

Travis pulls my covers down. "She cares a lot about you. Like I do."

"I know. You've been so amazing, Travis. I can't thank you enough."

He closes his eyes and then opens them. "You don't have to thank me. I'm your boyfriend. My job is to worry about you." He lets out a breath and looks at me directly in the eyes. His eyes soften. "You had me so worried, Hayden. When I couldn't wake you up, and then when you passed out. You really scared me."

Tears prickle my eyes. If you only knew the full story, Travis. I couldn't imagine if he knew the full extent. Cori and Brennley seemed more worried about my hospitalization knowing about my HIV. The stress it would have put on Travis would have been too much. It does make me feel really guilty, like a part of me is lying to him. After all this, he deserves to know the truth.

I make it a plan to figure out a way to tell him when I return home. After that it becomes his decision if he wants to take on every piece of me, knowing the added risks.

"I'm sorry, Travis." A tear slips down my cheek. I'm not just sorry for getting sick. I'm sorry for not having the courage of telling him the full truth. Of wanting extra time to be able to trust him.

Travis lifts his hand and wipes away the tear. I grab onto his hand and keep it close, holding his hand on my cheek.

"You have nothing to be sorry about. I'm just glad you are going to be okay."

"How did I get so lucky, running into you on that first day?"

He laughs. "I thought you said I attacked you."

I cringe. "I don't like that version of the story. It's not romantic."

"You don't think getting shat on the face by a bird is romantic?"

I laugh, and it triggers another coughing attack. "No, definitely not. Can we please come up with another story of how we met? So, when people ask how we met we can tell them this amazing, romantic story?" I give him a coy smile. "I have some ideas."

"Okay, well how about you get some rest, and you can tell them to me tomorrow."

"Okay. Goodnight, Travis."

"Goodnight, Hayden." He leans forward and kisses me on the forehead.

The next day, I get discharged from the hospital. I have some discharge medications to help treat my pneumonia which I can take at home. Travis stayed the whole night, and even slept in that awful, uncomfortable chair. He gets bonus boyfriend points for that one. Travis drives me home back to my house. I still feel quite tired, so we decide to put on a movie in the living room. I try to convince Travis to go to work, but he still refuses. I feel bad, but also am quite happy because I love cuddling up on the couch with him. I'm surprised he hasn't gotten sick yet. Both my parents have called, and Cori and Brennley keep blowing up my phone with texts almost every hour asking how I'm doing. Even Lauren calls, super angry that I didn't inform her I was in the hospital. Sorry, Lauren.

I email my professors at schools to let me know I couldn't write some of my midterms as I was in the hospital. They said as long as I have a doctor's note, I can make the exams up, so that's a relief. I even force myself to return to school a few days later, although Travis wasn't too happy about that.

It takes me a couple of weeks to fully get over my pneumonia. I follow up with Dr. Shields, as she requested to see me just to make sure everything is back to normal. At the appointment I confide in her that I am ready to tell Travis about my HIV, and she's happy for me, and tells me he can always come to my next appointment if he has any questions or concerns.

Apparently, she appreciates her patients asking her questions as opposed to googling them. Funny.

Travis has been amazing and checks up on me every day. He comes over almost every day. One day when my appetite improved I surprised him with lunch at his work. I walked in on him assisting this senior woman with some exercises. Man, did he look cute helping a frail elderly woman. He was extremely grateful for the lunch. I told him it was the least I could do for how amazing he's been over the last couple of weeks. We haven't done anything these last couple months, including kissing. I was so paranoid he was going to get pneumonia, but he surprisingly didn't.

Saturday morning, I invite Brennley over for a pancake breakfast. Cori joins us. I've decided I want to tell Travis about my HIV, so I thought since Cori and Brennley know, they would be able to give suggestions on how I should broach the subject.

We are eating our pancakes at the kitchen table. This time Brennley joins Cori and I by wearing pajamas. Because if you have the choice to wear normal clothes or pajamas, why wouldn't you choose pajamas? I tie my hair up in a ponytail and add some syrup on my plate.

"So, I was thinking about telling Travis about my HIV?"

Brennley swallows a bite of her pancake. "That's great, Hayden. You'll feel so much better when you do."

I use my knife and fork to cut off a piece of my pancake. "Yeah, I'm just still nervous about his reaction. But, I have concluded he is not Kyle. How he took care of me in the hospital, and after, really showed me how caring he can be."

Cori nods, because her mouth is full. She swallows. "Yeah, I really like Travis. It was so cute how he fussed over you. You can really tell he cares about you, Hayden."

I glow. "Yeah, I am lucky. How should I break the news? I guess I'm more concerned about the delivery aspect. I can't take the approach of just ripping off the band aid. When I did that with Kyle he freaked and wouldn't let me finish explaining."

Brennley gives me a reassuring smile. "Just do whatever feels right to know. You always say, one of the best things about Travis is, he is a good listener. I have yet to see him loose his cool."

She's right. He is relatively calm. Even when we did fight at the cabin, he never frightened me, or I was never worried he was going to blow his top.

"Yeah, maybe this time I shouldn't prepare a speech. I think last time I was too prepared and had this idea of how the night was supposed to go. If I don't have any expectations, maybe I won't be so disappointed if things don't go well."

Cori groans. "No, definitely *have* expectations. The least you can expect is that he acts like a respectful, mature human being. You deserve respect."

Cori is right. I sip my glass of orange juice. "You are right. I deserve respect."

Cori's smile widens. "See? You're finally learning!"

I swallow another bite of my pancake. "I also asked Travis to get tested."

Brennley nods. "That's good, Hayden. That's being a responsible adult."

I wince. "That's what I probably should have done before I had unprotected sex with someone who was HIV positive."

Brennley puts down her utensils. "But now, you've learned. Now, you can do that. A lot of people don't ask their partners to get tested, and it just happens that they luck out and don't catch anything. You can't beat yourself up over this forever."

"I know, I know. It's just hard."

Cori acknowledges my worries. "You're braver than you think you are."

I smile. "Well, I feel safe, and I fully trust Travis now."

Cori nudges my arm. "See? Didn't I tell you, life has a funny way of working out?"

"It hasn't worked out yet."

"But it will. Don't freak out until the moment happens. You're most likely worrying for nothing," Brennley reassures me.

I take another sip of my orange juice. "I hope you are right."

Chapter Fifteen: Hayden

After Cori and Brennley leave, I text Travis asking if he wants to come over to my place after he's done work for dinner. It takes him half an hour to respond but he agrees to come. I ask him if he has any dinner requests, and he messages me back saying 'surprise me'. Cori knows Travis is coming over, so she's promised to stay over at Erik's house, but to call her if tonight doesn't go as planned so she can be over with some ice cream and eggs stat. Eggs, initially I thought was weird. It took me a second but then I thought about it more and the eggs are probably to egg Travis's apartment if reacts poorly. God, I love Cori sometimes.

I head to the grocery store and decide that maybe I should make a chicken dinner with rice and a salad. I then remember I made stuffed chicken the night I told Kyle. I put the chicken back. Nope, definitely not chicken. I decide on making a lasagna with a salad. When I was over at his place for dinner he told me how much he loved Italian food, so I think he would like lasagna. I walk down an aisle and see a bag of cheddar and caramel popcorn mix. I smile to myself recalling how he stated he'd love a cheese flavored popcorn when we went to the movies. I decide to pick it up.

When I get home, I start prepping the lasagna. While I am waiting for the lasagna to cook, I go upstairs to get ready. I decide on some dark skinny jeans, with a red dressy top, that has a sweet heart neckline, and I curl my blonde hair into loose curls. I add a red lipstick that matches my top, and spray on some light perfume that I think smells good. I head back downstairs to the kitchen and open a bottle of red wine. I pour myself a small glass, just to calm my nerves a little. After I check on the lasagna, the doorbell rings.

I walk swiftly over to the door and open it to see Travis's beautiful face. "You don't have to knock anymore; you can just walk in."

"Noted." He replies. He dips down and gives me a quick kiss on the lips.

"How was work?"

Travis takes off his shoes. "It dragged on. I couldn't wait until it was over. As soon as you texted me I wanted to come right then."

"Such a sweet talker you are," I give him a flirty smile.

"Only for you." He gives me another quick kiss.

"So what smells amazing?"

I clasp my hands together. "I hope you like lasagna."

He wiggles his eyebrows. "I do. I also brought you something."

Oh man. Please don't be flowers. Please don't be flowers. Kyle brought me flowers *that* night. "What?"

"Close your eyes."

Okay? I close my eyes.

"Now you can open them."

I open my eyes. In his hands he is holding two slices of cheesecake.

My mouth hangs open and I lick my lips. "Travis, you know how much I love cheesecake. Let's skip dinner and just eat that." I reach out to try to take the cheesecake away from him.

He pulls the cheesecake away from me, behind him. "Nope, you have to be a good girl and wait."

I lick my lips again. "Well I never liked being a good girl." I try again to reach behind him to grab the cheesecake. With his other hand he grasps my hand. "Nice try, but it isn't working on me."

I give up. "Fine. I guess we can have dinner first."

He laughs. I lead him to the kitchen and he places the cheesecake in the fridge. Okay, I'll admit it. I was checking out his behind when he bent over to place the cheesecake in the fridge. It's just a nice view. I can't not. He turns around and catches me.

"Were you checking me out?" he asks.

Since I am working on being brave, I decide to act confidently instead of like my old self which would have been blushing. "What if I was? Got a problem with that?"

He strolls over to me. "No. No problem at all."

He bends and kisses my lips. He licks my lips, and I don't hesitate to give him full access to my mouth as I part my lips. After a couple minutes he places kisses down my neck. I lean back to give him more of my neck. I immediately put my hands on his head and run my fingers in his hair. His hair is really soft. He uses his other hand to grab one of the straps on my top and tugs it down. I immediately retract and pull the strap back up. He stops kissing me and pulls away. He looks a bit worried.

"Sorry." I blush. I know I am probably as red as my top. "After dinner, okay? If you start now, I won't be able to stop."

The worried look on his face disappears. "Okay. I understand. Would be a shame to let your wonderful masterpiece of dinner go to waste."

Not exactly what I was concerned about, but okay.

After chatting a while, I pour Travis a glass of wine, and we make our way out to the dinner table to eat. Travis take a generous bite of the lasagna.

"Hayden, this is amazing. You have to cook for me all the time now."

I giggle. "Definitely not."

"Does Cori make you cook for her all the time?"

I bite my lip. "Actually, I made a pancake breakfast for Brennley and Cori this morning."

He pretends to look hurt. "Where were my pancakes?"

I roll my eyes. "You were at work."

"If I knew there were pancakes I would have skipped work."

I lean forward. "That's why I didn't tell you. I can't be the reason you keep missing work."

Travis winks. "I don't mind missing work."

I point my fork at him. "Nope. You need to work so I can afford to make you dinner's like this."

Travis folds. "I guess you have a point."

I decide to be cheeky. "I always do."

After our amazing dinner, we wait a bit before we indulge in some cheesecake. It's all very cute. Travis feeds me cheesecake off his fork, and even smears some on my face, stating it was payback for the pasta sauce. Although instead of wiping off the cheesecake with a napkin, he licks it off with his tongue. I giggled, and had shivers running down my spine.

We then head to the couch in the living room. So many good memories here with Travis. I sit next to him, almost on top of him. He puts an arm around me and I cuddle into his shoulder. "Remember when Penelope caught us together on the couch?" he utters.

I giggle. "Yeah, that was kind of funny, but also kind of embarrassing. Talk about having an awkward conversation with Brennley."

"Was she mad?"

"No, she wasn't mad. She actually was kind of happy. She likes you. She was rooting for us."

He holds me tighter. "I'm glad."

I swallow a lump that has formed in my throat. "I was rooting for us too. Even when we weren't together."

"Me too." His voice comes out, barely a whisper.

I decide it's finally time to tell him the truth. I remind myself I trust him, and I feel safe enough to tell him. I sit up, out from under his hold, and move so I'm sitting a bit away from him, but still facing him. I look down at my hands, and then back at him. When I look in his eyes, I can see my reflection in them. This time, I don't look weak. I look strong. His eyes are more brown today. He doesn't say anything, he just swallows and stares at me. He stares at me with admiration and care. Not concern or worry.

Not the way Kyle did when I was about to tell him. He really broke a part of me. I used to be this confident girl who didn't care what people thought of her. If I wanted something in life, I would go out and get it. I wouldn't hesitate. Learning I was HIV positive changed the way I saw myself. It also made the way I thought people saw me change, even when they had no idea I had HIV. HIV was this dark cloud that hung over me. HIV made me hesitant. Hesitant about how I saw myself. Hesitant of what I said to people, or how I thought people saw me. Hesitant to tell people I made a mistake. Hesitant to tell people what that mistake cost me. Hesitant to go after what I thought I deserved.

Looking up at Travis, and seeing my reflection in his eyes, I realize I deserve him. I deserve someone who cares about me and is willing to hear me out. Someone who values what I have to say, and actually listens. Someone who will understand that HIV is a part of me, but isn't *just* who I am. I can finally say I am no longer hesitant. I am brave.

"I have something to tell you..." I start.

"Okay, what is it?" he asks.

His gentle expression helps me continue.

"The thing I'm about to tell you is really hard for me to say. But getting to know you, I've decided I fully trust you. I feel safe enough to share this part of my life with you."

He grabs on to my hand, but I gently release his hold. He doesn't look hurt, when I let go. I know his touch will make me more emotional as I tell the story, and I need to be strong when I tell him. "When I was twenty-one years old I made a poor judgement call."

He nods. His full attention is on me.

"Back when I was in high school, there was a guy who was a year older than me. His name was Trey, and he was probably the most attractive guy I had ever met."

"Except for me, right?" Travis pretends to look hurt.

I laugh. "Yes except for you. Now I've met you, I realize how unattractive Trey really was. He is nowhere as close to attractive as you."

Travis nods seriously. "Glad we clarified that. You can move on with the story."

I giggle and give Travis a shove on his shoulder. He starts laughing. "Why do you always make me laugh?" I ask him.

"Because I love making you laugh. Every time you laugh your eyes squeeze shut and you can barely see them and.."

I shove him again. "Please do not talk about how unattractive I look when I laugh."

He laughs again. "No, I'm being serious. I love your laugh."

I roll my eyes. "Okay, anyway. There was a guy in my high school who was super attractive. Almost every girl at the school wanted to date him. He was popular, athletic, charming, had a great body, and could speak multiple languages. You know the type..." I wave my hand. "Anyway, I wasn't popular, but I wasn't unpopular in school. I would say I was average looking. Definitely not the type to get Trey's attention. I knew in high school he would never go for me. He slept around a ton, which at the time was a turn off for me. When I was in University, I found out he attended the same University as me. Fast forward a couple years to when I was twenty-one. Cori and Lauren had forced me to go to this University party off campus. Apparently, *everyone* was going to be there and I would be lame if I missed it. I wasn't really the party girl. I mean I did fine in social situations, but I still get nervous if I don't know many people. Because it was a party, I thought it would help if I had a couple of drinks. A couple turned into about four drinks and four shots of vodka. I was hammered. I honestly, haven't ever, had that much to drink. "

Travis is still listening attentively. He doesn't look worried, so I continue.

"Cori had met up with her at-the-time boyfriend, and Lauren had gone off with some other guy she met. I was sort of hurt, because what was I supposed to do? I didn't know anyone else. Because I was drunk, it gave me courage I never knew I had. I made some friends and started dancing with someone. When I was on the dance floor, some guy caught my attention. It happened to be Trey. He looked just as good as I remembered him to be in high school, maybe even better. He had grown more into his body. Anyway, he recognized me and came over to dance with me. After a few dances, he pulled me off the dance floor and we started catching up. At first, I couldn't believe he was talking to me. There were tons of girls at this party. When we were talking, I felt this connection. Or at least I thought I did." Tears began to pool in my eyes, but I force them back.

Travis doesn't interrupt. He lets me continue on. I notice he has one hand clenched in a fist, but his face is hard to read.

"Trey offered me another drink, and we continued to chat. One thing led to another and we started making out. It was nice. I felt so good about myself at the time that this guy I always had a crush on was giving me so much attention. Anyway, we didn't stop at the making out. Trey lived down the street from this house, so I followed him there. It was really stupid. I knew what was going to happen, but honestly, I wanted to sleep with him. I really liked him. I was never reckless. I always made good decisions. I never drank too much. I never slept around. But you see so many of your friends and classmates do it, that for a second, I thought, 'why can't I be reckless for one night?' I didn't want the opportunity to pass. I really liked Trey. At that moment I trusted him. I knew not to expect a relationship, but I thought there was no harm in being with him for just one night. People have one night stands all the time."

Travis nods his head, but still doesn't say anything.

"Trey and I had sex a few times that night. The first time we had sex, the condom broke. I freaked out at first, but Trey had reassured me he was clean. I was on birth control, so I thought everything would be fine. I *trusted* Trey. I thought I knew him, so I thought I could trust him. The next few times we had sex we didn't use a condom because after the first time we thought there was no point. I know, stupid right?"

I look at Travis, and he has the same softness in his eyes.

"After that night, I never saw Trey again. A couple months later, I started not feeling well. To be honest, I just thought I had a cold. I hadn't slept with anybody since Trey. When I went to get a pap test at my doctor's I confided in her what happened, and she made me get tested. I was shocked when one of the tests came back positive for HIV.

I knew it had to be from Trey, because after I'd broke up with my last boyfriend I'd been tested right away and was deemed clean. Trey was the only one I slept with, not to mention I had unprotected sex with him. I had to tell Trey, and he got tested. It turns out he was also HIV positive. When I confronted him, he swore he had no idea he was HIV positive. He was so shocked, that I believed he didn't know he was HIV positive. My doctor says it is possible to not know you have HIV. Trey had told me he slept with a handful of people, so god knows how many people contracted it or who he contracted it from. It's scary to think about."

Travis blinks his eyes.

"So that is my secret, and why I hesitated to tell you. I'm HIV positive."

Travis just blinks his eyes again. I can't read his facial reaction. He looks stiff, like a statue.

I look down at my hands. "I found out after I turned twenty-two that I was HIV positive. I was immediately started on medication. I take my medications every day religiously. HIV isn't curable, but with the medications I take, it greatly reduces the risk of transmitting it to another person. That is also why I was hesitant to become sexually active with you. HIV is not transmitted through saliva, so kissing is okay, but before we took the next step, I needed you to be aware of my status before we did anything."

I decide if I am telling him all this, there's no point in holding anything back. "When I was twenty-three I tried to tell my then boyfriend Kyle, who we ran into, that I was HIV positive before we got involved. He panicked and freaked out and refused to talk to me or come near me. He looked at me like I was some sick disease. It really hurt my feelings. It was why I was scared to tell you. I didn't want you to freak out and react the same way Kyle did."

I've been so strong telling him, but I can't hold it in anymore. The memories of telling Kyle are just too fresh. I let out a sob.

Travis doesn't say anything. He just moves closer to me and wraps me up in a tight hug.

"I am so sorry, Travis. I fully regret that night. I will regret it for as long as I live. I have come up with numerous different ways in my head how that night should have gone, but there's no point now. I *can't* change it. I want to, but I can't. " Tears run down my face faster. Travis soothingly rubs my back. After a few minutes, we let go.

"I understand if you don't want to be with me." I whisper.

Travis finally speaks. "I can't believe that happened to you. I'm shocked. What you told me is awful. But I am glad you did tell me. It makes things that have happened between us more understandable."

I squeeze my eyes shut to prevent tears falling down, but it's no good because they keep coming.

"You think I wouldn't want to be with you because of that?"

"Kyle didn't. I would understand why."

Travis runs his hand over his face. "I don't know much about HIV."

I try to reassure him. "I know. I don't expect you to. I'm being honest when I said that since I take my medications properly the risks of transmitting it to you are not high. I know that probably doesn't help, but if that's what you are scared of, I understand. Do you remember that doctor who came to visit me in the hospital?"

"Yeah."

"That's Dr. Shields. She is an internal medicine doctor who specializes in HIV. I see her a couple of times a year. She's the one who treats me. If you wanted, she'd be able to answer any questions you have."

Travis looks focused in thought. "When you were in the hospital..."

"Cori and Brennley were worried, because with HIV it could affect my ability to fight off an infection, including pneumonia. Which is why, I think, Dr. Wells wanted me to stay overnight. Just in case."

Travis runs his hand through his hair. "And I had no idea. Does everyone know?"

I shake my head. "No. Dr. Shields, Trey, and Kyle obviously know. I just told Brennley and Cori a few weeks ago. Brennley found the medications in my purse when we went camping and she confronted me, so I told her."

Travis folds his hands. "What about your parents?"

I shake my head again. "No, they don't know."

His eyes widen. "Really?"

I nod. "I'm embarrassed, okay? You saw how my mom reacted when I was in the hospital. She worries about me. Knowing would break her heart. I can't do that to her. And I can't fathom telling my dad. Especially *how* I contracted HIV. They both will be so disappointed."

Travis just nods his head again.

I really want to know what he's thinking. "What are you thinking about?"

Travis wipes his hands on his jeans. "I'm just trying to process everything you just said."

I wipe my forehead. "It's a lot to take in. I know that. If you need more time to process everything, I totally understand."

He looks around the room and back at me. "If I took some time to think about things, I don't want you to think it's because..."

I hold up my hand to stop him. "You don't have to explain anything to me. Take a few days to think it over, and then we can make a decision together on where we go from here."

"It doesn't change the fact that I still really care about you, Hayden," he says solemnly.

I give him a weak smile. "I know."

I stand up from the couch, and he follows me to my front door. We don't say anything. He picks up the hint that I want him to go home and think about everything I've told him tonight. He quickly puts on his shoes, and I pass him his jacket when he's done.

"Good night, Hayden. Thanks for dinner. We'll talk soon." He bends down and kisses my cheek.

Well at least he isn't disgusted enough that he refuses to touch me. I lift my hand and hold it onto my cheek where he kissed me.

"Thanks for the cheesecake. Good night, Travis."

As he opens the door, I remember the popcorn I bought; I never got to show him. "Wait, I forgot to give you something."

I run back to my kitchen, grab the cheddar and caramel popcorn bag and pass it to Travis. "Cheese flavored popcorn."

He grabs the bag from me and looks at the picture. "No way, this is awesome. Thanks."

I half smile. "No problem. It reminded me of the night we went to the movies, so I couldn't resist."

Travis gives me a smile and walks out my apartment door. I close the door and lean back on the door after I've closed it. I let out a relieving breath. I think that went the best it could. He didn't freak out. But maybe he was just acting? I almost got the opposite reaction from him as I did Kyle. Kyle was easy to read and obvious where he stood, whereas Travis? I'm not so sure. I decide I'm just going to see how this plays out. No point in worrying until the time comes. Easier said than done though.

Chapter Sixteen: Travis

I can't believe what Hayden told me—she's HIV positive. I'm shocked.

Of course, I know what HIV is, and know you can contract it through having unprotected sex. It's one of those things people don't normally talk about. You know it's out there, and some people must have it, but because it's not talked about often you like to pretend it doesn't exist. I know that's not the best way to think about it. But now I know Hayden has it, it's weird. Something I've never considered or fathomed, and now it's a reality. Something I have to consider. I think one of the problems is that even though I know what HIV is, I don't know that much about it. Hayden said there wasn't a high chance of her transmitting it to me, but I don't know if that's true. I know you aren't really supposed to use Google to get health care information, but this isn't something I can exactly talk to my brothers about.

I sit on my bed and open my laptop. I type in HIV in the search bar and a ton of links pop up. I spend almost half the night, reading articles and information on HIV. I realize that there's a lot on the subject that I didn't know, or even considered.

The next day I meet up with both my brothers at a local diner for lunch. Trevor brings Noah, to give Savannah a break from the baby. Trevor talks to us about his new life as a dad, and the countless nights where he's had basically no sleep. The three of us also talk about the wedding, and Tristan briefly talks about his honeymoon—the places he saw, not the other activities.

"So, are you still together with Hayden?" Trevor asks me.

Are we? I think we are. I guess we are on a type of break, but we didn't break up. I don't want to break up with her. "Yeah, we're still together."

"Savannah and I really like her. She seems genuine..." Noah begins to fuss in his car seat so Trevor takes him out and gently rocks him in his arms.

"Yeah, she's amazing. Not only hot, but she is also super intelligent. She is getting her master's and wants to get her PhD."

Tristan pipes up. "That's important, that she actually wants to do things in life. My last girlfriend was basically a freeloader and wanted to stay home while I worked my ass off every day. She wouldn't even split rent." He cringes.

Noah has now fallen asleep in Trevor's arms. "Yeah and if you want to get married you really have to like the person. Looks is one thing, but marriage is a whole different game. You have to make a ton of decisions together and spend a lot of time with that person. Not everything is rainbows and sunshine. You have to see that person at their worst. Looks fade after a while, so it's important you enjoy spending time with that person."

I want to eventually get married, but not right now. "Whoa, guys. Hayden and I are just dating. It's still early. Marriage is not exactly on our minds yet."

Tristan takes a sip of his drink. "That's what I thought too when Addison and I started dating, but sometimes when you know, you just know."

I used to think Tristan was crazy, but now I'm not so sure. I can relate a tiny bit more to his situation with Addison. I still don't want to rush things though. I think about Hayden. Since the three of us are all older, I decide maybe I can confide in them. "Can I ask you guys something. Did Addison or Savannah ever keep a really big secret? Well, I don't want to say secret, but kept something about a part of their lives that you found out after dating them for a while?"

Tristan frowns. "Like what?"

I can't exactly tell them. "I'm not sure, like a health thing, or a family thing, or a financial thing?"

Trevor shifts Noah gently in his arms. "Well actually, yes. After a couple months of dating I found out Savannah was adopted when she was four. She always referred to her adoptive parents as 'mom' and 'dad', so I just assumed they were her biological parents."

I never knew that. "Were you mad when you found out?"

Trevor puts Noah back into his car seat. "I wasn't mad. It wasn't like she was keeping a secret from me. I never asked or inquired...I guess from her perspective she just saw her adoption as a part of her life she only wanted to share with people who she could trust, or the people who were going to stay in her life. I think for some reason she felt like she would be judged for being adopted, even though I think it was silly that she worried about people judging her. Girls are just more self-conscious about that sort of thing I guess. Plus, she did end up telling me when she was ready. It's not like she kept this secret forever."

As I make my way back home, I process what Trevor said. *'She only wanted to share with people who she could trust.'* Hayden and I have had a lot of conversations about trust. I broke up with her because I thought her not confiding in me was her basically saying she couldn't trust me. But now, I realize that her telling me was her way of proving she fully *does* trust me. I am nervous to be with her knowing she has HIV. To be honest, it does scare me a little. I think it has to do more with the fact that I don't know enough about HIV. Do I want that tiny bit of fear to be the cause of our break up? No. Hayden's a great girl and honestly, I couldn't imagine walking away with her and not being with her. It's crazy in these last couple of months how attached I've grown to our interactions. I love when she shows up and surprises me with lunch at work. I love when she texts me good morning when I wake up. I love how last night, she gave me cheddar flavored popcorn, remembering how much I wanted to try it.

It's a weird idea, picturing her in my life, but it's now becoming habit. It's becoming natural to me. Which is freaky because I haven't even slept with her yet. Maybe that's why I like her so much. We connect on a deeper level. Oh god, now I am turning into a chick. It gives me a lot to think about. I don't do relationships for this reason.

But I think this time is different.

* * * *

Hayden

On Sunday afternoon, Cori comes back from Erik's. Brennley comes over and the three of us decide to do yoga, from a beginner's yoga DVD I bought. Brennley and I keep laughing because we can't do all the poses, whereas Cori is a complete natural and has no problem following along with the instructor on the DVD.

"So how did Travis take the news?" Brennley asks.

I let out a breath, as the instructor instructs us to do. "Aren't we supposed to be relaxing?"

Brennley giggles. "I definitely don't feel relaxed right now. I'm stressed because I can't do half these poses."

I try to glide into the next position the instructor wants us to do, but one of my legs gives out and I fall over.

Brennley guffaws, while Cori goes and turns the DVD off. "You guys are awful. I'm doing this by myself next time."

I grab a pillow from the living room couch and throw it at Cori's head. "Sorry, Ms. I'm-a-natural and can-do-everything-perfectly-the-first-time."

Cori gives me the finger. Brennley and I both laugh. The three of us grab some water and sit back on the couch. Brennley taps my leg. "So, the news? How did he take it?"

I take a sip of my water. "I think it went well. He didn't freak out. I told him the whole story and at first, he seemed shocked. After that he was hard to read, but I think it's because he didn't know what to say. He did reassure me he still cares about me. I gave him the opportunity to go home and think about it. It's a lot to take in."

Brennley taps my head with her hand. "Well, I'm proud of you Hayden. It takes a lot of guts to admit you made a mistake, and to tell him the truth."

"Yeah," Cori adds. "I'm proud of you too."

"How are you and Erik?" I decide to change the subject. I don't want to get in the mind frame of thinking about how Travis is doing and what he's thinking about. It will drive me crazy.

"We are just so hot and cold. It drives me crazy. One moment we are great, and I love him, and we have fun together. But then the next day we fight over stupid stuff, and he turns into an asshole. Our fights don't last long, but it's really draining."

"Have you spent time with Jesse again?" Brennley asks her.

Wait! What?

Cori answers Brennley's question. "Yeah, I have. I mean we're just friends. Erik hangs out with other girls. I should be able to hang out with my guy friends, too."

"Wait! How come I didn't know you were hanging out with Jesse? As in Jesse who is Travis's best friend, Jesse?"

Cori gives me a nervous smile. "Uh, yeah, that one...sorry I didn't want to tell you in case things didn't work out with Travis. Jesse and I are strictly friends. He is just really easy to talk to. Not to mention really easy on the eyes. I'm in love with Erik, so you don't have anything to worry about."

I'm somewhat hurt that she didn't tell me, but I can't really call her out on it because I didn't tell her about a lot of things. Plus, I did have a few conversations with Jesse. I'll admit he was easy to talk to. Damn.

"Well you always tell me things will work out, so I'm sure that applies to you as well."

Cori looks at me confidently. "I'm sure it will."

Is she talking about the situation regarding Travis and I? Or about her and Erik?

Monday night after school, my mom shows up expectedly at my front door.

"Uh...hey mom. Come on in. What are you doing here?"

My mom takes off her shoes and tucks her hair behind her ears. "Well, I would have texted you, but I lost my reading glasses, so I couldn't read my phone."

It's probably a good thing my mom didn't text me. I showed her how to send emoticons a couple months ago, so now when she text messages you always get about fifteen emojis after the message.

"Wow. My mom is getting so old. Needing her reading glasses. Do you need a notepad to write on, so you can remember where you put things too?" I tease.

"Hey, watch yourself. I'd like to think I'm still somewhat young. You're getting old too. Next year when you turn twenty-five; you'll be halfway to fifty."

Damn. That's a scary thought.

I decide to be cheeky. "Well, I'll always be younger than you."

My mom chuckles and gives me a kiss on the head. "I wanted to come see how my daughter is doing. She said she would check in with me at least once a week, which she has not."

I go with my classic, "Sorry, I've been busy with school."

My mom throws her hands up. "You always say that!"

I laugh. "It's true though," I promise. "Come in. Let's sit on the couch in the living room."

My mom digs through her purse. "That reminds me. I brought you something to cheer you up now since you are all better." She hands me some homemade banana bread. Ever since my hospitalization, mom has been baking my favourite treats. I absolutely love it, although I don't think my midsection is loving it.

"Aw, thanks mom. I knew I kept you in my life for a reason." I joke.

My mom rolls her eyes at me. We walk into the living room and sit on the couch. "Where's Cori?" She asks.

"School. Her classes run late tonight."

"Are you guys still getting along?"

"Yes, mom." I say firmly.

"I was just asking. It's easy to be friends with someone. But sometimes when you live with them, it's more difficult than you think."

I pinch my brows together. "Mom, we've had this conversation years ago when I moved in. Why are you really here?"

My mom gasps. "Can't a mom see her daughter every once in a while?"

"Well yes. But you are acting weird. What's up? Is it about dad?"

My mom rubs my shoulder. "No. Your father and I are still divorcing. Everything between us is still civil, so you don't need to worry. How is Travis?"

I pout. "Is that why you are here?"

She laughs. "Of course, I want to hear all the latest gossip. My eldest daughter rarely talks to me, so I need to get the scoop from someone."

I rub my forehead with my hand. "Mom, you need a hobby."

"I do have a hobby. It's more like a job. It's called being a mom."

"Ha, ha...very funny. So back to my original point, why are you here?"

She winks at me. My mom *actually* winks at me. "You tell me about Travis, and then I'll tell you."

"Mom, I'm not a child anymore, you can't bribe me."

My mom crosses her legs. "Sure, I can."

Okay maybe it will work this one time.

"Well Travis and I are good."

My mom's jaw drops. "That's all I get? C'mon Hayden you can do better than that."

Do you ever wonder sometimes how you and your mom got paired up in life? Millions of people in the world, and you're paired up with one who is to be your mom.

"Fine. I really like Travis. We have a great time hanging out. He's respectful. He's a good listener, and he's easy on the eyes."

My mom points her finger at me. "Remember Hayden, looks aren't everything."

This is why my mom bothers me. She always tries to lecture me. Could you imagine if I told her about my HIV? That would be a never-ending lecture that I wouldn't want to hear.

"That's why I said he's respectful and a good listener." I argue.

"Are you guys being careful?"

"Mom!" I yell.

She looks at me innocently. "What? I want grandchildren, just not now. Maybe in a couple years."

"Anyway, subject change *now*."

My mom uncrosses her legs and shifts in her seat. "Well I wanted to ask you first because I respect your opinion and didn't want to catch you off guard again..."

"Okay" I nod, not knowing where she is going with this.

"Well, I met this guy the other day, and he sort of asked me out on a date."

A date? Oh, my goodness. This is weird. My parents were together for my whole life and now my mom is asking if it is okay if she can date other people? I don't even know what to think. It's just weird. But I do have to be supportive.

"Well mom, it's up to you. How do you feel about dating?"

She shifts again in her sit. "I don't know. I'm excited but also scared. I mean I haven't dated anyone besides your father in over thirty years. It's weird."

It's me this time who rubs her shoulder. "Well mom, that's a normal feeling. But if you want to start dating, I'm happy and will support you no matter what. You deserve to be happy. You deserve another shot at finding love. You won't know how you feel until you try."

My mom crinkles her face. "When did you get to be so smart."

"I've always been the smart one. It's Lauren you should really worry about."

My mom laughs. "What should I be worried about this time? What mess has she got herself into?"

I giggle. "I don't know. I haven't talked to her recently. But honestly you probably don't want to know."

My mom laughs again. "You're right. I probably don't. I don't know who that girl gets it from."

I try to help my mom out. "Adopted. I think she's adopted. Or hospital switch. I wouldn't rule that one out until the DNA results come in."

My mom slaps my leg. "Hayden!" she scolds.

"What? It's funny." I smile mischievously. "Well I definitely didn't get my humor from you."

"You're right. You definitely got that from your father."

Chapter Seventeen: Hayden

Friday after I finish classes I text Travis, asking if he wants to come over. He suggests picking up some Chinese food takeout for dinner after he's done work, which I agree to. He comes over with the takeout and we eat the dinner in the living room. I'm still in the same clothes I wore to school, skinny jeans and a black t-shirt. Travis is wearing basketball shorts, with a white-t shirt.

"So how was work?" I ask.

"Work was work. How was school?"

"It was okay."

Awkward silence.

I look down at my plate. "I don't want there to be awkward tension between us."

Travis shakes his head. "There's not. Well at least I don't feel it."

I smirk. "Okay, good."

After dinner I clear our plates, and the two of us sit back down on the couch. Out of nowhere, Travis leans forward and kisses me on the lips. Not a quick kiss. An 'I want to make out with you' kiss. Travis plunges his tongue in my mouth, and I automatically reach up and run my hands through his hair. My stomach muscles tighten, and I feel an ache start to develop down low. Travis pulls me onto his lap, so I am straddling him. As I get more into the kiss, I naturally rub up against Travis. The rhythm between us makes my ache grow even stronger. I can feel his erection against me, and it's in that moment I know I want to physically move forward with him, yet I don't know where his mind is at. Travis runs in hands up my curves, and I lean into his touch. As he runs his hands back down, his hands slide beneath my shirt. I know I have to stop this, because if he continues I won't be able to stop. It takes everything in me to pull away and remove myself from his lap. When he opens his eyes, I can see they are glossed over. I touch my finger against my lip.

"Sorry, Travis. I really like you, and I am ready to move forward, but I don't know where your head's at. I know I won't fully relax, unless I know for certain that you are okay with this."

He runs his hand through his hair. "Sorry, I got carried away. I find it hard to control myself when I'm around you."

I smile. "I know, me too. I feel bad because I keep being a tease around you. It's been months and I haven't been able to give you much. You probably walk around with constant blue balls." I frown. "But I can't have you regret anything that goes on between us. You have to make a choice. If you still have questions or concerns, you can tell me."

He tucks a piece of my hair behind my ear. "Honestly, I really like you Hayden. Yes, I've had to have a lot of cold showers lately, but I'm not a fifteen-year old boy anymore. I know how to take care of myself." He smirks. "I've thought about it. I don't want to lose you. I understand your HIV is important and we have to be extra careful, and aware of it, but I also don't want it standing in the way of being with you. You're not worth losing over this virus. When you told me, I was nervous because I don't know much about HIV. But for you, I am willing to learn more about it. I want to educate myself so both you and I can be protected. I'm willing to do this for you."

Tears creep in my eyes. "You're okay with it?"

He squeezes my hand and wipes away the tear that has snuck out. "Yes. But I want to take you up on your offer. If it's okay with you, maybe we can meet your doctor, so I can ask a few questions. That way we both can be one hundred percent comfortable when we finally take that leap."

I frantically nod. "Yes, I can make that happen. Thanks for taking this seriously and respecting me when I told you."

"You deserve to be respected." He entwines my hands with his and puts them onto his lap. "And I want you to know something, because I don't think anyone's told you this. You deserve to forgive yourself for your mistake."

I shake my head. "I was wrong. I regret what I did. I *always* will."

"Learn from this but forgive yourself Hayden. The negative feelings are probably eating you alive. I know from the panicky way you act, to you not being about to tell anyone about your HIV. The embarrassment comes from making the mistake, not the HIV itself. I don't want you to feel bad about yourself."

I look away. "But I..."

He cuts me off. "Nope. No buts. Forgive yourself. You'll feel better. Trust me."

"Do you forgive yourself for believing Courtney's lies, and not being able to figure out she was cheating on you?"

"I didn't at first. But after I did, I felt so much better. That's how I know you will too."

He smiles at me. The smile I love. Those wondrous dimples shine through. It makes my heart beat fast in a good way. I can't help but smile back at him. When I first got diagnosed with HIV, I felt like an overused, dead car battery. It drained me from my happiness. Drained me from life. But right now, the way Travis is smiling at me, I think he just jumpstarted me back to life.

I'm able to book an appointment with Dr. Shields, but it isn't until next week. Travis and I are having a hard time keeping our hands off each other, and because we can't act on it, it drives us even more crazy. I don't think I've ever been this horny. I just want to be able to touch Travis with no restriction. I mean I'm sure we can get away with doing other things, but I don't trust myself to stop. I can do this. Only a couple of more days. I mean we've not been doing it for months, a week shouldn't be too hard right?

During the next week, I meet up with Lauren. We do a margarita night and catch up. She shows me her new shampoo commercial that came out. I have to admit, she's a better actress than I thought. She informs me she's landed a part on another commercial. Apparently, a toilet paper commercial. I have to tease her and ask her if this means we get free toilet paper. That earns me a solid punch on the arm. But to be honest, since Lauren works as a makeup artist at a high end cosmetic store, she gets me really good deals on makeup. Toilet paper isn't exactly something I want to spend my hard earned money on, so if we get free toilet paper, then I'm happy.

I tell Lauren about mom wanting to start dating. She agrees it's weird, but she's also happy for mom. Lauren tells me about this new guy she's met. Apparently, he's from Australia and has an accent. The day Lauren actually introduces me to a guy as her boyfriend is the day I'll actually believe she has a boyfriend. But who knows? Maybe Lauren has finally grown up.

Although when her next story ends in 'And I couldn't remember where I was when I woke up', I decide that Lauren has definitely not grown up. Her behavior scares me, but If I say something, she'll freak out at me.

On Tuesday night, the gang asks for Travis and me to join them in couples' bowling, since it's half-price night. Do people actually still go bowling? Apparently so. We showed up and it was pretty packed. I was awful of course because bowling is basically a sport. Travis was pretty good. Who am I kidding? He was basically *our team*. I cheered for him as I sipped my beer on the side, though. See? I can be supportive.

On Wednesday night, my dad asks me to go for dinner. It would be weird if he asked me if he could start dating, although he didn't ask me—much to my relief. He asked me how I was doing and asked about school. He's one of the few people who is interested in what I'm studying, so I can talk to him about school for hours. He says he misses me and wants to take Lauren and me to Las Vegas for New Years. He even offered to pay, so being the broke student I am, I agreed. Although since he's a pilot, I bet he won't have to pay for the flight there and back. After I agreed to go, I remembered that Travis and I are dating. He probably wants to spend time New Years with me.

Oh, well. Future Hayden problem...

Thursday night, I head to group. I even tell Cori that's where I am headed before I go there. It feels nice to not have to lie. I feel more energized at group, and even Mason notices. I'm brave enough to share the story of how I told my boyfriend about my HIV. Everyone in group was supportive, and it made me feel not so hopeless and useless.

On Friday, Travis takes the day off work, and we head to my doctor's appointment. We sit in the waiting room. I'm nervous. Which is silly, because he'll probably ask basic, common sense questions. I hold his hand in the waiting room. His hand is a bit sweaty; but I mean, even him just being here for me means a lot. Also, he's sitting in a waiting room where people know Dr. Shields specializes in HIV. He doesn't seem embarrassed, and he hasn't tried to run or hide, so that's good.

"You nervous?" I whisper in his ear.

"Nope." He says confidently.

"You just want to get laid, don't you?" I whisper again.

He smirks at me. "I think it's *you* who can't wait," he says quietly.

I give him a flirty smile. "You're right. I can't wait." I run my hand up and down his thigh.

He immediately grabs my wrist. "You're driving me crazy."

"Good." I lick my lips. He shifts in his seat. I wink at him. I love driving him crazy.

Dr. Shields greets us with a radiant smile. She lets us sit down and listens to our concerns. She answers all mine and Travis's questions. I know most of what she is going to say, because I've asked her the same questions, but it's also reassuring. Plus, I'm here to support Travis. He actually asks really intelligent questions in a professional manner. He also uses some HIV terminology. He must have done some research. That thought warms my heart. It's little things like that which he does for me, that makes me feel loved.

Loved.

Loved...

Do I love Travis? I know I really care about him. He is my boyfriend. I'm not waiting for some miraculous moment where I discover he loves me. Thinking back on all the time we've spent together, I'm realizing it' is the small things that have added up, that make me really love Travis.

There! I said it. I admitted it. I *love* Travis.

After we leave the appointment, Travis drives me back to school, so I can make my late afternoon class.

"So, how do you feel after talking to Dr. Shields?" I ask.

He keeps one hand on the steering wheel, and with his other hand he grabs my hand and brings it up to his lips to give it a quick kiss.

"Well, it definitely wasn't as awkward as I thought it would be."

"So, it wasn't as bad as those sex talks we got in school, or the sex talks we got from our parents?" I joke.

He grimaces. "No, definitely *not* that bad. "

"So how do you feel about us if we were to...further our relationship?" I look out the passenger window.

"Hayden, I told you. Your HIV is not scaring me away. I feel a lot better after talking to Dr. Shields. It was a good idea.

Now you and I will be able to be comfortable. It's amazing how far the medications for HIV have come. Plus, I'm trusting you. Trusting that you take your medications every day and are doing your part to keep your viral load of the virus to undetectable levels."

"Look at you, picking up on the HIV terminology. " I'm impressed. "You *can* trust me Travis. I'll always be honest with you. I don't want to hide this condition from you anymore. I'm not embarrassed anymore."

"You showed me that today, by trusting me enough to come to your appointment."

Travis pulls up outside my University. "So tomorrow, I was thinking you could come over to my place. I want to make dinner for you this time."

"That sounds fantastic." I take my seat belt off and lean in to give him a kiss on the lips. He tries to deepen the kiss, but I push him back. "I really can't be late for class. I've got to go."

He smirks. "Okay, okay."

As I turn to get out of the car, he smacks my ass. I turn back around and frown at him.

"Sorry, I couldn't help myself."

I just roll my eyes, trying to hide the smile that's creeping up on my face. "See you tomorrow, Romeo."

Travis gasps. "Romeo? Both him and Juliet died."

He's right. I think it over. "We're more like Noah and Allie from *The Notebook* anyway. Destined to be together."

"They died too." Travis points out.

"After spending many years together." I argue.

"*If you're a bird, I'm a bird*", he directly quotes.

I laugh, but cringe as well. "One, I can't believe you can quote *The Notebook*. Secondly, I've changed my mind. We are *not* like Noah and Allie. I will not let us be compared to birds."

He clutches his heart dramatically. "But babe, I thought you loved birds."

"Fuck off. You've officially ruined *The Notebook* for me." I shut the car door and begin to walk to class, probably looking like a weirdo. I've probably got a ridiculous grin on my face, as I'm trying not to burst out laughing. Stupid birds...

Saturday morning, I get up early to go for my morning run. I don't want to be the one to jump him this time at the track. I don't see Travis, which is good. My body is already too excited to see him. Probably because it's assuming I'm going to be getting laid tonight. I wipe that thought from my brain. I can't be thinking of him right now. The wait is driving me crazy. I'm a bit anxious. It makes me worry slightly. What if we're incompatible in the bedroom? All this build up to be nothing but disappointment? I push that thought away. I need to focus on something else. I change the song on my iPod to a more upbeat tempo song and push myself hard for the last few minutes.

After I get home, and I'm showered, I decide to go shopping at the mall. I'm not a big shopper, but I want to wear something tonight that Travis will like. I know he won't really care what I wear, but for some reason I have this need to try to impress him. I know he wears a lot of black, so my eyes get drawn to black fabrics. I find a couple of black dresses and try them on. One of them fits extremely well. It is long sleeved on one side and is strapless on the other. Down the sides of the dress are neat triangle cut outs that show skin. It's sexy. It reminds me of how Travis runs his hands up my curves. I definitely need to buy it.

I get home and complete my homework for the weekend. Well, as much as I can handle doing. You never really get caught up in post-secondary. I'm somewhat distracted about tonight. I don't know why I am putting so much pressure on myself. I guess I just don't want to disappoint him.

Why do I have these thoughts?

'It's because you really like him' my subconscious reminds me.

I head to the bathroom and shave. I clip my nails to make sure they aren't too long and dirty. I apply some makeup, giving myself more of a natural look. I curl my hair because I know Travis likes it when I curl it. I brush my teeth, probably about three different times. I just want to make sure my breath doesn't stink. Talk about mood killer. I think I'm more nervous than the night I lost my virginity and believe me was I nervous. I clench the edges of my bathroom counter and look at myself in the mirror. "You can do this Hayden." After my very lame and very simple pep talk, I'm ready to head over to Travis's.

On the way to my front door, Cori surprises me by entering the apartment.

"Hey. You look hot!" Cori eyes me down.

I blush, slightly embarrassed. "Too much?"

Cori furiously shakes her head. "No, definitely not!"

"I'm going out with Travis tonight, so don't wait up."

Cori gives me the knowing look. "Okay, have fun kids. Be safe."

"I'm not making that mistake again." I joke, but Cori and I both know, it really isn't a joke.

I give Cori a quick side hug, and then head down to my car to drive over to Travis's.

I take a few calming breaths and knock on Travis's apartment door. He opens the door all the way to let me in, and greets me with a quick, soft kiss. I hand him the wine I brought, because I may have a small wine obsession. You can't show up to someone's house for dinner without wine. Okay, maybe in certain circumstances you shouldn't. This is not one of them.

"Wow, you look beautiful." he admires my dress.

I try not to blush, but I'm sure I do. I can feel it. "Thanks."

"So, I've got some bad news."

My face drops. "Oh no, what is it?"

Travis must read the worried look on my face, because he quickly states, "No, not awful news. I just attempted to make a dinner. I might have been too optimistic with what I chose. I burned it terribly in the oven, so I may have had to order a pizza. I hope you're not mad. Good news though is, that my oven is okay, and I didn't burn the place down."

I laugh. "Pizza is fine. What were you trying to make?" I take off my coat, and Travis takes it from me to hang up.

"I don't want to tell you. You'll just make fun of me."

I smirk. "Valid."

After we sit down in his kitchen, and make small talk, his doorbell rings. The pizza is here. He brings over the two boxes and we dig in. After the pizza, Travis opens the wine I brought, and we bring our glasses into his living room, and sit on his couch.

"So, my dad might have bribed me to come with him on a trip to Las Vegas during New Years. "

Travis's brows furrow. "Really?"

I bite my lip, then release it. "Yes, so now you have to help me come up with a good excuse to let him down gently."

"Do you want to go?"

I take a sip of my wine "I do, but if we're still together I'd want to spend New Years' with you."

His eyes brighten. "Well if you want to go, you can go. Don't let me hold you back."

I place my wine glass back on the table and cross one of my legs over the other because I'm wearing a dress. "No, I just have to find a nice way to tell him I want to go away with him, just not on New Years'. Maybe I should ask your dad. He's a psychologist. He'll know how I should tell him."

"I'm sure he will. Although he'll probably make you work it out yourself how you're going to tell him. He doesn't just give straight advice. He wants you to come up with these things on your own. He just guides you there."

I tilt my head. "You didn't want to become a psychologist?"

He laughs. "No. Definitely not my thing. Although my eldest brother Trevor just graduated not too long ago. He's a psychologist. " He takes a sip of his wine. "You didn't want to become a pilot?"

"That's cool that your brother followed in your dad's footsteps. And no, I never wanted to be a pilot. Too much physics."

"What about Lauren?"

I let out a guffaw. "It took her seven times to pass her driver's license. I wouldn't trust her as a pilot."

Travis's eyes dance with laughter. "Seven? I thought Tristan had it bad taking it three times."

"It sometimes is beneficial to have a sister like Lauren. Makes you look better."

Travis chuckles. "God, I love you."

Travis's eyes are wide, and I'm shocked for a second. We haven't said the 'L' word yet, but I've definitely thought it. Even though I know what he meant, I decide to take the opportunity to be brave, since that's my new motto these days.

"I love you, Travis. I'm been thinking about it lately, and I realize I've loved you for a long time. It took me a while to figure it out, but I do love you. It's the small things that you do that make me love you. You respect me, appreciate me, and make me feel loved. You don't say it necessarily, but I can tell from your actions how much you do love me. When you call me asking how my day was, how you took care of me in the hospital... You slept in that god awful chair for goodness sake. Not everyone would do that." Travis is smiling so I continue on. "When I was upset learning that my parents were divorcing, you wrapped me up in your arms and in that second, I knew I had found someone special. Someone who could read me well. I never had to explain anything to you. You just knew. You pushed me. I set such a narrow boundary for myself, but you made me want to get up, cross the line and leave that safety net I set up for myself. You most importantly taught me how to trust, when there were times I thought I'd never be able to trust a guy again."

Travis's eyes stay locked on mine. "I'm glad you feel that way Hayden, because I feel the same. I keep imagining you in my life. My future revolves around you, and I find myself mapping you out in all areas of my life. You make me happy. I can't help but call you every day because you're always on the forefront of my mind. You made me believe in the reasons why I wanted a relationship in the first place. This indescribable feeling, or connection. Whatever it may be, I don't want to let it go. I love you too, Hayden. I'm willing to take that next leap with you."

How perfect was that? There's no doubt now, that I can fully trust Travis. He's everything I hoped for, even better than my mind could have created.

I lean forward, and before I know it our lips are connecting. We start to stand up from the couch as we continue kissing. Travis bends down and wraps his arms under my thighs, lifting me in his arms. He then carries me down a hall which, I assume, leads to his bedroom. My eyes are closed so I don't really know, nor do I really care at this point. Travis breaks the kiss for a short second to open his door. As soon as we enter, he closes it with his foot and continues to kiss me. He walks back with me still in his arms, until he hits the end of his bed. He sits down on the edge with me straddling his lap. I lock my hands around his neck and continue to kiss him, as he takes his hands and starts stroking my inner thighs. My muscles are taut with need. A throbbing ache starts to develop down there. He continues to move his hands up and down my thighs. On the down strokes, my body curses. I start rubbing up against him, and I can feel his erection against my stomach. As I rub up against it, Travis lets out a moan that comes out more of a grunt. It's sexy. His hands then reach up higher on my thighs until he hits the bottom of my panties.

"Please," I beg against his mouth.

He chuckles between kisses. "You like this." He teases me as he continues to stroke up and down.

On the next upstroke, I grab his hand and hold it tightly against my upper thigh, so he can't move it. "Don't go back down. Go up." I instruct against his lips.

He moans deeply in response, and I release my hold on his hand. Ever so carefully, he dips his hand beneath my underwear. I let out a high-pitched sigh. As he inserts a finger in me, I gently bite down on his earlobe. We both let out simultaneous moans. I begin to ride his hand, and he inserts another finger. I tilt my head back, and I'm in such complete bliss that no sounds manage to come out of my open mouth. I continue to ride his skillful hand. While I'm doing this, he plants an open mouth kiss on my neck, and it's too much. I let out a blissful moan as I hit my climax.

After I come back down from the amazing high, I reach down and grab onto the bottom of Travis's shirt. I tug at it and lift it up to pull over his head. I break the kiss for a second to pull the shirt off. I look at Travis's beautiful bronze chest right in front of me. Of course, he has a six pack. I always knew he was toned, but I didn't know he was this ripped. I immediately place my palms on his chest. He feels taut. I bend down and place kisses on his neck. I place kisses just below his collarbone. Because of the way I'm sitting on him, I can't continue to kiss him further down his chest, to admire his fine abs. I step back off his lap to admire him, as I stand in front of him. Because I'm all about being brave these days, I grab hold of the hem of my dress, and lift it over my head; I'm just in my black strapless bra, and black panties.

Travis's lips are slightly puffed and swollen, and his eyes appear darker and more seductive. He stands up and undoes his jeans and pushes them down to the floor so he's just in his boxers. Travis turns me around and guides me back onto the bed. He slightly lifts us up so we are positioned higher on the bed, so my head hits the pillow. He runs his hands up my sides and whispers in my ear, "I've wanted you for so long. You have no idea." I tilt his head back to me to continue to kiss him. I arch my back into his touch, and he uses it as an opportunity to unhook my bra. Once it's off me, he throws it onto the floor. He leans down so we are skin to skin. It's indescribable. I guide my hands down his chest, so I can finally feel his firm abs. My wandering hands continue lower until they hit the band of his boxers. I dip my hand in and begin to stroke him. Travis stops kissing me and bends down to place his mouth on one of my breasts. It's electric as the sensations move throughout my body. I let go of him, and my hands lift up so that they are in his hair. I arch my chest into him, and gently tug on his hair. As soon as he is finished exploring my left breast, he moves on to my right one. I squeeze my legs tighter, as the throbbing down there becomes unbearable.

When he's done with my right breast, he reaches to his side drawer and pulls out a condom. He places it on the pillow beside my head. Travis reaches down and pulls my underwear down my legs, and I fling them off when they hit my feet. Travis lifts each of his legs, one at a time as he pulls down his boxers. I let out a deep breath. He is breathtakingly gorgeous. I watch him intently as he puts on the condom. When he is finished, he leans down over me, using his forearms for support. He nudges my legs open with his knees to where he wants them spread. He gives me a quick kiss on my lips and whispers against them "I love you."

Before I can say 'I love you' back, he thrusts into me, and I let out a glorious moan. As soon as he is fully in me, he checks on me as he asks, "You good?"

I can feel his warm breath on my face. "Yes", I answer him. I'm more than good.

He begins moving in and out of me. I wrap my legs up around him and keep up with his movements. He begins at a slow and steady pace, and then picks it up to where we are both comfortable. As he is rocking against me, I can't begin to explain the feeling, besides complete bliss. It feels natural, like this isn't our first time together. He reads my body well, and before I know it, I hit my climax. A couple of seconds after I go off, he goes off and joins me in the abyss of complete and utter bliss.

Chapter Eighteen: Hayden

We're currently in Travis's bed, facing each other, a few mere centimeters away from each other. Travis reverently runs this hand over the bridge of my nose.

"I love your freckles. They're faint, but when you really look you can see them. I love them." He leans over and kisses each of my freckles. I have about five or six, give or take, mostly on the bridge of my nose where he touched.

When he leans back, I scrunch my nose. "Don't say that. My freckles are my least favourite part of my body. Every morning I try to cover them up with foundation, but they always manage to creep through, especially in the summer."

"Well they are *my* favourite part of your body."

I arch my brows and mutter "Really?"

He gives me a coy smile. "Well they are *one* of my favourite parts of your body."

I laugh. "If you asked me what my favourite part of your body was, honestly it wouldn't be something on your face either."

He chuckles. "I can't believe you said that!" He starts to tickle me, and I giggle.

"I thought you loved how blunt I was."

We begin a wrestling match, but I'm defeated, and pinned on the bed soon enough—I really didn't have a shot of beating him and his outrageously muscular body.

"Gotcha," he exclaims. He has my arms pinned over my head. "Now, you're mine."

I giggle. "Yes, now I'm yours."

He bends down and kisses me. I take full advantage as he relaxes his grip when he kisses me. I manage to get my hands out of his and attempt to push at his shoulders to try to flip him over and pin him on his back. There's no hope. He's way too muscular and heavy, so I am not able to move him. At all.

He laughs. "Nice, try."

I let out a groan. He starts kissing his way down my body and that groan soon turns into a moan.

After we have sex a couple more times, I'm completely exhausted and drained. I need to head home now if I want to stay awake on the ride home. "I think I should think about heading out soon."

Travis looks at me like I have three heads. "Umm, no. You aren't going anywhere."

I giggle, but sit up, so the covers of his bed fall down slightly. I look at his bed side table. His alarm clock says it's almost one in the morning. "I have to go. It's late. Or early— however you want to look at it."

Travis sits up slightly and begins planting kisses on the back of my shoulder. "No, don't go. It's late. Stay here. With me."

"Are you sure?"

He kisses my shoulder again. "More than sure."

"What does more than sure mean?"

His eyes twinkle. "It means you are staying put in *my* bed." He gently pulls on my shoulders and brings me back down so we're lying back down on his bed facing each other, our lips almost touching.

"Tell me a secret," I whisper.

"This could back fire on me," he chuckles.

"Please." I beg.

"What do you want to know?"

"I don't know. Anything. I just want to learn more about you."

"I have a peanut butter addiction. It's actually really bad. I put it on everything."

I giggle. "Really? That's not a bad thing. Peanut butter is really good, so I can't fault you."

"Now you have to tell me a secret."

I lean closer, so our noses are touching. "Yours wasn't a real secret."

"Yes, it was."

I lick my lips. "No, it was a fact about yourself. Not a secret."

He almost whispers as he says, "No, it was a secret that was *also* a fact."

I roll my eyes. "Nope, it was a fact."

"Are we arguing over the difference between a fact and a secret?"

"Yeah, because apparently you didn't learn the difference."

He squeezes my side and I let out a high pitch scream. "Fine, I'll take it. I guess I did ask you to tell me anything about yourself."

"Exactly." He looks proud of himself. "I win. Now tell me a secret."

I arch my brows. "What do you want to know?"

"Anything. I just want to learn more about you."

I smile when I realize he's responded in the same way as I had. "Remember when I told you I didn't want to be a pilot because I hated physics?"

He nods.

"It's actually because I'm scared of flying."

He looks caught off guard. "Really? You do so much travelling."

"Yeah, but I usually have to take a few Gravol before I fly."

"I never would have guessed."

I wink. "That's why it's a secret."

We stay quiet for a couple minutes still facing each other.

"I'm glad I bumped into you."

"What?"

"That night at the bar. When you took off after we met, I thought I'd never see you again. So, I'm glad I bumped into you that night."

"Why are you telling me this?" I whisper.

"It's my secret."

I lean in and softly press my lips to his for a second. My eyes keep fluttering closed. I'm super tired, but I like being this close to him.

"You're tired, aren't you?"

I run my hand down his shoulder. "A little bit."

"Turn around." he instructs.

I do, so my back is facing his chest. He places his arm around me and pulls me so I'm right up against his chest.

"Good night, Hayden." He kisses my temple.

"Goodnight, Travis."

Trust

I wake up feeling a bit chilly. I open my eyes and realize Travis is not in the bed. Did he leave? He got what he wanted and just left? Wait, no. This is his apartment. He wouldn't have left me in his apartment. I get up out of bed and find one of his dark grey t-shirts folded on his dresser. I pick it up and put it on. Travis is so tall that the t-shirt comes down to my knees.

I quietly tip toe down the hall, when this amazing aroma hits my nostrils. What is that delicious smell? The light is on in the kitchen. I walk in to Travis flipping pancakes in just his boxers.

"Oh, my goodness! Dreams really do come true. Beside the fact that we aren't in Hawaii, my lifelong dream has come true."

Travis turns only his head around. "Which is?"

"Having an insanely attractive man, preferable shirtless, cook me breakfast, while I get to sleep in, and be woken up by a succulent aroma where he has breakfast waiting for me. Also, coffee already made. Can't forget the coffee. You didn't forget the coffee, right? " Travis points to the pot of coffee and I grin. "Although in my dream we're in Hawaii, but because you are so amazing, I'll take being in your apartment."

I walk over and squeeze Travis in a hug from behind. "You are the best boyfriend ever. Have I told you that?"

"You can tell me that every day." He turns around and kisses me on the lips. He lifts me up and places me on the counter beside where he is stirring scrambled eggs.

"How did you sleep?" He pauses stirring the eggs to kiss my forehead.

"Really well actually. Your bed is comfy."

Travis goes back to stirring eggs. "So, it was the bed that made you sleep well?" He picks up a mug of coffee beside the stove that I hadn't noticed and takes a sip.

"No, I don't think it was necessarily the bed. I think it's because you fucked me into a sleep coma."

Travis almost spits out his coffee. His body starts shaking because he is laughing so hard. "I didn't expect that to come out of your mouth."

I bat my lashes at him. "Well, it's the truth."

Travis comes up between my legs and kisses me again on the forehead. "Well, I'm glad you think that."

Travis goes back to finish stirring the eggs. He turns off the element and places the frying pan off the heat. He finishes flipping the last two pancakes and places them onto a plate. I watch as he places the scrambled eggs on another plate and brings them to the kitchen table. I jump off the counter and help him get forks and knives out.

"I always thought of you as a cereal type of guy."

"I am. But I have to impress my girlfriend by cooking for her. Especially because last night at dinner I wasn't able to."

I give him a flirty smile. "You definitely did impress me, just not with your cooking abilities... Oh, by the way, I hope you don't mind that I borrowed your shirt."

He looks me up and down. "No, I like it."

I take a bite of my pancake. "Good." When I finish my bite, I ask him. "Did you know Cori and Jesse were hanging out?"

Travis almost drops his fork. "No."

I nod. "Yeah, I found out the other day from Brennley. Cori says they're just friends, but I worry about her. She has a hard time being 'just friends' with a guy. Mostly because they don't want to be 'just friends' with her."

"Jesse's not like that."

I swallow another bite. "Yeah, I know. I was speaking of guys in general. Don't tell Cori, but Erik isn't really my favourite person."

"No?"

"Nope. I just get bad vibes from the guy."

"Did you get bad vibes from me when you met me?"

I stand up and sit on his lap. "Nope, I only get good vibes from you." Since it is early in the morning, I realize if I was back home I'd be leaving for my run. "I just realized, we missed our early run this morning."

Travis smirks, and kisses my neck. "I have a different way we can both get in our daily exercise."

After our post breakfast sex, I'm in dire need of a shower. "Do you mind if I take a shower?"

Travis eyes darken. "Only if I get to come with you."

"Absolutely."

Trust

Travis and I are in his shower. I discover Travis is a water hog. "Hey, let me under the water. I'm freezing here." He moves out of the way, and I crank up the hot water. I like my showers hot. "Whoa, way too hot." he exclaims.

"Sorry, I forgot you are used to having cold showers." I tease.

He pushes me up so fast against the shower wall, I barely have time to blink. "What was that?" his voice comes out gravelly.

I start to giggle. "I'm sorry." I lean forward and kiss him. Before he deepens the kiss, he places his hand outside the shower curtain, to grab something. I look down and notice it's a condom. Does he just have them lying down everywhere in his apartment? He puts on the condom expertly and lifts me up from under my thighs and positions us, so he can slide into me. He starts thrusting, and my head falls back and hits the shower wall, while he places his mouth on my breast. I'm so content right now I don't feel it hurt when my head hits the wall. All I can feel is the pleasure he's giving me by rocking into me, while water pours down on us. When we both hit our releases, he lowers me. We both take the time to reverently wash each other's body, making sure not to miss anywhere. As I wash his back, I give him a slight back massage. In response, he grunts his appreciation. Best morning ever.

Chapter Nineteen: Hayden

On Sunday night, Travis is disappointed when I inform him I have to leave, as I have to be up early Monday morning for class. I let him know I'll be able to come back over after he's finished work. The rest of the week flies by, and by the time I realize it, it is finally Friday. Lauren's birthday is tomorrow, and she is throwing a huge party at our parents' old house. They haven't sold the place yet, but somehow Lauren manages to work her magic charm and get them to both agree to let her throw a party. I'm sure she just told them that a few close friends were coming over. My parents are so naive. Lauren's parties tend to be pretty wild, and sometimes get shut down because hundreds of people decide to show up. Because she is my sister I have to make an appearance, at least for a short while. I convince Travis to come with me. My sister invites Cori and Brennley to come, and I'm sure they'll bring Cooper and Erik.

Travis and I pick up Cori and Erik from Erik's place, so only one of us has to be the designated driver. I volunteer to be 'it' on the way home, so if Lauren bothers me I can leave whenever I want. I'm dressed in skinny jeans and a pink, somewhat low-cut shirt, with my hair down and straightened.

As we make it to my parents' street, I know we are going to be in for a treat. There are already tons of cars parked on the street, and I can hear music blaring from my old house. Travis holds my hand as the four of us walk up to the house. As we walk in, I'm glad all my important stuff is at my apartment. There are a ton of people here. The music is blasting, and people are dancing, and drinking from red plastic cups. How old is my sister again?

I have to pull on Travis's hand and squeeze behind people in hunt of my sister. I don't know how I'm going to find her with this many people here. Travis and I walk by a group of Lauren's friends playing beer pong. They say hi to me and ask me to join, but I politely decline. I ask them where Lauren is, and they say she's outside on the deck.

I make it out on the deck and spot Lauren. She's standing with a couple of her girlfriends, drinking wine. She looks up and smiles when she sees me. She looks gorgeous. She is wearing a burgundy short dress with a sweet-heart neckline. I let go of Travis's hand to give her a big hug. "Happy birthday, Lauren!"

Lauren squeezes me back. "Thanks, Hayden. Glad you could come. Thanks for the present."

I had given Lauren a gift certificate for her and I to do a spa day. I gave it to her early, as I knew if I gave it to her tonight, I wouldn't know if it would make it home safely with her.

Lauren beams when she sees Travis. She gives him a hug. "Hi Travis. Thanks for coming."

"Happy birthday!", he tells her as they pull away.

"There are drinks in the kitchen if you want." Lauren nudges her head in the direction of the kitchen.

"Okay, thanks." I respond.

Travis and I head back to the kitchen, and I give him a beer to drink. We meet back up with Cori and Erik and chat for a couple minutes. After some time, Brennley and Cooper show up. I give them each a hug, and they join us in conversation.

Lauren surprises me as she hugs me from behind. "Come dance with me. It's my birthday, you can't say no."

Oh wow. She's pulling the birthday card. I frown at her, but grab Brennley and Cori to join us, as the boys stay back to chat. We dance for a couple of songs, but it's all I can take, as it's way too hot. "I need air. It's too hot." I have to yell over the music at Lauren. She nods in response, but continues dancing with her friends. Cori, Brennley and I head outside to the backyard There is more room outside, and it is cooler than inside.

I update Cori and Brennley on how Travis took the news and how we are closer than ever. Once I am done, I follow Cori's gaze to see the three guys coming outside. Travis comes up to me and I snuggle up against him. Erik begins telling some animated story, but I don't bother listening. His stories aren't exactly good or funny to be honest. I politely nod at the right times and laugh when everyone else does. As he continues the story, a guy in the distance catches my eye. He has blond hair and is holding a red plastic cup. I notice he bends down and kisses a girl who is wearing a super short dress and has brown hair. When he turns around, I realize it is Kyle.

Holy shit! The last person I want to see!

I turn myself and Travis to angle ourselves out of Kyle's line of vision, so he doesn't notice us. I want to suggest going back inside, but I don't want to come off as rude and interrupt Erik's story. I keep glancing back to keep tabs on Kyle. Travis notices me glancing back, and whispers in my ear, "Who are you looking at?"

His eyes follow my gaze, and he spots Kyle. "Your ex, Kyle?"

I nod. "Can we please leave? I really don't want to run into him."

Just the sight of Kyle angers me. I clench my fist, the one that's not holding on to Travis. I hate that smug look on Kyle's face. Like he thinks he's too good for everyone.

Travis nods. We wait for Erik to finish up his story, but just before we're going to leave, the music shuts off. Maybe the party is going to get shut down, so we can all leave. But nope, I'm wrong.

One of Lauren's best friends Mia, stands on a chair and announces, "Tonight is Lauren's birthday. We're going to sing happy birthday to her!" Mia points to Lauren who has made an appearance outside.

After we all sing happy birthday to Lauren, the music restarts and I pull on Travis's arm. I really want to leave. Kyle has moved from the backyard up onto the deck. I notice he approaches Lauren and pulls her into a hug. For some reason it angers me. I don't know how Travis and I are going to leave without walking past Kyle. Travis whispers in my ear to wait to see if Kyle leaves.

Cori must have noticed something off with me, because when our eyes meet she mouths a 'What's wrong?' I just nudge my head up to the deck where Kyle is. Cori notices Kyle, and I see her eyes narrow, and fists clench.

"I'm going to kick his ass!" Cori announces.

Erik looks down at Cori. "Whose ass are you going to kick baby? Hopefully not mine."

I let out an awkward laugh because Erik is oblivious sometimes. Although now is definitely not the time for Cori to approach Kyle. I let go of Travis and stand in front of Cori. "No, Cori. Please, don't cause a scene."

After Kyle and Lauren hug, Lauren spots me and gives me a wave.

Shit! Don't bring attention to me, Lauren. Kyle turns to see who Lauren is waving at.

Fuck! He sees me.

Lauren and Kyle make their way down the deck steps onto the grass area where we're standing in the backyard. Now it's too late to make a quick escape.

Damn Lauren.

Lauren and Kyle approach us. Both of them are staggering as they walk. They both have glazed over eyes. I can smell the alcohol on them as they approach us.

Great. Not only do I get to run into my ex, but I get to run into my ex who is drunk.

"Hayden, look who it is!" Lauren exclaims.

I don't have a good explanation why Lauren would think it's a good idea to bring my ex over to me and my current boyfriend. Why the hell would she think I want to see my ex? The only logical explanation is that the alcohol has fried my sister's brain from reasonable thinking.

"Hey, Hayden." Kyle snarls.

Kyle walks towards me and I immediately step back. "Don't fucking touch me." I tell him.

Kyle has the smuggest look on his face. I want to rip his face off. The smell of alcohol on him makes me scrunch my nose. He lifts up his hand that's not holding his drink in a defensive stance. "Don't worry, Hayden. You know I wouldn't want to touch *you*."

I can feel Travis tense, but as I dart out to Kyle, Travis grabs me by the waist to hold me back. I try to get out of Travis's arms, but he just holds me tighter. "Fuck off, asshole. Get out of my house!" I shout at Kyle.

"Hayden!' Lauren shouts. "Don't be rude." Lauren looks at me and she must be able to tell how angry I am. Lauren looks back at Kyle. "Maybe it would be best if you leave."

I shake Travis's hold off me.

Kyle nods. "Are you *positive* you want me to leave?" he asks Lauren. Now, he's doing this on purpose.

I can't help the anger that takes over. I bolt forward and swing my right hand and punch Kyle right in the face. I can hear the snap, as Kyle's nose breaks. He falls back, spilling his drink, and blood begins coming out of his nose.

"You fucking bitch!" Kyle shouts at me. People nearby have now stopped what they're doing and are staring at us. Kyle lifts a hand and holds it to his nose.

Cooper picks Kyle up by the shirt and throws him backwards. "Get the fuck out—now, man."

I look down at my hand and notice my knuckles are starting to bleed. My hand isn't exactly hurting. It must be the adrenaline still racing through my body. Before Kyle turns to leave he notices my hand bleeding.

"Don't worry, I'm leaving. Wouldn't want to get infected HIV blood on me anyway. Right Hayden? "

I hear many people gasp, including Lauren. I look around… Everyone is staring directly at me. I feel completely naked.

Out of the corner of my eyes, I see both Cooper and Travis grab a hold of Kyle, to I assume escort him out of the house.

I freeze. I can't believe what just happened. My heart is hammering against my chest, and I can't get any air into my lungs. I'm out in the fresh air, yet I'm gasping for air. I cannot believe he said that. In front of a ton of people.

Brennley pulls out a wet wipe from her purse and gives it to me to put on my knuckles. She hugs me in a protective shield and guides me to the fence at the side of my house that leads to the front.

"Nothing to see here everyone. Obviously, Kyle is drunk, lying and acting like a dumbass. Carry on!" I hear Cori shout at everyone.

As Brennley escorts me out front, we climb into the back seat of Cooper's car. I begin crying, and Brennley holds me in a tight hug.

"Forget him, Hayden. No one will believe him anyway. Everyone could tell how drunk he was." Brennley's comment doesn't help.

I continue to sob. "Please take me home." I beg.

Cori comes to Cooper's car. Brennley somehow passes her the car keys. She must have a spare set. "Drive back to your apartment now."

I hear the car start up, but I hear Lauren's voice in the distance shouting my name.

Holy fuck! Now Lauren is going to start asking questions. I hear the passenger door open up.

"Hayden, I'm so sorry. I didn't know Kyle was going to act like that. I thought you guys were still friends. Why did he accuse you of having HIV?"

Cori reaches over and pushes Lauren out of the car. "Lauren, you need to get out. Now is not the time. She's obviously upset. "

Lauren gets out of the car. "I love you Hayden. I'll call you tomorrow." I hear her shut the car door. Cori pulls out onto the street and we begin heading home. After a couple of seconds my cell phone starts ringing. I look at it; it's Travis's number.

"Oh no, we left the guys." I cry.

Brennley lets go of me for a second. "Don't worry. I'll call Cooper and tell him where we are going. They can take Travis's car back."

After we get back, I wrap up my knuckles and get changed into my pajamas, then crawl into my bed. Cori and Brennley lie down next to me.

"I can't believe he said that in front of everyone. So many people know now." I sob.

"Hayden, Kyle was so drunk. I honestly think people won't believe him." Brennley tries to reassure me.

"What if they do?" I cry.

"Then it isn't your fault. You can't control how people react. People will believe whatever they want to believe. Just hold your head up and show them it doesn't bother you. Lots of people were drunk, so many of them won't remember tonight. If you show them you aren't affected by what Kyle said, then it will blow over." Cori reaches over and squeezes my hand.

A couple of seconds later, there's a knock on the door. Cori stands up. "It will probably be the guys. Do you want me to ask Travis to leave, or do you want to see him if he asks?"

"No, I want Travis." I reply.

Brennley gets up off the bed. "I'll give you some privacy. Call me if you need anything."

"Thanks." I mutter.

"And, Hayden? Don't worry what other people think. All the important people in your life still care about you."

"Cooper knows now." I mumble.

"I'll talk to him. He won't care, Hayden. He's a good guy. I promise." Brennley hugs herself.

I just sniffle.

"I'll talk to you tomorrow."

Just as Brennley leaves, Travis blasts through the door. "Hayden?"

I let out a weak, "Yeah."

Travis climbs onto my bed and lifts me up and places me on his chest. He wraps his arms around me. "You okay?"

"No." I mumble. He squeezes me tighter.

"Don't worry about what everyone thinks. They were all drunk. Kyle was drunk..."

I cut him off. "Don't worry, Brennley already gave me that speech."

"Why did you go after Kyle? He wanted you to react like that. He was hoping you would, so he could keep egging you on."

"I know, I'm an idiot." I cry into his chest.

He lets out a breath. "I didn't mean that. I just hate that you let him hold so much power over you."

I lift my head up. "He told everyone I was HIV positive!"

"I know, but if you could have stayed calm, everyone would have just assumed he was lying out of his ass and was intentionally trying to get you rattled up."

I push off Travis's chest and get off my bed. I cross my arms. "Wow, well, if you want to go take Kyle's side, he lives just a couple of minutes away." I say sarcastically.

Travis gets up out of the bed. "You know that's not what I meant."

"Well, what did you mean? Are you just mad because now everyone knows you're with someone who's HIV positive? It was okay if just you knew, but now everyone knows, you're embarrassed to be with me." I shout.

Travis looks surprised. "Hayden, I don't care *who* knows. I just want you to think before you act. You can't go around punching people. "

I'm angry. He obviously *isn't* taking my side. He obviously doesn't understand how much Kyle's comments hurt me.

I raise my voice. "So, you're embarrassed because you don't want to be with an impulsive hot headed girlfriend? Is that it?"

"Hayden, you're making these accusations up, that I haven't said."

I shrug. "You might not have said the words exactly, but that's you are implying."

Travis takes another breath. "Look, I'm sorry, okay? It's been a long night. Let's just sleep, okay?"

I'm too angry right now. I don't need Travis lecturing me. I want him to comfort me and just reassure me he loves me, and everything is going to be okay.

"I think it's best if you just leave." I say.

Travis looks confused. "What?"

I nod my head. "You were right. It's been a long night. I have some things I need to think about. I'll call you tomorrow."

"Hayden?"

I interrupt him. "Just go."

Travis looks defeated. He turns and walks out of my bedroom door, not saying anything as he leaves.

My dignity might not be the only thing I lost tonight.

Chapter Twenty: Hayden

The next morning, I wake up feeling un-refreshed. My eyes are red and puffy from crying all night. I walk into the kitchen and I'm surprised when I don't see Cori. Her bedroom door was open, so she must have left. Just as I sit down with a bowl of cereal, my doorbell goes. I really don't want to see anyone right now. I groan as I get up and answer the front door. When I open it, I see Lauren.

"I'm surprised to see you this early in the morning, after your birthday last night. I am surprised you aren't hung over." I say.

Lauren steps into my apartment. "Believe me, I am hung over, but I had to see you."

I walk back into my kitchen while Lauren follows me. I sit at the table and continue eating my cereal. Lauren pulls out a chair at the table and sits beside me.

"How are you?" she asks.

"Fantastic." I say sarcastically.

"Look, I'm sorry. I didn't know there was so much tension between you two. Kyle said you guys were still friends. I didn't mean any harm."

I don't really blame Lauren. "It's okay, Lauren. You weren't the asshole last night."

Lauren wipes her hands on her jeans. "About last night...about what Kyle said..."

I cut her off. "Kyle is a lying asshole, who made me look bad in front of all those people. I will never forgive him."

Lauren looks at me with sympathetic eyes. "Why did he accuse you of having HIV?"

I take a huge bite of cereal, talking with my mouth full, because I don't care at this point. "I don't know. Because he's an asshole."

Lauren looks at me like she doesn't believe me. "It was a very specific insult."

I finish chewing. I really don't want to have this conversation with Lauren, especially because I'm in a terrible mood. It makes me lose my temper.

"I don't know Lauren! I don't know why he is the way that he is! All I know is that he's an asshole who doesn't know how to keep his mouth shut!" I aggressively scoot my chair back to put my bowl and spoon into the dishwasher.

Lauren nervously wraps a strand of her blonde hair around her index finger. "Well you're not, right? HIV positive, I mean?"

I drop my bowl and it hits the ground with a thud. I am about to explode. Angry doesn't even begin to explain what I'm feeling. I tightly grip on the edge of the kitchen sink. I take a few breaths to calm myself before I answer her.

"Why would you ask me that Lauren?"

Lauren shrugs. "Because if it's true I want to know."

I grab the bowl from the ground and put it in the dishwasher. "If it was true, it would be none of your business."

Lauren's jaw drops. "I'm your sister. I'm your family. Of course, it would be my business. What if I needed to know for an emergency?"

"Family doesn't need to know everything about each other. Every family has their secrets. Mom and dad having troubles in their marriage is a prime example," I clearly state.

"And how devastated were you when you found out *after* the fact?"

"Lauren, I don't really want to argue about this right now. Obviously what Kyle said upset me, but it will blow over. Just forget that he said anything at all. I can't believe you even remembered, considering your state last night."

"Of course, I want to get the facts straight! I'm your sister. If you would have told me what was going on, I would have been the first to kick Kyle's ass."

I smirk. "Like you tell me everything? You hide so much stuff from me, Lauren. And *that's* okay. We *don't* have to tell each other everything."

Tears begin to form in Lauren's eyes. "I didn't know you felt that way. I don't tell you everything because I don't want you to be disappointed in me. You are Ms. Perfect. You make all the right decisions..."

Boy if she only knew...

"I tell you all the important things though, I promise." Her voice comes out a bit shaky. "I just thought...I just thought...you trusted me."

I explode. "It's kind of hard to trust you, when you told me the other week that you woke up one morning and didn't even know where you were."

Lauren stands up from her seat. "Talk about trust. I tell you these things in confidence, and you throw them in my face first chance you get! It's you who can't be trusted."

I feel defeated. I just want to curl up in bed. I have no more energy to fight with Lauren, so I just give up.

"Maybe you're right, Lauren."

Lauren doesn't say anything. She just quietly picks up her purse and heads for the front door. I hear the door close when she leaves.

I suddenly feel nauseous. I run to the bathroom, and barely make it before the vomit comes out. I rinse out my mouth. I drag my feet back to my room, curl up on my bed and self-pity myself back to sleep.

Stupid Kyle...

* * * *

The next day I receive a call from my mom. I guess Lauren talked to her, because she called saying Lauren called her, because she was worried about me. I tell my mom we fought because I was being irrational because I was on my period. She believes it and stops asking questions. After a couple of minutes reassuring her, and promising to go out with her for dinner one day this week, she leaves me alone, and we hang up.

I don't hear from Travis all week, which is not like him. I replay our conversation in my head over and over again. I have come to realize—I shouldn't have hit Kyle. It's not attractive to be unable to control oneself. I am more mature than starting fights.

I still wished he was on my side, even when I don't make the right choices. I really miss Travis, so I decide the right thing to do is stop by his apartment to apologize.

Trust

On Saturday morning, I knock on Travis's front door. He opens the door, standing in just his sweatpants with no shirt on. I hold up the bagels and coffees I stopped for on my way to his apartment. "Breakfast?" I ask.

He opens his apartment door wider and I walk in. I follow him to the kitchen, and hand him the coffee cup. He takes a sip. "Thanks."

I put the bagels on the kitchen table. "So, I came over because I wanted to apologize. I realize now, I shouldn't have punched Kyle. It was a poor decision on my part. I was hurt by what he said, but I should have just walked away and ignored him. I'm sorry I put you in that position."

He puts his coffee cup down on the counter. "Look, I accept your apology. I should be apologizing too. Even if I didn't agree on how you handled the situation, I should have supported you, not lectured you."

Sometimes an apology can go a long way. That's all the reassurance I need. "So, we're good?"

He smiles. "We're good...Also...are there bagels in there?" He nudges his head in the direction of the bagels sitting in the bag on the table.

I giggle. "Yes, there are. But first, I want to finish my apology."

Travis pinches his brows. "Okay..."

I place my coffee cup on the kitchen table and walk over to where Travis is leaning against the kitchen counters. Just as I approach him, I pull down his sweatpants and boxers, as I make my way down on my knees before him.

Travis looks down at me kneeled in front of him. "I think I'm going to like this apology."

I give him a flirty grin. "I think you will too."

The next morning I'm woken up by Travis planting kisses down my spine. I smile into the pillow as I lie on my stomach. I stayed the night at Travis house, as we spent the day apologizing to each other in the best of ways.

He reaches under my stomach and pulls me up onto my hands and knees. I know where this is heading, and I can't wait. Travis makes his way behind me, and the next thing I know is he is slamming into me from behind. I grip tightly on the bed and push back against him, as he thrusts into me. We continue at a quick pace, and the moment he whispers in my ear that he loves me, I lose it.

Best way to start a morning.

Travis and I head out for a morning run and return to his place to shower. After we get out of the shower and get dressed, we enjoy a cup of coffee at his kitchen table.

"So, Lauren asked me if what Kyle said about me was true?" I bit my lip.

"About being HIV positive?"

"Yup." My hands tighten around the coffee mug.

"Did you tell her the truth?"

I scratch my head. "No, I didn't. We ended up fighting, and I haven't spoken to her since."

Travis takes a sip of his coffee. "Don't you think maybe this is the perfect opportunity to tell her?"

I groan. "It's not fair. I wanted to tell her on my *own* accord. Not have my ex blab my medical history. This is the worst way she could possibly find out."

Travis reaches over and rubs my hand with his thumb. "But you can't change things now. It's already happened. Do you trust your sister?"

I think about what I said to Lauren. I told her I didn't trust her, which was not entirely true. The truth is, I know Lauren wouldn't tell a soul if I told her the truth. Sure, we fight and bring up funny stories to embarrass one another in fun, but she is my sister. Lauren has always been there for me, and I know she always will. Having a sister is like having a permanent best friend. I know she isn't going anywhere, and she does know how to keep a secret. I mean if my parents knew half the things she did in her teenage years, she would be disowned by now.

"Yes, I guess I do trust Lauren. I just don't know how to tell her."

"Tell her, in the same way you told me."

I find this ironic, since I planned on telling Lauren before Travis, so Lauren could give me advice on how to tell Travis. Now Travis is giving me advice on how to tell Lauren.

"Yeah, I guess you are right." I stand up and sit on his lap. He tilts his head slightly and I bend down to give him a kiss. I break the kiss for a brief second. "I'm not going to tell her today though. I have plans." I say against his lips.

"What kind of plans?" he asks.

"Plans that involve just me and you. And maybe a bed. Maybe not. Plans I think you are really going to like."

He raises his brows. "Yeah, I think I'd like that."

I smile as I press my lips back to his.

Tuesday night, I offer to look after Penelope for Brennley. We're currently sitting on the couch in the living room, watching a documentary on penguins.

"Do you know what I want be when I grow up?" Penny asks me out of the blue.

She changes her mind all the time, so I am not sure what she's chosen this time. Last time she told me she wanted to buy a bookstore and sell books; at the time she was into reading. I definitely approved of that idea.

"What do you want to be when you grow up?"

"I want to be a veterinarian. That way I can help all the sick animals get better. I want to buy a farm where I have lots of animals." She counts on her fingers. "Dogs, cats, bunnies, lions, penguins, tigers, dolphins, chickens, lambs, and cows. Lots of animals."

Wow, that was an eclectic variety of animals. There wasn't really a specific theme going on. I look into Penelope's brown eyes. "How are you going to have a dolphin on your farm?"

"It's not going to be on the farm. It will live at the aquarium." She looks at me like I'm the stupid one. Kids are so weird sometimes.

"Oh, I see. What about the lions? What if they eat your chickens?"

"They won't, because they'll all be friends. The lions will be in a cage too, so they don't run away."

Oh, well that makes perfect sense. "Oh, I see."

"When you work at the aquarium I'll let you look after my dolphin."

I laugh. "Well it sounds like you've thought of everything."

I comb my hands through Penelope's soft brown hair. "Also, Travis can work at the Aquarium too if he wants."

I laugh again. "Okay, I'll be sure to tell him."

Penelope turns to me. "Are you and Travis going to get married?"

"Why are you so obsessed with marriage?"

Penelope pouts. "I used to think Brennley and Cooper were going to get married. But now they fight all the time."

That's interesting. Brennley hasn't mentioned anything about having problems with Cooper. Although lately, things have been about me. Man, I've been a bad friend lately. "Don't worry, Penelope. Sometimes grownups fight, but it doesn't mean they don't love each other. I'll talk to Brennley, okay?"

Penelope nods. "Auntie Hayden?"

"Yes?"

"Are you going to get sick again?"

I squeeze Penelope tightly. I have no idea where this is coming from, but kids always ask unpredictable questions. "I hope I don't get sick again, but sometimes it just happens. I'll do my best to take care of myself, so I don't, okay?"

I can feel Penelope nod against my chest. "My mom got so sick she died and went to heaven. But it sucks for Brennley because she doesn't get to have a sister anymore."

The sadness in Penelope's voice, devastates me. Everything she said is true. Her mom was sick. Her mom had an addiction, so bad it ended her life. I can't imagine the way it affected both Penelope and Brennley.

"Brennley will always have a sister. Her sister will always be in her heart. She won't ever forget her."

"Do you like having a sister?"

"Yes, I love having a sister."

Penelope pouts again. "I wish I had a sister to play with. My friend Melody at school has a sister and they play together all the time."

"Well, you have Brennley. She's almost like a sister. Plus, you have the coolest aunts ever. Aren't Cori and I fun aunts?"

"Yes. I like when you guys take me out for rainbow ice cream. Or when you braid my hair."

"I'll talk to Cori and see if maybe soon we can go out for ice cream."

"Okay." Penelope turns back and continues to watch the documentary. Her question about having a sister made me a little more emotional than I thought. Lauren and I were super close growing up. We used to have tea parties and play with Barbies. We would spend hours at the beach in the summertime. As we got older we spent less time together, but I couldn't imagine my life without her.

Penelope's comment made me realize just how lucky I am to have a sister. I pick up my cell phone and text Lauren to see if she wants to meet up tomorrow after I finish classes. I'm surprised when she responds almost immediately, agreeing to meet up. I gulp. I think the anticipation of waiting to tell her might be worse than actually telling her.

Chapter Twenty-One: Hayden

Wednesday morning, I receive a text message from my mom asking if we can do dinner tonight. Guess she found her glasses. Before I respond, I remember I'm meeting up with Lauren. I think maybe I should tell both my mom and Lauren at the same time. Two birds, one stone, and all that.

Birds...

Damn, Travis has officially ruined birds for me. I text Lauren asking if we could do dinner with mom, to which she is agreeable. I offer to pick her up on the way to mom's.

Lauren and I are silent on the drive to mom's new apartment. We're both excited when we arrive at my mom's new apartment, and discover she's making chicken fajitas. My favourite dinner. I show mom the wine I brought, and the three of us catch up in the kitchen as we sip on wine. Mom also fills us in on how her date went. She says it went well enough to go on a second date, which is good. I'm proud of my mom for putting herself out there.

After dinner, the three of us sit down in mom's living room. There's a halt in the conversation. It's the perfect opportunity to cut in and tell them. But how? I'm so nervous. My palms are literally dripping with sweat. The wine has made me feel a bit braver.

I can do this. I will do this.

"So, I have something important I have to tell you guys," I begin.

Both Lauren and my mom's eyes find mine. "What is it, honey?"

"The thing I have to tell you is really hard to explain." I say with a shaky voice. Looking at my mom, and being afraid of her disappointment, makes this way harder to say. I've always wanted my parents to be proud of me. It sounds silly, but I also want them to like me. I want them to think I can take care of myself and support myself. The way I take care of myself is almost a reflection of how well of a job they did in raising me. I don't want my mom to think I'm some irresponsible, immature child who makes rash decisions. I'd do anything, for them to think highly of their daughter.

A knock on the door interrupts my thoughts.

My mom has a guilty look on her face. "Sorry girls, I forgot to tell you I invited your dad. I thought tonight since we could all be together that it would be the perfect opportunity to discuss the divorce and how we are going to move forward, and the changes we are making. You both said how upset you were that you weren't involved in the decision of divorcing, so I wanted you to be involved in how we are going to make this work."

Wow, mom. Way to make this awkward.

Couldn't she at least have given Lauren and me a heads up. She probably knew we'd bail if we knew.

Sneaky mom.

Mom gets up, and before I know it dad walks into the living room, and sits down on a chair, near where Lauren and I are sitting on the love seat. My dad's green eyes beam at Lauren and me.

"How are my girls?"

Lauren and I briefly catch him up on our lives. My mom joins the conversation. It's weird because in some ways it feels like nothing has changed, but in some ways it feels awkward, like we've all being forced to communicate with each other. After we discuss the divorce, and make decisions as a family, my mom turns to me.

"I'm sorry Hayden. I forgot that you had something important to tell us."

I look at my dad. Well, I guess there's no holding back now. I guess I could tell my dad too. I was wanting my mom to break the news gently to my dad after I told her, but I guess it is best if he hears it from me.

"Well, what I am going to tell you is difficult for me to say. I don't want you guys to be mad at me. Just remember what I am going to say, is over with and nothing you guys do at this point can change that fact. I'm dealing with the consequence of a mistake I made."

My mom looks directly at me. "I would never be mad at you honey. Disappointed, but never mad."

A parent being disappointment is way worse than being mad.

"That's what I was afraid of mom. You being disappointed in me, and you lecturing me."

My mom crosses one of her legs over the other. "I promise I won't lecture you."

I look over at me dad. He holds his hands up and reassures me, "I won't lecture you either."

I don't want to tell them the whole story necessarily. Because I don't know how to approach it with my parents, I just go for it. "I got diagnosed with HIV."

My mom gasps loudly, while my dad has a puzzled look on his face. Lauren is nonchalant; I think she figured this was coming.

"How did you get diagnosed with HIV?" my mom asks.

"The doctor diagnosed me." I reply.

My mom crinkles her face. "That's not what I meant. What I mean is *how* did you get HIV?"

This is probably the worst part of explaining this to them. I know I just have to do it. "I had unprotected sex, with a partner who didn't know he had HIV."

I can't look in my dad's direction at all. This is the very definition of uncomfortable. I look down at my hands and wished I was anywhere but here.

I hear my mom let out a sob. "Oh, Hayden..."

"Mom, please. Don't cry."

"I can't help it. How did this happen?"

I groan. "I already told you *how* it happened."

"But you are always so responsible. You always make good decisions. You have good judgment. This isn't you, Hayden." My mom cries.

My dad is silent, and I have yet to look at him.

"This is what I was afraid of. I'm not going to sit here and get a lecture about how stupid I was, or how poor my judgment was. I already know that. I tell myself that every day. You guys can't make me feel any worse than I already feel about myself. But you know what? Everyone makes mistakes."

I stand up and head for the door because I don't want my family to see me cry. I hear footsteps from behind, so I turn around. Lauren wraps me in the tightest tug.

"I love you Hayden, no matter what."

This makes me cry harder, because it was all I wanted to hear from my family when I told them. No lectures, no fighting, just support and reassurance that they'll always love me. No matter what. My mom's voice breaks Lauren and I from our hug.

"I'm sorry Hayden. I'm just shocked, that's all. I will always want what is best for you."

I wipe a tear that has escaped from my eyes. "I know mom. I know I've disappointed you, and that's why it's taken me so long to tell you, because I knew you would react poorly."

My mom sinks her shoulders. "How long have you had it?"

I look away. "Two years."

"Two years? And not once did you think to tell me?"

"Mom, I told you! I was embarrassed! I don't want my HIV affecting the way you treat me. I saw your face just a couple of minutes ago when I told you. That's what I was afraid of."

Tears stream down my mom's face. "I still wished you would have told me, honey."

I finally am brave enough to look at my dad. He has tears in his eyes. Honestly, I've only seen my dad cry once; when his mom died.

"Dad..."

"Who was it?" he asks.

Who was what? It takes me a second, but I figure out he wants to know who I contracted HIV from.

"At this point, does it really matter? That person is out of my life."

My dad nods his head slowly. I guess he understands my point.

"This is not what I would have wanted for you, but I'm glad you finally told us. I can't believe you were scared to tell us. Nothing you do would make me love you less."

I bite my lip to hold back tears. "Are you sure, dad?"

He laughs, "Of course. Just like I wasn't mad when you tried to back out of the garage with my car that one time, without checking to make sure the garage door was up."

Man, I totally remember that. He had to spend a good chunk of money fixing the bumper. I laugh through my tears.

"It's not the same thing though. I can't fix my diagnosis."

My dad holds up his hand. "Doesn't matter. Point is, that it doesn't matter how many mistakes you make, I'll always be here for you."

"Thanks, Dad."

"Me too, honey. I never would have imagined this would happen to you, Hayden, but I want you to know that I still love you."

A weak smile manages to find its way to my face. "Thanks, mom. I know you guys probably have a lot of questions, but I was hoping we could save that for another day."

"Sure, honey."

I give her a weak smile that doesn't reach my eyes. "Okay, well...I'm going to head out now. I'll talk to you guys later."

Lauren pipes up. "I'm coming with you."

Oh, right. I totally forgot for a second, I drove her.

I'm driving Lauren home. We haven't spoken much, just listened to the radio. Lauren reaches over from the passenger seat and turns the radio down.

"I know you said you didn't want to discuss it, but can I just ask why you didn't tell me when you found out?"

Before I can remind her that I'd just told her and my parents I was embarrassed, she cuts me off.

"I know you said you were embarrassed, but why would you be embarrassed with me? If I'm not embarrassed by your awful singing voice, why would I be with your HIV?"

I reach over as I am driving and smack her with one hand. "My singing voice is angelic. Very soft and gentle. Natural."

Lauren lets out a genuine laugh.

"You're just jealous of my awesome range and pitch." I'm obviously being sarcastic. I'm just as bad at singing as I am at sports.

Lauren dramatically rolls her eyes. "If you say so. But besides your singing, I have never judged you. I always tell you things I'm not proud of. I guess, I just thought I was different because I'm your sister. I feel like, as a sister I should get a free pass. I should know what's going on in your life, no matter how embarrassing it is; because at the end of the day you're stuck with me. And if we can't laugh at each other when we screw up, what is the point?"

"But when I got diagnosed with HIV, it was the opposite of funny." I tell her seriously.

"Okay, bad example."

"So, your point is...?"

"Just know this: I will always be your sister, and you can trust me."

"Okay, loser."

It's Lauren this time who smacks me.

"Ouch."

"We were having a moment."

"That's the point. Siblings are always supposed to ruin moments. We're not supposed to have dramatic, movie-like moments."

Lauren doesn't believe me. "Says who?"

I ignore her comment and turn up the radio. "Are you ready to hear my amazing pitch on this next song?"

Lauren covers her ears. "Please don't."

I point my finger at her. "You promised you can't be embarrassed by me."

She just groans as I start singing in my horrible singing voice.

Chapter Twenty-Two: Hayden

Over the next couple of months, my parents and Lauren have accepted the fact I live with a chronic illness. It's a part of me, but I'm not going to let it change me completely. I've met with each of them, individually, and they've asked me questions about my HIV.

My dad even showed me an article with a new HIV research study going on. I think it's his way of supporting me. Lauren has been super understanding and admits that she's a tiny bit glad she isn't the only one in the family who's made some less than ideal choices. My mom probably had the most questions. She says that if she didn't worry about me, then she wouldn't be doing her job as a mom.

After a couple weeks my HIV news is considered old, so it rarely gets brought up in conversation when I see my family. The four of us have actually managed to hang out a few times. We were even able to spend Christmas morning together, which was nice. Christmas morning Lauren surprised us by announcing she's landed a small role in a Christmas movie. All four of us sat down and watched the movie together. Lauren looked gorgeous in the movie, and I admit she did a good job. When I complimented her she brushed it off and gave credit to Brennley who gave her some acting tips.

I spend boxing day with Travis's family. Besides Addison, they're all welcoming, and made me feel included. Also, Travis's nephew Noah is too cute for his own good. Travis is just as good with Noah as he is with Penelope, not that I was surprised. Speaking of Penelope, Travis thought it would be hilarious to get Penelope a book on birds for Christmas. Penelope brings the book over every time she visits, as Travis has convinced her it was my favourite book. I complain the whole time we have to read the story. Obviously, my dislike for birds has continued.

I was able to convince my dad to move our Las Vegas trip to after New Years'. It was nice to go away with Lauren and my dad for a few days. Although of course Lauren wins big at the casino, whereas I was just feeding the casino my money. Remember when I talked about life being unfair?

The second week of January is Travis's birthday. I'm excited, because after talking to my dad I have the perfect birthday gift for him. It's an exciting time for me because this is officially my last semester of school, and if I pass my classes I'll graduate with my master's degree.

The day before Travis's birthday, I stay over at his place, so we can do some early celebration. I wake up extra early and sneak down to his kitchen to make him breakfast. I go all out for breakfast, making eggs, bacon, hash browns, crepes, and fruit. When I finish setting the table, I walk down the hallway back into his bedroom. I stand for a second and watch him sleep. He's sleeping on his back with half the covers on him, so it gives me a great view of his abs. His chest simply rises and falls as he breaths.

I suddenly have a naughty plan that I decide to put into action. I climb gingerly onto the bed, trying hard to prevent any squeaking noises. I want to surprise him. Just as I am about to swing my leg over his body, he wakes up.

"No, I was going to surprise you!"

He chuckles. "How were you going to surprise me?"

I wink. "It's a secret. But now you've ruined it."

"I can go back to sleep," he suggests.

I exaggeratedly collapse on top of him. "Not the same." I mumble into his chest. After he tickles my side, I jolt up, screaming and laughing. "No, please don't."

"Tell me." he demands.

I ignore his comment. "Happy birthday, babe!" I lean down and kiss him. After a couple seconds, he tickles my side again, causing me to break the kiss as I jolt again. "No, stop!"

"Tell me." he tries again.

I huff. "Fine." I lean back down to lie flat on his chest. He wraps his arms around me. "I was going to wake you up by giving you a birthday blow job."

He lifts me up, so he can look at me. "And I ruined it?" He looks disappointed.

"Yes, you most certainly did."

Travis closes his eyes. I tap his shoulder. "Wake up, birthday boy."

No response.

"Wake up, birthday boy."

No response.

I lean down and give him a quick kiss.

No response.

"Travis are you going to wake up? I made you breakfast."

No response.

"Okay...fine!" I give an evil laugh.

I slowly scoot down his body and give him the birthday morning wake-up call he was wanting.

As we're indulging in his birthday breakfast, I tell him, "I have another present for you."

Travis's eyes light up. "You do?"

"Yes." I feel my eyes glisten.

"You're just full of surprises, aren't you?"

"Yup." I nod my head. "I like surprising you."

Travis puts his fork down. "Okay, what is it?"

"You have to wait until after breakfast."

He frowns. "That's torture."

"It creates anticipation."

"I better not have to take a birthday photo."

I laugh. "No, but that would be a wonderful idea. I did bring my camera."

After breakfast, we make our way to the couch. I pass him an envelope. He takes it gladly. He opens the envelope. He reaches and pulls out a card.

"Dear Travis..." he reads.

I stop him. "No, don't read it out loud."

"Why not?"

"Because you'll embarrass me."

"But I love embarrassing you."

I groan. "Fine."

"Even though meeting you was one of the most embarrassing moments of my life, I'm so glad I got to meet you. When we met on that day in the park, I thought I'd never see you again. I was almost grateful I wouldn't have to see you again, because I was so embarrassed by what happened. However, life has a funny sense of humor, and thought it would be a good idea to bring us back together—for me to embarrass myself in front of you a million more times."

Travis pauses for a second. "A million times?"

I wave my hand. "That's just a rough estimate."

He laughs, but continues...

"It's now, that I don't know what I would do if I'd never got to see you again. Even though we have been together less than a year, I want you to know how much you mean to me. I love when you kiss my forehead. I love when we sit on the couch and you stroke my hair. I love when you hold my hand while driving. I love the way your eyes beam when I bluntly tell you how attractive you are. But most of all I just like spending time with you. I look forward to each day because of you. Even the simple days when we sit on the couch and you watch T.V while I do my homework. Or when we go for morning runs together. I love how you listen to me, and care for me. But most importantly, I love and will never forget the way you taught me how to believe in myself and trust myself, and the others around me. I love you Travis. You deserve the best birthday ever. Love, Hayden."

Next thing I know Travis is pulling my hands away from my face, where I've covered my eyes. "So, did you like your card?"

He smiles. "I loved it. I love you too. You mean a lot to me. That won't ever change."

"Well, I can't wait until you see the present. You'll love that more."

"Not a chance."

I point to the envelope. "The present is also in the envelope."

Travis shakes the envelope and two tickets fly out. He picks them up and reads them. "Are these what I think they are?"

"If you think they're two plane tickets for you and I to go to Japan after I graduate in April then you're correct."

Travis places the tickets on the table and basically blows me over as I fall back onto the couch as he gives me a hug.

"You like?" I ask.

He nods. "I like. But you shouldn't spend this much money on me."

I give him the 'really' look. "Yeah, because you didn't spend hundreds of dollars on me at Christmas?"

He shakes his head rapidly from side to side. "That's different."

"No, it's not! But don't worry. Since you know my dad is a pilot, he may or may not have been able to use his connections for this trip."

"Oh, I see." Travis bends down to kiss me. "I love you, Hayden. And for the record, meeting you was the best day of my life, *not* the most embarrassing."

I smile widely. "Glad you made that clear."

He bends down and gives me another kiss. "I can't wait to go on this trip with you."

"Me too." I respond. "You like your present?"

Travis nods mischievously, but presses his lips to mine. "Yes, and I can't wait to show you just how much."

* * * *

Thursday night, I attend group. Even though I've become more comfortable with myself, I still enjoying going to group for the support. I don't think it's possible to have too much support. Mason announces there is a new member joining our group tonight.

The girl looks close to my age; light brown hair and brown eyes. She introduces herself as Amelia. She dives right in and tells us her story of how she contracted HIV. I'm amazed by her bravery, considering this is her first group and she doesn't know anybody. She talks about how her boyfriend cheated on her and ended up contracting HIV from the woman who he cheated with, and then passed it to Amelia. I feel awful for Amelia. When she talks about her boyfriend, and not knowing he was HIV positive, it literally hurts my heart. She continues to explain her rationale for not getting tested right away, and it hits close to home. She tells us it took her a while before she found out she was HIV positive.

My heart pounds against my chest. I'm worried it's going to beat right out of my body. I place one of my hands over my heart. Then I think of the moment Travis told me he loved me and wouldn't let my virus get in the way of being with him. The thought makes my heart beat calm right down. But, I'm not done just yet.

I know I need to talk to Amelia. I don't want her to feel the way I felt about myself. There is nothing worse than feeling horrible and thinking poorly about yourself. As everyone is packing up, I wait until they leave, so that it is just Amelia and I.

"Hey, Amelia, I'm Hayden." I approach her cautiously.

She gives me a warm smile. "Hi."

"Your story. It reminded me a lot of mine."

She looks surprised. "It did?"

I nod.

Amelia flinches. "My boyfriend is an asshole. I'm never going to forgive myself for trusting him."

I'm never going to forgive myself for that mistake...

"Do me a favor Amelia. Forgive yourself. You deserve to forgive yourself. If you don't, the guilt will consume you. Life feels better when you forgive yourself."

Amelia doesn't say anything. I pick up my purse, and just as I am about to leave I look back at Amelia. "Don't lose trust in people completely. There are some people in your life worth trusting."

Epilogue

6 Months Later

"Hey babe, have you seen my swimsuit?" I yell, frantically looking through my clothes to find it.

"Yes, it's hanging up in the laundry room."

"You did laundry?" My voice comes out sounding surprised.

"Well, now that my girlfriend lives with me, I can't be a slob." Travis appears in the doorway to our apartment bedroom. We moved in together just over a week ago. I had this awful realization that I have way too many clothes.

"That's true." I squeeze by him and smack his butt as I leave the bedroom to head to the laundry room. As I walk down the hallway to the laundry room, I can't hide the smile that forms on my lips as I walk past the picture hanging up in the hallway of us together in Japan. Travis *finally* let me take his picture. He only let me take two, in which, thank goodness, I looked decent in both. I find the bathing suit I was looking for and change into it. I put on a bathing suit cover-up and tie my hair into a messy bun.

It's summer, so we're meeting our friends down at the beach. I'm in dire need of a tan—although with my porcelain skin, I'm sure it will be a burn. I walk back to our bedroom and see Travis in his swim suit bottoms. Have I mentioned I love it when my boyfriend wears a swim suit? It's unfair because he tans easily, turning his chest into a nice bronze color. Travis throws on a shirt. Damn, no.

"I lost my view." I complain.

"What view?" Travis asks.

"Never mind." I find my sunglasses on the floor of the bedroom. Maybe I'm the slob. I bend over to pick them up and stand up.

"I lost my view!" Travis exclaims.

"What view?" I ask. And then I figure it out. "I thought we'd be able to control ourselves better now we live together."

Travis shakes his head. "No, I definitely think it's made it worse."

I laugh, but I walk over and kiss him. "Ready to go?"

Travis pulls up my cover up. "Almost. Give me a few minutes."

"We can't be late. Our friends will wonder where we are."

Travis laughs as he plants kisses on my neck and undoes the ties on my bathing suit top. "Oh…and you can't be late to meeting friends at the beach…"

I think it over. He has a point. "I guess we could be a couple minutes late…"

Travis and I meet our friends Keegan and Kelsey, and Dominick and Cassie at the beach. We sit, chat, tan, and go in the water to cool off. On the other side of the beach is a cliff from which you can jump off into the water. I don't know how high it is, but it's quite the drop. I've never been able to do it. I've always been too scared. I've seen numerous people do it. I suddenly have the urge to do it—to jump off the cliff.

"Travis, I want to show you something." I announce.

He stands up and we walk around the beach, as our friends watch our belongings. "So, ever since I was a little girl, there has been this cliff I wanted to jump off from, into the water."

Travis smiles. "I have a feeling I know which one you're talking about."

"Good. Then will you help me live my lifelong dream and jump off it into the water with me? I can't do it by myself. I'll bail."

"If that's what you want to do."

"I do."

There isn't anyone on the cliff, which is good. It's in a hidden area, so many people don't know about it. I grab hold of Travis's hand as we walk to the edge, and immediately look down.

"Oh, my goodness, never mind. I can't do it." I panic.

"Yes, you can. It really isn't that high."

I squint at him. "Are you trying to say that to make me feel better?"

"Yes and no?"

I nervously laugh. "Well it isn't helping. Please can we just go back? Forget I mentioned this."

"You said it was your lifelong dream." He points out.

"No, I said having an insanely handsome boyfriend cook me breakfast, while I slept in, was my lifelong dream, and it's already happened."

"Well, now both your dreams can come true," he assures me.

"I don't know..." I hesitate.

"C'mon, you can do this."

I close my eyes and open them, hoping the drop would appear lower. Nope, it didn't work. My hands are shaking, but I manage to grip Travis's tightly. "Okay, let's do this."

Travis and I walk up to the edge of the cliff. Okay, so maybe Travis dragged me to the edge of the cliff.

Semantics.

Travis turns his head to the side, as we stand beside each other, facing the water, hands intertwined.

"Do you trust me?" he asks.

"Always."

And with that reassurance it's enough for me to take that leap.

THE END

About the Author

Avery Woods lives in beautiful, but sometimes rainy Vancouver, BC, Canada. In addition to writing, Avery works as a full time Registered Nurse.

When she's not writing or working as a nurse, you can find her consuming books by the minute. Trust is her first book.

https://authoraverywoods.jimdo.com/

Made in the USA
San Bernardino, CA
14 March 2018